Asa Gray, William S. Sullivant

The Musci and Hepaticae of the United States East of the

Mississippi River

contributed to the second edition of Gray's manual of botany /by William

S. Sullivant. With eight copper-plates illustrating the genera.

Asa Gray, William S. Sullivant

The Musci and Hepaticae of the United States East of the Mississippi River
contributed to the second edition of Gray's manual of botany /by William S.
Sullivant. With eight copper-plates illustrating the genera.

ISBN/EAN: 9783337302160

Printed in Europe, USA, Canada, Australia, Japan

Cover: Foto ©Andreas Hilbeck / pixelio.de

More available books at **www.hansebooks.com**

THE

MUSCI AND HEPATICÆ

OF THE

UNITED STATES

EAST OF THE MISSISSIPPI RIVER.

CONTRIBUTED TO THE SECOND EDITION OF

GRAY'S MANUAL OF BOTANY,

BY

WILLIAM S. SULLIVANT.

WITH EIGHT COPPER-PLATES,
ILLUSTRATING THE GENERA.

NEW YORK:
IVISON, BLAKEMAN, TAYLOR, & COMPANY,
138 & 140 GRAND STREET.
CHICAGO: 133 & 135 STATE STREET.
1871.

THE following pages are designed to contain brief descriptions of all the MUSCI and HEPATICÆ hitherto detected in that portion of the United States lying east of the Mississippi River. A few species found elsewhere, either new, or having a geographical range hertofore unnoticed, or for some other special reason, have also been described; namely, those from Texas and New Mexico, and also several from near our northern boundary, and likely to occur within it.

The territory within the limits adopted—extending, as it does, from 25° to 47° North Latitude, and traversed for nearly its entire length by mountain ranges, reaching, at several points in their northern and southern terminations, an alpine elevation—presents conditions favorable to a copious and varied muscological vegetation. And if the number of species here recorded is not so large as that found in an equal area similarly situated on the Eastern Continent, it must be borne in mind that our Bryology and Hepaticology (particularly the latter) have thus far been very imperfectly investigated. Scarcely any portion of our country, excepting Central Ohio, has been carefully examined. The mountain ranges have only been cursorily visited by a few interested in these branches of Botany. In the northern section, notwithstanding numerous discoveries made by the late Mr. OAKES, and the more recent ones (among them a *Dichelyma,* a *Tetrodontium,* and an *Atrichum*) by THOMAS P. JAMES, Esq., there will doubtless yet be detected many other well-known European species, not a few of which have already been collected in British America by DRUMMOND.

The southern section has been even less carefully explored, and offers a promising field for future discoveries. Among the recent accessions to our Flora from this quarter are an *Orthotrichum*, a *Fissidens*, and several *Bruchiæ* and *Fabroniæ*, gathered by H. W. RAVENEL, Esq.; also some fine *Sphagna*, an *Anomodon*, a *Fontinalis*, and a *Macromitrium*, brought thence by our friend, the excellent bryologist, M. LEO LESQUEREUX.

No portion of our territory has contributed so little to our Bryology and Hepaticology as the Florida peninsula, which in this respect still remains almost a *terra incognita:* its only known species, *Pilotrichum cymbifolium*, like *Meteorium pendulum* from Western Louisiana (whence novelties may also be expected), is thoroughly tropical in all its characters, and gives promise of new and interesting forms to reward future explorers.

W. S. S.

COLUMBUS, OHIO, *July,* 1856.

MUSCI AND HEPATICÆ

OF THE

UNITED STATES

EAST OF THE MISSISSIPPI.

ORDER 139. MÚSCI. (Mosses.*)

Low, tufted plants,.always with a stem and distinct (sessile) leaves, producing spore-cases which open by a terminal lid (except in Nos. 1 – 4), and
contain simple spores alone. Reproductive organs of two kinds : † 1. The
sterile (*male*) flower, consisting of numerous (4 – 20) minute cylindrical
sacs (*antheridia*) which discharge from their apex a mucous fluid filled with
oval particles, and then perish. 2. The fertile flower composed of numerous (4 – 20) flask-like bodies (*archegonia, pistillidia*), each having a membranous covering (*calyptra*), terminated by a long cylindrical funnel-mouthed
tube (*style*). The ripened archegonium (seldom more than one in a flower maturing) becomes the *capsule*, which is rarely indehiscent or splitting
by 4 longitudinal slits, but usually opens by a lid (*operculum*) : beneath the
operculum, and arising from the mouth of the capsule, are commonly 1 or 2
rows of rigid processes (collectively the *peristome*) which are always some
multiple of four : those of the outer row are called *teeth* ; those of the
inner row, *cilia*, their intermediate smaller processes, *ciliolæ*. An elastic
ring of cells (*annulus*) lies between the rim of the capsule and operculum.
The powdery particles filling the capsule are *spores* or *sporules*. The
thread-like stalk (*pedicel*) supporting the capsule is inserted into the elongated torus (*vaginula*) of the flower. The pedicel continued through the
capsule forms the *columella* ; when enlarged uniformly under the capsule, it
forms an *apophysis* ; when protuberant on one side only, a *struma*. The
calyptra separating early at its base is carried up on the apex of the capsule ; if it splits on one side it is hood-shaped or *cuculliform*, if not, it is
mitre-shaped or *mitriform*. Intermixed with the reproductive organs are
cellular jointed filaments (*paraphyses*). The leaves surrounding the antheridia are called the *perigonial* leaves ; those around the archegonium or
pedicel, the *perichætial* leaves.

Artificial Analysis of the Genera.

I. ACROCARPI. Fruit terminal.

A. Capsule without a deciduous operculum.

    • Capsule dehiscing by irregular ruptures.

3 ARCHIDIUM. Calyptra torn irregularly at the middle.
5. BRUCHIA. Calyptra circumcissile at the base. Capsule apophysate.
4. PHASCUM. Calyptra circumcissile at the base. Capsule not apophysate.

    • • Capsule dehiscing by 4 longitudinal slits.

2. ANDRÆA. Capsule sessile on a pedicellate vaginula.

B. Capsule dehiscing by a deciduous operculum.

    • Mouth of the capsule naked.

    ← Capsule sessile on a pedicellate vaginula.

1. SPHAGNUM. Calyptra irregularly torn, persistent.

    ← ← Capsule on a proper pedicel : vaginula not pedicellate.

6. GYMNOSTOMUM. Calyptra cuculliform. Antheridia terminal.
25. POTTIA. Calyptra cuculliform. Antheridia axillary.
56. APHANORHEGMA. Calyptra mitriform. Antheridia axillary.
55. PHYSCOMITRIUM. Calyptra mitriform. Antheridia terminal.
40. HEDWIGIA. Calyptra conic. Antheridia axillary.

    • • Mouth of the capsule furnished with teeth.

    ← Peristome single.

    ↔ Teeth of the peristome 4.

26. TETRAPHIS. Calyptra mitriform. Plants with a conspicuous stem.
27. TETRODONTIUM. Calyptra dimidiate-mitriform. Almost stemless plants.

    ↔ ↔ Teeth of the peristome 16. Calyptra mitriform.

    a. Calyptra plicate.

85. PTYCHOMITRIUM. Teeth deeply bifid ; their segments adherent.
88. COSCINODON. Teeth cribrose.

    b. Calyptra not plicate.

37. GRIMMIA. Teeth entire, cribrose or 2-3 cleft at the apex.
86. SCHISTIDIUM. Teeth as in No. 37. Columella adherent to the operculum.
89. RACOMITRIUM. Teeth filiform, 2-3-cleft to the base.
57. SPLACHNUM. Teeth in pairs, reflexed when dry.
18. CONOMITRIUM. Teeth truncate, very short, more or less perforated.

    ↔ ↔ ↔ Teeth of the peristome 16. Calyptra cuculliform.

    a. Leaves 2-ranked.

17. FISSIDENS. Teeth cloven half-way into two unequal segments.
24. EUSTICHIUM. Fruit unknown.
23. DISTICHIUM. Teeth usually entire ; if cloven, their segments equal.

    b. Leaves spreading every way.

    1. Capsule cernuous-inclined, unequal.

14. DICRANUM. Teeth as in Fissidens. Leaves furnished with a costa.
16 LEUCOBRYUM. Teeth as in Fissidens. Leaves destitute of a costa.
15. CERATODON. Teeth deeply bifid. Capsule with a short struma.
12. TREMATODON. Teeth cleft below. Capsule with a long and linear apophysis.
52. CONOSTOMUM. Teeth united at the apex. Capsule ribbed.

    2. Capsule somewhat pendulous on an arcuate pedicel, equal.

13. CAMPYLOPUS. Teeth deeply bifid. Calyptra fringed at the base.
11. DICRANODONTIUM. Teeth deeply bifid. Calyptra not fringed at the base.

3. Capsule erect, oval or somewhat pyriform.

9. **SELIGERIA.** Teeth lanceolate, obtuse. Capsule globose-pyriform.
7. **WEISIA.** Teeth lanceolate, acute. Capsule oval, smooth.
8. **RHABDOWEISIA.** Teeth subulate. Capsule oval, striated.
10. **ARCTOA.** Teeth split half-way down. Capsule somewhat turbinate, striated.
31. **DRUMMONDIA.** Teeth truncate, erect. Capsule globose-oval.
54. **ENTOSTHODON.** Teeth lanceolate, horizontal. Capsule globose-pyriform.

4. Capsule erect, oblong or cylindrical.

21. **DESMATODON.** Teeth deeply bifid, erect. Operculum elongated-conic, obtuse.
29. **SYRRHOPODON.** Teeth entire, horizontal. Operculum subulate-rostrate.
58. **TETRAPLODON.** Teeth in fours, reflexed when dry. Operculum conico-convex.

↔ ↔ ↔ ↔ Teeth of the peristome 32. Calyptra cuculliform.

19. **TRICHOSTOMUM.** Teeth more or less united in pairs, with a narrow basilar membrane.
22. **DIDYMODON.** Teeth as in the last, but without any basilar membrane.
20. **BARBULA.** Teeth very long, once or twice twisted around the columella.
43. **ATRICHUM.** Teeth adherent by their points to the flattened top of the columella. Calyptra spinulose at the apex.
44. **POGONATUM.** Teeth as in the last. Calyptra densely hairy.

↔ ↔ ↔ ↔ ↔ Teeth of the peristome 64. Calyptra cuculliform.

45. **POLYTRICHUM.** Teeth adherent as in No. 43. Calyptra densely hairy.

← ← Peristome double ; its teeth 16.

↔ Capsule symmetrical, erect : inner peristome of 16 cilia.

33. **MACROMITRIUM.** Teeth when dry erect. Calyptra campanulate, plicate.
28. **ENCALYPTA.** Teeth when dry erect. Calyptra campanulate, not plicate.
34 **SCHLOTHEIMIA.** Teeth when dry revolute. Calyptra campanulate, not plicate.
32. **ORTHOTRICHUM.** Teeth when dry reflexed Calyptra campanulate, plicate.
30. **ZYGODON.** Teeth when dry reflexed. Calyptra cuculliform.

↔ ↔ Capsule unsymmetrical and inclined to one side.
= Inner peristome a plaited cone.

41. **BUXBAUMIA.** Capsule gibbous, ovate, plano-convex, pedicellate.
42. **DIPHYSCIUM.** Capsule gibbous, ovate, not plano-convex, sessile.

= = Inner peristome a membrane cut into 16 cilia.

51. **BARTRAMIA.** Capsule globose, ribbed when dry.
47. **AULACOMNION.** Capsule oblong, ribbed when dry.
49 **MNIUM.** Capsule oblong : male flower discoid.
48. **BRYUM.** Capsule elongated-pyriform : male flower gemmiform.
50 **MEESIA.** Capsule elongated-pyriform. The outer peristome the shortest.
53. **FUNARIA.** Capsule short-pyriform. Teeth oblique, united at the apex.

= = = Inner peristome a membrane cut into 64 cilia.

46. **TIMMIA.** Capsule obovate-oblong. Cilia united at their apex in fours.

II. PLEUROCARPI. Fruit lateral (with operculum and peristome).

A. Calyptra cuculliform.

● Peristome single : teeth 16.

67. **CLASMATODON.** Teeth irregular twice or thrice divided to the base. Annulus large, imperfect.
70. **FABRONIA.** Teeth regular, approximated in pairs. Annulus wanting.

● ● Peristome double : the outer of 16 teeth ; the inner of 16 cilia, with or without ciliolæ ; or an irregular membrane.

← Capsule erect, equal.

a. Leaves papillose.

69. **MYURELLA.** Cilia from a broad base : ciliolæ present. Foliage glaucous-green.
66. **LESKEA.** Cilia from a broad base : ciliolæ none. Foliage dark-green.

65. ANOMODON. Cilia from a narrow base. Foliage yellowish green.
69. THELIA. Cilia obsolete : a broad annular membrane present Foliage glaucous-green.

  b Leaves not papillose, complanate.
76. NECKERA. Cilia from a narrow base. Leaves undulate.
75. CYLINDROTHECIUM. Cilia from a narrow base. Leaves smooth
77. OMALIA. Cilia from a broad base : ciliolæ present.

  c. Leaves not complanate.
  — Inner peristome a membrane adherent to the teeth.
62. LEUCODON. Perichæth very long. Calyptra smooth.
68. LEPTODON. Perichæth very long. Calyptra hairy.
72. PYLAISÆA. Perichæth short. Calyptra smooth.

  — — Inner peristome free, divided to the base into 16 cilia.
71. ANACAMPTODON. Teeth of the peristome reflexed when dry.
74. PLATYGYRIUM. Teeth of the peristome broadly margined. Annulus large.
64. ANTITRICHIA. Perichæth long. Ramification pinnate. Pedicels flexuose.
79. CLIMACIUM. Perichæth long. Ramification dendroid. Columella exserted.
60. DICHELYMA. Perichæth long. Inner peristome as in Fontinalis, No. 59.

  ← ← Capsule inclined, unequal.
73 HOMALOTHECIUM. Inner peristome a membrane adherent to the teeth. Calyptra hairy
80. HYPNUM. Inner peristome a plicate membrane divided half-way into carinate cilia : ciliolæ present. Calyptra smooth.

  B. Calyptra mitriform. Peristome double ; its teeth 16.

  * Capsule immersed, erect.
59. FONTINALIS. Inner peristome of 16 cilia connected by cross-bars.
61 CRYPHÆA. Inner peristome of 16 free and subulate cilia.

  * * Capsule exserted, horizontal.
78. HOOKERIA. Inner peristome of 16 carinate cilia : ciliolæ absent.

Suborder I. SPHÁGNACEÆ.

1. SPHÁGNUM, Dill. Peat-Moss. (Tab. 15.)

Calyptra irregularly ruptured in the middle. Operculum convex, depressed. Capsule subglobose, sessile on the pedicellate vaginula. Peristome none. Inflorescence monœcious or diœcious : antheridia roundish, with a long pedicel, lodged singly in the axils of the perigonial leaves at the clavate extremities of short branches. — Large, soft, flaccid, and usually pale-colored plants, inhabiting bogs and swampy places ; stems erect, mostly simple, capitate at the summit by the crowded branches which elsewhere are (3–7 together) in distinct fascicles ; branch-leaves 5-ranked, between broad-ovate and linear-lanceolate, convolute-concave, with a peculiar reticulation, composed of two kinds of cellules, one kind (utricles) large, sub-fusiform, colorless, perforated, and lined with a spiral filament (fibrillose), except in No. 10 ; the other kind (ducts) much smaller, linear, chlorophyllose, running between the contiguous walls of the utricles and forming the angular-serpentine network. (Σφάγνος, the ancient name.) Cross-sections of the leaf (see Sulliv. in Mem. Amer. Acad. IV. p. 174. t. 4. B.), showing the form and relative position of the utricles and ducts, are of service in determining the species, as follows : —

* Ducts somewhat elliptical, situated centrally between the angular-rotund utricles and not extending to either surface of the leaf.

1. **S. cymbifólium,** Dill. Diœcious; stems robust, $6'-18'$ long; branches $4-6$ in a fascicle, tumid, mostly obtuse; stem-leaves spatulate, not fibrillose; branch-leaves imbricated, ovate, cucullate and entire at the apex; capsule with stomata in its wall. — Bogs, &c.; common. — A large species, distinguished from its congeners by the sharp papillæ on the back of the leaf near the apex, and by the striæ on the walls of the cortical utricles of the branches. (Tab. I.) (Eu.)

2. **S. compáctum,** Brid. Diœcious? stems erect, $2'-5'$ high, densely cæspitose, with one layer of cortical utricles; branches $2-3$ in a fascicle, short, crowded, erect; branch-leaves ovate-acuminate, recurved-spreading, broadly margined, truncate and toothed at the apex; utricles with small pores, those at the point of the narrowly acuminated perichætial leaves not fibrillose. — (S. strictum, *Musc. Alleghan.*, No. 201.) — Springy places on high mountains, Southern States, *Lesquereux, Curtis, Buckley.* (Eu.)

3. **S. contórtum,** Schultz. Somewhat stiff and dark-colored; stems $4'-6'$ high; branches attenuated, more or less contorted; branch-leaves rather secund, ovate-lanceolate, of a firm texture; utricles very narrow, with a row of small pores on each side. — Cranberry marshes, Northern Ohio, *Lesquereux.* (Eu.)

4. **S. Lescûrii,** Sulliv. (Musc. Bor.-Amer., No. 6.) Aspect same as that of small forms of No. 1; ramification and mode of growth loose; branches $2-3$ in a fascicle, distant; stem-leaves lingulate, obtuse, the utricles fibrillose; branch-leaves elongated-ovate, truncate and dentate at the apex, the ducts cuneiform-elliptic, approaching the convex surface of the leaf; perichætial leaves quite large, when flattened oval-ovate; capsule oblong-globose, blackish, much exserted. — Wet sandy places among the mountains of Alabama; also Dismal Swamp, Virginia, *Lesquereux.*

5. **S. ténerum,** Sulliv. & Lesqx. (Musc. Bor.-Amer., No. 11.) Stems $2'-3'$ high, cæspitose; branches crowded, deflexed; stem-leaves large, ovate-lanceolate, the utricles fibrillose; branch-leaves ovate-lanceolate, imbricated; utricles ample, with a few large pores; ducts nearly cuneiform-elliptic, approaching the concave surface of the leaf; perichætial leaves ovate-subulate, undulate on the convolute margins above, the utricles mostly not fibrillose; capsule scarcely emergent. — Margins of rivulets; Raccoon Mountains, Alabama, *Lesquereux.*

6. **S. húmile,** Schimper. Cæspitose; stems $1'-2'$ high, with 3 layers of cortical utricles; branches crowded, spreading, $2-3$ in a fascicle; branch-leaves ovate-lanceolate, the upper half horizontal, truncate and dentate at the apex, narrowly margined; utricles broad, with large pores. — Tallahassee, Florida, *Rugel:* among the Lookout Mountains, Alabama, *Lesquereux.*

7. **S. cyclophýllum,** Sulliv. & Lesqx. (Musc. Bor.-Amer., No. 5.) Stems $2'-3'$ long, thick, turgid, flaccid, with only one layer of cortical utricles, mostly simple, rarely with a few scattered branches, not in fascicles; leaves pale greenish-white, narrowly margined, somewhat constricted at base, closely imbricated, oblong-rotund, entire at apex; ducts as in No. 5; flowers and fruit unknown. (S. cymbifolium, var. turgidum, *Hook. & Wils. in Drum. 2d Coll. No. 17.*) — New Orleans, *Drummond:* mountains of Alabama, *Lesquereux.* — (This

and No. 8 may be sterile forms or incomplete states of two species yet unknown. They approach nearer to S. cymbifolium than to any other species; but their leaves have a closer reticulation, and are not papillose on the back near the apex, nor are the cortical utricles of the branches marked with striæ, as they are in the last-named species.)

8. **S. sedoìdes,** Brid. Form and ramification of the stem and cross-section of the leaf same as in the last, but a somewhat smaller plant, and not so flaccid; leaves mostly of a dark vinous red, oval, entire at the apex, not margined; when dry absorbing moisture with difficulty; flowers and fruit not seen — Springy places, on Table Rock, S. Carolina, *Gray, Lesquereux*: Mt. Marcy, New York, *Torrey.* — (In the first-mentioned locality occurs an olive-green variety, (?) — perhaps S. Pylæsii, *Brid.* — smaller in all its parts; branches somewhat numerous, short, mostly single, and with closely-imbricated leaves, much smaller than the distantly placed stem-leaves. — (Musc. Bor.-Amer., No. 4.)

* * *Ducts oval, situated centrally between the rotund utricles, and extending to both surfaces of the leaf.*

9. **S. squarròsum,** Pers. Monœcious; stems 8'-12' long, robust, rigid; branches deflexed, attenuated, 5 in a fascicle; branch-leaves ovate-acuminate, squarrose; stem and perichætial leaves oblong, obtuse, not fibrillose. — Bogs, &c.; common in the Northern and Middle States, and westward. — A large species. (Eu.)

10. **S. macrophýllum,** Bernhardi. Stems slender, stiff, reddish, 4'-6' long; branches short, flat, flabelliform, 2-3 in a fascicle; branch-leaves long, subulate, straight, spreading, dentate at the apex; utricles elongated, with 7-9 large pores in a line along the centre, and remarkable for the absence of a spiral fibre; capsule oblong, concealed by the perichætial leaves. — Swamps near the sea-coast, New Jersey to Florida: also Raccoon Mts., Alabama, *Lesquereux*.

* * * *Ducts triangular, situated between the rotund utricles next the concave surface of the leaf.*

11. **S. acutifòlium,** Ehrh. Monœcious; stems 5'-10' long, slender; branches crowded, elongated, attenuated, mostly pendent; stem-leaves lingulate, obtuse, not fibrillose; branch-leaves ovate-lanceolate, tapering to a narrow truncate point, erect-patent; capsule much exserted. — Frequent; variable in size: foliage often tinged with red. — S. rubellum, *Wils.* (common in Europe), closely resembling this, but a smaller species, with elliptical leaves and diœcious inflorescence, may be looked for within our limits. (Eu.)

12. **S. fimbriàtum,** Wils. Monœcious; much like and formerly confounded with No. 11, but a more delicate species, with fimbriated stem-leaves, and large, conspicuous, obovate, obtuse, and cucullate perichætial leaves. — British America, *Drummond.* (Eu.)

13. **S. tabulàre,** Sulliv. Stems 2'-3' high, closely cæspitose; branches densely crowded, short, erect-patent; stem-leaves large, oblong, obtuse or acute, fibrillose; branch-leaves ovate-acuminate, the upper half spreading and undulate on the margins; perichætial leaves lanceolate, acute, broadly bordered above; sporules golden-yellow. — (S. acutifolium, var.? *Musc. Alleghan.*) — Table

Mountain, N. Carolina; near Mobile, Alabama. — A small species, with foliage mostly of a pale brownish or yellowish hue, resembling S. molluscum, but that has a cross-section of the leaf like No. 15 and 16.

14. **S. mólle,** Sulliv. Densely cæspitose; stems 2'–3' high, fragile, concealed by the crowded and short patent branches; branch-leaves oblong, ovate-acuminate, recurved-spreading; perichætial leaves orbicular-ovate. — Mountains of N. Carolina, *Gray:* Tallulah Falls, Georgia, *Lesquereux.* — Has remarkably soft whitish foliage.

* * * * *Ducts triangular, situated between the rotund utricles next the convex surface of the leaf.*

15. **S. cuspidátum,** Ehrh. Monœcious; stems 6'–10' long; fascicles of 4–5 deflexed branches distant; stem-leaves lanceolate-acuminate, recurved-patent, when dry flattened and undulate on the margins (the best distinctive mark of the species); perichætial leaves broad-ovate, acute. — Var. RECÚRVUM, leaves oblong-lanceolate, when dry much recurved. — Var. PLUMÓSUM, growing in water, more elongated and attenuated in all its parts. — Not uncommon; New England to Louisiana. Foliage pale green or yellowish-white. (Eu.)

16. **S. Torreyànum,** Sulliv. Stem stiff, a foot or more in length; branches 4–5 in a fascicle, 12''–15'' long, 2''–3'' wide, flat, linear-lanceolate; leaves elongated-lanceolate, spreading, straight, broadly margined, erose-dentate at the apex; fruit unknown. — Ponds and slow-flowing streams; pine barrens of New Jersey, *Torrey.* — A large robust species: foliage drab-colored, of a firm texture.

SUBORDER II. **ANDRÆÀCEÆ.**

2. ANDRÈA, Ehrh. (Tab. 15.)

Calyptra mitriform. Operculum none. Capsule oblong-oval, dehiscing by four longitudinal fissures, and sessile upon the pedicellate vaginula. Inflorescence monœcious or diœcious. — Small alpine or subalpine mosses, of a dark brownish or blackish color, growing on rocks; stems ascending, rigid, dichotomously divided; leaves with or without a costa, of a firm texture, the areolation above angular-rotund and small; below oblong and large. — (A personal name.)

1. **A. petróphila,** Ehrh. Monœcious; stems 4''–10'' long, filiform, leafless below; leaves ovate- and oblong-lanceolate, concave, spreading-incurved from an erect base, without a costa, papillose on the back, the point oblique, often with a hyaline crenulate margin. (A. rupestris, *Hedw.*) — High mountains; a variable species. (Eu.)

2. **A. rupéstris,** Turner. Monœcious; leaves spreading or secund from an ovate base, linear-lanceolate, smooth, concave; costa continuous. (A. Rothii, *Web. & Mohr.*) — White Mts., New Hampshire, *Oakes.* (Tab. 15.) (Eu.)

3. **A. crassinérvia,** Bruch. Monœcious; near the last, but the leaves are shining, falcate-secund, subulate from an oblong base, cuspidate by the large, terete, excurrent costa, which is papillose at the point. — With No. 2. (Eu.)

Suborder III. BRYÀCEÆ.

Div. I. Acrocárpi.

Fruit terminal on the main stem, or rarely terminal on short lateral branches.

A. CLEISTOCÁRPI. — Capsule without an operculum, rupturing irregularly.

Tribe I. PHÁSCEÆ.

3. ARCHÍDIUM, Brid. (Tab. 15.)

Calyptra irregularly ruptured in the middle; the lower part persistent. Capsule globose, sessile on the short vaginula, immersed. Columella none. Spores large, few (8 - 15). Inflorescence monœcious : male flower naked or 2-leaved, axillary. — Minute terrestrial plants, of a structure more simple than any of the suborder, hence its name ('Αρχίδιον, a beginning).

1. **A. Ohioénse**, Schimp. Stems at first erect, 1″ - 2″ high, afterwards decumbent, and lengthened by innovations; leaves lanceolate, cuspidate by the excurrent costa, slightly denticulate above, the perichætial much larger; capsule terminal on a short lateral branch. (A. phascoides, *Musc. Alleghan.*, *No.* 213.) — Meadows and waste fields, Central Ohio, and N. Alabama. (Tab. 15.)

4. PHÁSCUM, L. (Tab. 15.)

Calyptra campanulate or cuculliform. Capsule roundish, more or less apiculate, shortly pedicellate, usually immersed. Columella present. Spores numerous, muriculate : inflorescence monœcious. — Diminutive species, mostly annual, growing on the ground, either stemless and bulb-like, or with a short stem, sparingly divided; leaves costate or ecostate. (Φάσκον, an ancient name for a moss.) — For convenience, the genus is here retained in its former extended sense ; the names of the genera, into which a natural arrangement requires the species to be distributed, being used for sections.

* *Plants growing from a conferroid thallus. Columella fugacious.*

⸹ 1. EPHEMÉRUM, Hampe. — *Stemless: leaves of a loose rhomboidal areolation . calyptra campanulate-conic : capsule globose-ovate, subsessile, apiculate : spores large : male flower gemmiform, at or near the base of the fertile stem.*

1. **P. serrátum**, Schreb. Leaves oblong or linear-lanceolate, ecostate, deeply serrate; capsule purple, shining. — Moist ground ; edge of woods. (Eu.)

2. **P. séssile**, Br. & Sch. Leaves lanceolate-subulate, nearly entire ; costa excurrent, more or less obsolete near the base. — Clayey soil, in thin woods, Central Ohio. (Eu.)

3. **P. crassinérvium**, Schwægr. Leaves linear-lanceolate, strongly and irregularly dentate near the apex ; costa continuous, not excurrent. — With the last. — Also with a var. ? having the leaves near the apex spinulose-dentate, (the teeth often recurved,) and papillose or cristate on the back ; spores much larger : — probably E. spinulosum, *Br. & Sch.*, mentioned in *Wils Bryol. Brit.*, p. 27.

4. **P. cohǽrens**, Hedw. Leaves oblong-lanceolate, strongly serrate; costa vanishing below the apex; capsule brownish-purple. — River-banks, Central Ohio. (Eu.)

* * *Plants without a confervoid thallus. Columella persistent.*

§ 2. PHYSCOMITRÉLLA, Schimp. — *Caulescent : leaves loosely areolated : calyptra campanulate-conic : capsule globose, apiculate : antheridia naked, axillary, with paraphyses globosely distended at the apex.* (Closely allied to Aphanorhegma among Funarieæ.)

5. **P. pàtens**, Hedw. Leaves subspatulate-lanceolate, serrate, costate nearly to the apex; capsule sometimes exserted. — Moist clayey soil, Central Ohio : rare. (Eu.)

§ 3. ACAÙLON, Mull. — *Stemless, bulb-like : leaves broad-ovate or obovate, very concave, recurved at the apex, with a lax areolation : capsule globose, entirely concealed by the 2 or 3 large subcucullate perichœtial leaves : calyptra minute, campanulate : inflorescence as in* § 1.

6. **P. triquètrum**, Spruce. Leaves 3-ranked, carinate-concave, shortly cuspidate by the continuous excurrent costa, the perichætial ones 3 and larger; capsule horizontal, with a curved pedicel. — On dry soil; rare. (Eu.)

7. **P. mùticum**, Schreb. Size of the last; leaves not carinate, costate, the perichætial ones 2; capsule erect; pedicel straight. — Moist ground. (Eu.)

8. **P. Schimperiànum**, Sulliv. (Musc. Bor.-Amer., No. 26.) Resembles the last two species, but the perichætial leaves near the apex are papillose on both surfaces, erose-dentate on the recurved margins, and cuspidate by the costa which extends scarcely ¼ of the way towards their base, the other leaves without any trace of a costa; capsule, pedicel, and calyptra as in No. 7. — San Marcos, Texas, *Wright.*

§ 4. PHASCUM Proper. — *Stems simple, or once or twice divided by innovations : leaves costate; areolation below large, loose, oblong, above minute, subquadrate, chlorophyllose : calyptra cuculliform : capsule globular, acuminate.* — (Resembles the Pottieæ.)

9. **P. cuspidàtum**, Schreb. Leaves elongated-lanceolate, cuspidate, more or less papillose on the back near the apex; costa excurrent; capsule immersed or exserted ; antheridia mostly naked in the axils of the perichætial leaves. — Old fields; not uncommon. (Tab. 15.) (Eu.)

§ 5. PLEURÍDIUM, Brid. — *Stems erect or decumbent : leaves subulate, costate, with a loose and oblong hexagonal reticulation : calyptra cuculliform or campanulate-conic : capsule globular or ovate, sometimes becoming lateral by innovations of the stem.*

10. **P. alternifòlium**, Brid. Lower leaves ovate-lanceolate, the upper much longer, subulate from an oblong base; costa excurrent, with the point more or less serrulate; capsule ovate, obtusely acuminate; calyptra cuculliform; male flower gemmiform, axillary. — Old fields, &c.; common. — In American forms the base of the leaves is usually more closely areolated than in the European

G. M.   2

ropean, and the point is more strongly serrulate : the capsule also is inclined to an oval shape. (Eu.)

11. **P. subulàtum,** Schreb. Very much like the last, but the base of the leaf not so suddenly dilated, more lanceolate, the point not so serrulate ; calyptra smaller ; the antheridia naked in the axils of the perichætial leaves.— Pennsylvania and Rhode Island : rare. (Eu.)

12. **P. palústre,** Br. & Sch. Distinguished from the last two species mainly by its campanulate-conic calyptra 4 - 5-lobed at the base : inflorescence as in No. 11.— Sandy soil, New Jersey, *James.* Louisiana. (Eu.)

13. **P. nervòsum,** Hook. Upper leaves more or less obovate-oblong, densely areolated above, serrate at the apex of the lamina, with a broad, long-excurrent costa ; the lower leaves much smaller, oblong, acuminate, closely appressed ;. capsule ovate ; pedicel short ; calyptra cuculliform ; male flower gemmiform at the base of the fertile stem.— Pennsylvania, *Drummond.*

§ 6. ÁSTOMUM, Hampe.— *Stems simple or branched, perennial : leaves elongated, costate, the terminal much larger, with a loose, hyaline areolation below ; above minute, subquadrate, granulose : calyptra cuculliform : capsule globose or ovate, more or less rostellate.* — (Allied to the Weisieæ.)

＊ Male flower gemmiform, axillary.

14. **P. crispum,** Hedw. Stems divided above, bearing several capsules on each branch ; leaves crisped when dry, shortly cuspidate by the strong excurrent costa, the lower ovate-lanceolate, the upper linear-lanceolate from an oblong base, the margins above strongly convolute ; capsule globose, apiculate, with a more or less obscure operculation. — It is uncertain if the species is truly American ; but specimens (imperfect) from Texas and Indiana appear to belong to it. (Eu.)

15. **P. Sullivántii,** Schimp. Resembles the last, but has shorter stems, not so much branched ; capsule solitary, shining, bright orange-colored ; calyptra and spores smaller. — Very common.

16. **P. nitidulum,** Schimp. Near No. 15, but a smaller species, with a shining, pale chestnut-colored, oval, obliquely rostellate capsule, its pedicel thrice as long as in the last ; calyptra minute, scarcely descending to the obscure line of operculation. — Central Ohio : rare.

＊ ＊ Male flower gemmiform, terminal on the main stem or its branches.

17. **P. Ludoviciànum,** Sulliv. Larger than No. 14 ; leaves very much the same in every respect ; capsule oblong-oval, obtusely rostellate, usually 2 - 3 in the same perichæth, borne on a branch arising from below the male flower. — (P. crispum, var. rostellatum, *Schwægr.? Hook. & Wils. in Drum. 2d Coll., No.* 10.) — New Orleans, *Drummond.*

5. BRÙCHIA, Schwægr. (Tab. 15.)

Calyptra mitriform, lobed at the base. Capsule obovate or oblong, rostellate, pedicellate : collum large. Columella present. Spores numerous, usually yellow, muriculate. Inflorescence monœcious : male flower gemmiform, term.-

nal on a short branch. — Minute terrestrial perennials, with mostly simple stems and lanceolate-subulate, continuously costate leaves of a loose oblong areolation at their base, elsewhere smaller, compact and roundish. (Named after *Bruch*, a distinguished bryologist.)

1. **B. flexuòsa**, Schwægr. ¿Stems flexuose-erect, simple; leaves distant, spreading from an oblong base, long-subulate, channelled, denticulate at the apex; capsule obovate-oblong, exserted, abruptly passing into a rather long slender and flexuous pedicel, covered for half its length by the calyptra. — Var. NIGRICANS : Whole plant longer; leaves shorter, appressed; spores larger, dark brown. — New England to Florida, and westward; the var. on Raccoon Mountains, Alabama, *Lesquereux*, and Cleaveland, Ohio, *Prof. Cassels*.

2. **B. Beyrichiàna**, Hampe. Has (according to Schwægrichen) the leaves and pedicel of No. 1, but a much shorter stem, and the calyptra entirely covering the oblong capsule. — Maryland, near Baltimore, *Beyrich*. (Not since detected.)

3. **B. brévipes**, Hook. Stems short; leaves as in No. 1, but erect, over-topping the globose-oval somewhat pyriform capsule; pedicel short; spores nearly twice as large as in the first species. — Louisiana, *Drummond*.

4. **B. brevifòlia**, Sulliv. Size of No. 3; leaves much shorter, broader, erect, reaching only to the base of the large obovate-oblong and short-pedi-celled capsule; spores as in No. 1. — (Bruchia Vogesiaca, var. 2, *Hook & Wils. in Drum. 2d Coll. No. 15 partly.*) — Louisiana, *Drummond:* South Carolina, *Rave-nel:* Texas, *Wright.* (Tab. I.)

5. **B. Ravenélii**, Wils. mss. Almost stemless; leaves lanceolate-subu-late; costa excurrent and with a scabrous apex; capsule globose-pyriform, ob-tusely apiculate, slightly exserted, short-pedicelled; calyptra strongly papillose, 8 – 10-lobed at the base. — South Carolina, *Ravenel.* — (Very near the Chilian B. Hampeana, *C. Mull.*)

B. STEGOCÁRPI. — Capsule dehiscing by a deciduous operculum.

Tribe II. WEÍSIEÆ.

6. GYMNÓSTOMUM, Hedw. (Tab. 15.)

Calyptra cuculliform. Operculum conic-rostrate. Capsule suboval, annu-late, exserted. Peristome none. Inflorescence diœcious : male flower terminal, gemmiform. — Rather small, densely cæspitose species, with linear-lanceolate cos-tate leaves of a close, opaque, rather quadrate areolation. (Name from γυμνός, *naked*, and στόμα, *a mouth*; no peristome.)

1. **G. curviróstrum**, Hedw. Stems fastigiately branched; capsule obovate, shining; operculum with a long oblique rostrum. — Frequent, in dense cushions, on wet limestone rocks. (Eu.)

2. **G. rupéstre**, Schwægr. Smaller than the last; capsule oval, and with an erect elongated-conical operculum. — In similar situations with No. 1 : variable. (Tab. I) (Eu.)

7. WEÍSIA, Hedw.   (Tab. 15.)

Calyptra cuculliform. Operculum rostrate. Capsule oval, annulate, exserted. Peristome single, of 16 linear-lanceolate articulated teeth, entire or perforated, without a medial line. Inflorescence monœcious or diœcious. — Small
species, growing on the ground; stems more or less fastigiately branched; leaves
linear-lanceolate, costate, of a dense and somewhat quadrate areolation. —
(Named after *F. W. Weis*, a German cryptogamic botanist.)

1. **W. viridula,** Brid. Leaves very much involute on the margins,
crisped when dry; costa slightly excurrent. — Old fields, meadows, &c. : very
common and variable. (Tab. 15.) (Eu.)

8. RHABDOWEÍSIA, Br. & Sch.   (Tab. 15.)

Calyptra cuculliform. Operculum with a long oblique rostrum. Capsule
short-oval, 8-striated, annulate, exserted. Peristome single, of 16 subulate or
lanceolate teeth, without a medial line. Inflorescence monœcious: male flower
terminal, gemmiform. — Size and aspect of the species very much as in the last
genus, from which it is separated by the striated capsule (hence its name, from
ῥάβδος, *a stria*, and *Weisia*).

1. **R. fúgax,** Br. & Sch. Leaves linear-lanceolate, carinate, costate to
the apex, nearly entire on the margins, crisped when dry, more or less papillose;
the areolation dense and quadrate above, larger, looser, and oblong below; teeth
of the peristome subulate, fugacious. — White Mountains, New Hampshire,
Oakes; rare. (Tab. 15.) (Eu.)

2. **R. denticulàta,** Br. & Sch. Very near the last, but rather larger;
leaves linear-lanceolate, approaching to lingulate, coarsely serrate at the apex;
areolation larger; teeth of the peristome lanceolate, not fugacious. — Crevices
of rocks, on high peaks of the Alleghany Mountains; not uncommon. (Eu.)

Tribe III. SELIGERIÈÆ.

9. SELIGÈRIA, Br. & Sch.   (Tab. 15.)

Calyptra cuculliform. Operculum large, obliquely rostrate. Capsule globose-pyriform, exannulate, exserted. Peristome single; teeth 16, lanceolate,
obtuse, without a medial line. Inflorescence monœcious: male flower gemmiform, terminal. — Very small, almost stemless mosses, growing on rocks; leaves
lanceolate-subulate, with a stout excurrent costa; the areolation dense, except at
the base. (A personal name.)

1. **S. tristicha,** Br. & Sch. Stems 2″–3″ high, 3-ranked, obtuse at
the apex. — (*Weisia calcarea, Musc. Alleghan., No.* 142.) — Limestone rocks, in
shaded ravines, Central Ohio. (Tab. 15.) (Eu.)

2. **S. recurvàta,** Br. & Sch. Resembles the last (and grows with it),
somewhat larger; leaves not 3-ranked, acute; capsule not so globose, pendulous on a longer curved pedicel, erect when dry. (Eu.)

TRIBE IV. DICRÀNEÆ.

10. ÁRCTOA, Br. & Sch. (Tab. 15.)

Calyptra cuculliform, inflated. Operculum large, obliquely rostrate. Capsule oval or somewhat turbinate, ribbed when dry, erect or inclined, annulate, exserted. Peristome single : teeth 16, lanceolate-subulate, cloven half-way, the divisions unequal. Inflorescence monœcious : male flower gemmiform. — Densely cæspitose alpine species, growing on rocks, with long lanceolate-setaceous falcate-secund costate leaves, of an oblong and compact areolation. (Name from ἄρκτος, *north*; found only in Northern latitudes.)

1. **A. fulvélla,** Br. & Sch. Leaves fulvous, with a strong continuous costa denticulate at the apex ; perichætial leaves large, sheathing. overtopping the capsule. — White Mountains, New Hampshire, *Oakes.* (Tab. 15.) (Eu.)

11. CAMPÝLOPUS, Brid. (Tab. 15.)

Calyptra cuculliform, fringed at the base. Operculum conic-rostrate. Capsule oval, regular or gibbous, annulate, ribbed when dry, on a decurved pedicel. Peristome single : teeth 16, linear-lanceolate, deeply bifid ; segments unequal. Inflorescence diœcious : male flower terminal. — Stems densely cæspitose, dichotomously branched ; leaves rigid, lanceolate-setaceous, with a broad excurrent costa ; areolation large, oblong or rhomboid at the base, elsewhere much smaller and subquadrate. (Named from καμπύλος, *curved*, and πούς, *a foot*, in allusion to the curved pedicel.) (Tab. 15.)

1. **C. flexuòsus,** Brid. Stems 1' - 2' high, radiculose ; leaves erect-patent or falcate-secund ; capsules aggregated at the apex of the stem, regular or gibbous. — Shaded rocks, Grandfather Mountain, N. Carolina. (Tab. 15.) (Eu.)

2. **C. leucótrichus,** Sulliv. & Lesqx. (Musc. Bor.-Amer., No. 73.) Stems densely leaved above, claviform ; leaves erect-patent, linear-lanceolate, with a long hyaline and denticulate hair-point ; costa very broad, strongly lamellose on the back. — On rocks, dry woods, Raccoon Mts., Alabama, *Lesquereux.*

3. **C. Leànus,** Sulliv. Stems fastigiately branched ; the branches terminated by dense heads of minute oblong bodies (probably abortive leaves) ; leaves lanceolate-subulate, erect, rather secund, the costa occupying nearly all the leaf. — Ohio and Pennsylvania : not rare ; on very much decayed stumps and logs. Resembles the young growth of Dicranum flagellare.

12. DICRANODÓNTIUM, Br. & Sch. (Tab. 15.)

Calyptra cuculliform, not fringed at the base. Operculum conic-subulate. Capsule elliptic-oblong, annulate, smooth, pendulous from an arcuate pedicel. Peristome single : teeth 16, linear-lanceolate, cloven to the base ; their divisions unequal. Inflorescence diœcious : male flower gemmiform, terminal. — Habit and aspect nearly as in the last genus. (Name from δίκρανος, *fo·ked*, and ὀδούς, *a tooth*.)

i. **D. longiróstre,** Br. & Sch.　Stem 1' - 3' high, with innovations from near the apex; leaves fragile, more or less falcate-secund, subulate-setaceous from a dilated base; costa broad, occupying all the upper portion of the leaf. — On rocks, Alleghany Mountains.　(Tab. 15.)　(Eu.)

13. TREMÁTODON, Rich.

Calyptra cuculliform, inflated.　Operculum subulate-rostrate.　Capsule oval-oblong, inclined, with a very long collum, annulate, long-pedicellate.　Peristome single : teeth 16, linear-lanceolate, perforated, or more or less cloven.　Inflorescence diœcious : male flower gemmiform. — Short-stemmed, gregarious plants, with long subulate-setaceous and continuously-costate leaves.　(Name from τρῆμα, a perforation, and ὀδών, a tooth.)　(Tab. 15.)

1. **T. longicóllis,** Rich.　Capsule with a narrow linear collum of twice its length; pedicel 1½' - 2' long, slender, flexuous, straw-colored. — Clayey and sandy soil, New England to Florida, and Ohio, Cassels.　(Tab. 15.)

14. DICRÀNUM, Hedw.　(Tab. 16.)

Calyptra cuculliform.　Operculum conic, long-subulate-rostrate.　Capsule oval, oblong or cylindrical, regular or somewhat gibbous, erect or cernuous, long-pedicellate.　Peristome single : teeth 16, linear-lanceolate, cloven half-way or more into two unequal segments.　Inflorescence monœcious or diœcious : male flower gemmiform, terminal. — Perennial plants, growing on the ground or on rocks; stems from a few lines to several inches in height, fastigiately branched and continued by innovations from near the apex; leaves mostly linear-lanceolate and lanceolate-subulate, continuously costate, often falcate-secund, with a minute, compact, roundish areolation above.　(Name from δίκρανος, forked, alluding to the teeth.)

§ 1. CYNODÓNTIUM, Br. & Sch. — *Leaves more or less papillose, crenulate-ser-rate at the apex; the areolation uniform at the base : calyptra inflated-cuculliform : capsule mostly strumose and erect : monœcious.*

1. **D. graciléscens,** Web. & Mohr., var. **tenéllum,** Bryol. Europ. Stems short, 4'' - 10'' high; leaves linear-lanceolate, scarcely papillose, the margins above plane, the costa vanishing at the apex ; capsule exannulate, oval, not strumose, obsoletely striate.　White Mts., New Hampshire, Oakes.　(Eu.)

2. **D. polycárpum,** Ehrh.　Stems 1' - 2' high ; leaves linear-lanceolate, variously curved, somewhat papillose on both surfaces, denticulate at the apex and at the base; capsule oval-oblong, erect, regular, or gibbous-inclined and strumose, ribbed when dry ; annulus conspicuous. — Northern shore of Lake Superior, Agassiz.　(Eu.)

3. **D. virens,** Hedw., var. **Wahlenbergii,** Bryol. Europ.　More robust than the last; stems often 3' high ; leaves spreading, flexuous, lanceolate-subulate, smooth, denticulate at the apex, the costa nearly excurrent ; capsule oblong, incurved, cernuous, prominently strumose, annulate. — Lake Superior, Agassiz.　(Eu.)

§ 2. DICRANÉLLA, Schimp. — *Small species: leaves smooth, more or less serrate at the apex; the areolation uniform at the base: calyptra not inflated: capsule mostly cernuous, seldom strumose: diœcious.*

4. **D. cerviculàtum,** Hedw. Densely cæspitose, yellowish-green; stems short, 4″–6″ high; leaves lanceolate-subulate, serrate at the apex, somewhat secund, with a broad costa; capsule gibbous, short, globose-oval, narrowly annulate, strumose. — Bogs, New Jersey, *Torrey.* (Eu.)

5. **D. vàrium,** Hedw. Stems 4″–5″ high; leaves lanceolate-attenuated, nearly entire at the apex, patent; costa slightly excurrent; capsule oval or oblong, more or less oblique and incurved, exannulate; operculum large, shortly rostrate. — Clay-banks, in loose patches: very common: variable. (Eu.)

6. **D. débile,** Hooker & Wilson. Resembles small forms of No. 5; stems 2″–3″ high, mostly simple, leaves erect; the lower short, ovate-lanceolate, rather obtuse; the upper linear-lanceolate, channelled, and with entire reflexed margins, costate to the apex; capsule oval, erect; operculum with a small conic base, and an erect subulate rostrum as long as the capsule; peristome small: teeth 2–3-cleft half-way, below red, strigillose, the segments scabrous; annulus very large, deciduous, triple; spores rather large; pedicel yellow. — Clayey soil, Mobile, Alabama?

7. **D. ruféscens,** Turner. Stem short, gregarious; leaves reddish, lax, linear-lanceolate, falcate-secund, the margins plane, obscurely denticulate; areolation loose; capsule erect, oval or somewhat obovate, exannulate; operculum large, with a short rostrum. —Wet clay-banks, Pennsylvania, *Lesquereux.* — Resembles No. 5. (Eu.)

8. **D. subulàtum,** Hedw. Loosely cæspitose; stems 5″–10″ high; leaves secund, somewhat falcate, long-subulate from a lanceolate base, entire; costa predominant; capsule ovate, gibbous, cernuous, striated when dry; annulus rather large; pedicel red. — White Mts., New Hampshire, *Oakes.* (Eu.)

9. **D. heterómallum,** Hedw. Somewhat larger than the last; leaves secund, slightly falcate, lanceolate-setaceous; costa heavy, vanishing at the subdenticulate apex; capsule cernuous or nearly erect, more or less obovate and gibbous, obliquely plicate when dry; pedicel pale yellow. — Var. ORTHOCÁRPUM has an erect cylindrical capsule. — Moist ground; very common. (Eu.)

§ 3. DICRANUM PROPER. — *Mostly large species: stems often densely tomentose for their whole length with radicular fibres: leaves with enlarged yellowish and diaphanous cellules at their basal angles: capsule cernuous or erect.*

* *Monœcious: leaves falcate: capsule cernuous.*

10. **D. Blýttii,** Bryol. Europ. Cæspitose; branches fragile; leaves soft, dull-green, flexuose, rather secund, crisped when dry, the costa slightly excurrent; capsule oval, when dry strumose; annulus simple. — Alpine and subalpine rocks, White Mountains of New Hampshire, *Oakes.* (Eu.)

11. **D. Stárkii,** Web. & Mohr. Stems 1′–3′ long, decumbent at the base; leaves long, subulate-setaceous from a lanceolate base, secund, not crisped when dry, the costa shortly excurrent; capsule oblong, gibbous, strumose, striated; annulus double. — With the last. (Eu.)

12. **D. montànum,** Hedw. Compactly cæspitose; leaves bright-green soft, patent, rather secund, crisped when dry, lanceolate-subulate, serrate on the margin, and papillose on the back at the apex; costa strong, percurrent; capsule oblong, sulcate when dry; annulus double. — On trunks of trees, Goat Island, Niagara Falls, *Lesquereux.* (Eu.)

13. **D. flagellàre,** Hedw. Near the last species, but distinct by its numerous fragile and short erect flagellæ, furnished with minute appressed lanceolate ecostate leaves; stem-leaves greenish-yellow, more falcate-secund; the capsule longer and narrower. — On decayed logs in woods; very common. (Eu.)

14. **D. interrúptum,** Br. & Sch. Stems 1'–2' high; leaves long, secund-falcate, or spreading every way, flexuous, subulately attenuated from a lanceolate base; costa broad, predominant, denticulate at the apex; capsule cylindrical, annulate, dark brown. — On rocks in mountain districts. — A rather harsh, dark-green species, somewhat larger than No. 12 and 13. (Eu)

15. **D. longifòlium,** Hedw. Loosely cæspitose, pale-green; stems elongated, slender, arcuate-ascending; leaves circinate-secund, very long, filiformly attenuated, with a remarkably broad costa, denticulate on the margins and the back at the apex; capsule elliptic-cylindrical. — Shaded rocks, Alleghany Mountains. (Eu.)

16. **D. scopàrium,** L. Loosely cæspitose; stems 2'–4' high; leaves secund or falcate-secund, lanceolate-subulate, carinate-concave, serrate at the apex; costa with prominent ridges at the back, dentate above; capsule cylindrical, slightly cernuous. — Var. PALLIDUM (Musc. Alleghan., No. 155) has narrower leaves, with a looser areolation, the lower areolæ not sinuous, the costa with ridges only near the point; pedicel pale yellow. — Alleghany Mountains; rare. — The variety in districts not mountainous, and very common. (Tab. 16.) (Eu.)

17. **D. elongàtum,** Schwægr. Compactly cæspitose; stems slender, 4'–5' long; leaves lanceolate-subulate, entire, erect-patent; capsule gibbous-ovate, striate, annulate. — High peaks of the Alleghany Mountains: north shore of Lake Superior, *Agassiz.* (Eu.)

18. **D. congéstum,** Brid. Loosely cæspitose; leaves spreading, subsecund, flexuous, lanceolate-subulate, denticulate at the apex, crisped when dry; costa·strong, excurrent; capsule oval-oblong, much incurved, striated. — On rocks, in mountainous districts; common. (Eu.)

19. **D. palústre,** Brid. Stems 3'–4' high; leaves spreading, linear-lanceolate, undulated, serrate on the margin and also the back at the apex; costa slender and vanishing below the point; capsule oval-oblong, slightly incurved, striated; annulus none. — In cranberry marshes, Northern Ohio, *Lesquereux.* (Eu.)

20. **D. Schràderi,** Web. & Mohr. Densely tufted; stems 3'–5' long; leaves crowded, erect-patent, oblong-lanceolate, rather obtuse, undulated, the upper half serrated on the margins and papillose on the back; costa ceasing

below the apex; capsule incurved-oblong, annulate. — Bogs, in mountainous districts. (Eu.)

21. **D. spūrium,** Hedw. Stems usually short, thick and condensed; leaves ovate-lanceolate, acuminate, undulated, serrate; costa serrated on the back above, ceasing below the apex; capsule cylindrical, slightly strumose and incurved; when dry strongly ribbed. — (D. pallidum, *Bryol. Europ.?*) — Dry sandy soil, Ohio, and Southern States. (Eu.)

22. **D. undulātum,** Turner. Loosely cæspitose; stems 4 - 6' long, robust; leaves widely spreading, the upper ones falcate-secund, linear-lanceolate from an oblong base, very much undulated, sharply serrate on the margin and the back near the apex; costa slender; capsule cylindrical, strongly arcuate, on long pedicels, 2 to 5 from the same perichæth. — On the ground, in dry woods; common. (Eu.)

23. **D. Drummóndii,** Mull. — Very like No. 22, but distinguished by its longer and narrower leaves, not so sharply serrate, papillose only on the back, and cirrhose-crisped when dry. — White Mountains of New Hampshire, *Oakes:* Lake Superior, *Agassiz.* (Eu.)

15. CERÁTODON, Brid. (Tab. 15.)

Calyptra cuculliform. Operculum conic, subrostellate. Capsule cylindrical, subcernuous, annulate, long-pedicellate. Peristome single: teeth 16, linear-lanceolate, cloven nearly to the base into two equal segments; their articulations prominent. Inflorescence diœcious, terminal: male flower gemmiform. — Densely cæspitose plants, with fastigiate ramification; leaves lanceolate or lanceolate-subulate, costate; the areolæ above dense, roundish and small, below larger and diaphanous. (Name from κέρας, *a horn,* and ὀδών, *a tooth,* the teeth of the peristome being nodulose like a goat's horn.)

1. **C. purpūreus,** Brid. Leaves oblong-lanceolate, carinate, the margins recurved; costa excurrent; capsule purplish-red, shining, ribbed and strumose when dry. — Very common everywhere: on the ground. (Tab. 15.) (Eu.)

Tribe V. LEUCOBRYEÆ.

16. LEUCÒBRYUM, Hampe. (Tab. 16.)

Calyptra cuculliform. Operculum with a long-subulate rostrum. Capsule oblong-cernuous, strumose, long-pedicellate. Peristome as in Dicranum. Inflorescence monœcious: male flower terminal. — White or pale-glaucous mosses, growing in dense compact masses; stems dichotomously branched; leaves lanceolate-subulate, ecostate, composed of two or more layers of large, pellucid, empty, rectangular-oblong, perforated cellules, with minute 3 - 4-sided intercellular chlorophyllose passages. (Name composed of λευκός, *white,* and βρύον, *a moss,* from its pallid color.)

1. **L. glaūcum,** Hampe. Stems 3' - 6' high, leaves fragile, crowded, convolute above; capsule reddish-brown, ribbed when dry. — (Dicranum glaucum, *Hedw.*) — About the roots of trees in moist ground, margins of swamps,

&c.; common : ripens its fruit (which is scarce) in October and November. (Tab. 16.) (Eu.)

2. **L. mìnus,** Hampe. Besides numerous discrepancies, singly of not much importance, this species differs from the last in its much smaller size, its preference for dry localities, and the time (May and June) of ripening its fruit. — On the ground, dry woods ; not rare.   (Eu.)

Tribe VI. FISSIDÉNTEÆ.

17. FÍSSIDENS, Hedw.   (Tab. 15.)

Calyptra cuculliförm, or conic-mitriform. Capsule oval or oblong, erect or cernuous, rather long-pedicellate. Operculum conic-rostrate. Peristome single : teeth 16, geniculate-inflexed : — otherwise as in Dicranum. Inflorescence various. — Frond-like plants ; the leaves exactly two-ranked, inserted on opposite sides of the stem, their proper lamina infolded-boat-shaped, producing from the keel an equitant blade, which forms the principal portion of the leaf ; areolation minute, hexagonal-rotund. (Name from the Latin *fissus*, split, and *dens*, a tooth.)

* *Fruit terminal.*

1. **F. hyalìnus,** Hook. & Wils. Stems 1″-2″ high, erect, simple ; leaves oblong-lanceolate, acute, without any costa ; areolation large and hyaline ; capsule erect, oval ; calyptra conic, entire at the base. — Damp earth, in shady woods, near Cincinnati, Ohio : found only by the late *T. G. Lea.*

2. **F. obtusifòlius,** Wils. Stems simple, 2″-3″ high ; leaves oblong-oval, very obtuse, costate nearly to the apex ; capsule obovate-oval ; operculum convex-conic, with a very short rostrum ; spores large ; calyptra cuculliform : diœcious ; male flower terminal. — Wet and shaded rocks, near rivulets ; Central and Southern Ohio.

3. **F. exìguus,** Sulliv. Size, inflorescence, and calyptra as in the last ; leaves oblong-lanceolate, costa ceasing near the apex ; capsule oval, somewhat oblique ; operculum rather short-rostrate. — Damp rocks in shaded ravines, &c.; common.

4. **F. minùtulus,** Sulliv. Size, inflorescence, and calyptra as in the two preceding species ; leaves linear-lanceolate, with a transparent wavy border ; costa vanishing near the summit ; capsule oval, erect ; operculum rather long-rostrate. — With the last.

5. **F. bryoìdes,** Hedw. Somewhat larger than the last three ; capsule and operculum same as in No. 4 ; leaves oblong-lanceolate, with a thickened border ; costa excurrent ; calyptra cuculliform : monœcious ; male flowers numerous, axillary. — Moist and shaded banks.   (Eu.)

6. **F. Ravenélii,** Sulliv. Size, calyptra, and inflorescence as in No. 2 ; leaves linear-lanceolate, costate to the apex, subpapillose, repand-dentute on the pellucid margins of the true lamina, denticulate on the blade ; areolation minute, opaque ; capsule elliptic-oblong, papillose. (*Mem. Amer. Acad.*, n. ser., 4, p. 171, t. 2.) — Damp ground, S. Carolina, *Ravenel, Curtis.*

7. **F. osmundioides,** Hedw. Stems erect, 1′-1½′ high, branched ;

leaves oblong, obtuse, apiculate, the costa vanishing near the apex; capsule oval-oblong, erect or oblique; operculum long-rostrate; calyptra subulate from a mitriform lobed base; inflorescence as in No. 2. — On the roots of trees, in swamps. (Eu.)

* * *Fruit axillary.*

8. **F. subbasiláris,** Hedw. Stems 5″–10″ high, densely cæspitose, radiculose, branched; leaves elongated-oblong, obtuse, apiculate, eroded-denticulate at the summit, near which the costa vanishes; capsule erect, oval-oblong on a pedicel arising from near the base of the stem; operculum long-rostrate; calyptra cuculliform. — On decayed logs and trees, near the ground.

9. **F. taxifolius,** Hedw. Stems 5″–8″ high, branched and fasciculate from the base; leaves elongated-oblong, minutely denticulate on the subpellucid margin, obtuse; costa shortly excurrent; capsule oblong or obovate, inclined or horizontal; operculum, calyptra, and origin of the pedicel as in the last ·· monœcious; male flower gemmiform at the base of the fertile stem. — Woods, in sandy soil. (Tab. 15.) (Eu.)

10. **F. adiantoides,** Hedw. Stems much branched, 1′–3′ long; leaves oblong-lanceolate, serrulate, 2 or 3 rows of the marginal cellules transparent; costa percurrent; capsule oval-oblong, inclined; pedicel from the middle of the stem; operculum and calyptra as in No. 8; inflorescence as in No. 5. — Shaded moist places, on the ground, and on wet rocks. (Eu.)

11. **F. polypodioides,** Hedw. Stems broad, 1′–2′ high; leaves ovate-or elongated-oblong; costa vanishing at the subdenticulate obtuse apex; capsule obovate-oblong; operculum subulate-rostrate from a large rather hemispherical base; pedicel short, flexuous, arising from the upper part of the stem; calyptra cuculliform; diœcious. — Wet rocks, Georgia, *Lesquereux.*

12. **F. grandifrons,** Brid. Stems erect, 2′–3′ high, sparingly branched; leaves linear-lanceolate, thick, composed of several strata of cellules, the costa ceasing below the apex; fertile flower gemmiform, axillary, containing 30–60 archegonia; male flower and fruit unknown. — Niagara Falls (American side), on the perpendicular faces of rocks, moistened by the spray. (Eu.)

18. CONOMÍTRIUM, Montagne. (Tab. 15.)

Calyptra small, campanulate-mitriform, lobed at the base. Operculum hemispherical, apiculate. Capsule immersed spherical, nearly sessile, exannulate. Peristome none. Inflorescence monœcious or hermaphrodite: paraphyses globosely distended at the apex. — A genus, by its feeble dehiscence, globose capsule, and the characters of vegetation, forming an intermediate link between Physcomitrella among Cleistocarpous, and Physcomitrium among Stegocarpous Mosses. (Name from ἀφανής, *unapparent,* and ῥῆ;μα, *rupture,* or *suture*; i. e. dehiscence obscure.)

1. **C. Juliàuum,** Mont. Stems 2′–5′ long, filiform, floating, much divided; leaves distant, linear-lanceolate, acute, costate to the apex; capsule obconic, tapering into a short pedicel, the two together scarcely longer than the operculum, whose rostrum only is covered by the calyptra. — Ohio and southward, attached to stones in shallow brooks, &c. (Tab. 15.) (Eu.)

Tribe VII. TRICHOSTÒMEÆ.

19. TRICHÓSTOMUM, Br. & Sch.   (Tab. 15.)

Calyptra cuculliform. Operculum conic-rostrate. Capsule oval or cylindrical, mostly erect, long-pedicellate. Peristome single: teeth 32, linear, approximate in pairs. Inflorescence various. — Plants growing on the ground or on
stones, of a rather rigid habit; stems simple or dichotomously divided; leaves
varying from lanceolate to lanceolate-subulate, costate to or beyond the apex;
areolation loose below, dense and roundish above. (Name from θρίξ, a hair,
and στόμα, a mouth, in allusion to the capillary teeth of the peristome.)

1 **T. tórtile,** Schrad. Stems mostly simple, 3″–5″ high; leaves lanceolate-subulate, spreading, often subsecund, reflexed on the margin; costa excurrent; capsule cylindrical; operculum shortly rostrate; annulus simple: diœcious;
male flower terminal. — Road-sides, clay-banks: frequent. (Tab. 15.) (Eu.)

2. **T. ténue,** Hedw. Distinguished from small forms of the last, which
it much resembles, mainly by its large double annulus, firmer and brownish-red
capsule, and the plane (not reflexed) margin of the leaf. — Pennsylvania, according to *Hedwig.* (Eu.)

3. **T. váginans,** Sulliv. Stems 6″–10″ high, slender; stem-leaves
erect, appressed, ovate-lanceolate; the perichætial leaves sheathing, suddenly
attenuated, spreading at the apex, the costa strong and excurrent; capsule
oval-oblong; teeth of the peristome short, anastomosing in pairs; annulus
double, very large, its width equal to half the length of the teeth; pedicel slender, flexuous; operculum elongated-conic, obtuse; inflorescence as in No. 1. —
Sides of ditches and roads, Pennsylvania and New England.

4. **T. pállidum,** Hedw. Stems short, 3″–4″ high; leaves long-seta-
ceous from a lanceolate base; costa broad, excurrent, denticulate at the apex;
capsule oblong-elliptic. — Clayey grounds; frequent. — Conspicuous by its numerous, long (1½′–2′ high) straw-colored pedicels; monœcious; male flower
gemmiform, in the axils of the upper leaves. (Eu.)

5. **T. glaucéscens,** Hedw. Stems densely cæspitose, 6″–10″ high,
fastigiately branched; lower leaves small, remote, lanceolate; the upper larger,
and crowded into a terminal tuft, linear-lanceolate, costate to the apex, the plane
margins denticulate above; capsule oval-oblong; operculum elongated-conic.
Shores of Lake Superior, *Agassiz.* — Remarkable for the glaucous hue of its
foliage. (Eu.)

20. BÁRBULA, Hedw.   (Tab. 15.)

Calyptra cuculliform. Operculum subulate-conic. Capsule oval-oblong or
cylindrical, long-pedicellate. Peristome single: teeth 32, very long, filiform,
contorted, connected at the base by a short or long tubular membrane. Inflorescence various. — In habit, ramification, texture, and mostly in the form of the
leaves, allied closely to Trichostomum: differing chiefly in the torsion of the
peristome. (Name a diminutive of *barba*, beard, in allusion to the capillary
peristome.)

* *Teeth of the peristome arising from a short basilar membrane.*

1. **B. unguiculàta,** Hedw. Stems ½'–1' high, branched; leaves erect-patent, oblong-lanceolate, rather obtuse, shortly cuspidate by the excurrent costa, revolute on the margins; capsule cylindrical, erect; annulus none: diœcious; male flower terminal. — Clayey soil, &c.; frequent. (Tab. 15.) (Eu.)

2. **B. cæspitòsa,** Schwægr. Stems short, condensed; leaves crowded, linear-oblong, shortly acuminate, cuspidate by the slightly excurrent costa, undulate on the margins; capsule cylindrical, erect or subarcuate; annulus none: monœcious; male flower axillary. — Woods, about the roots of trees. — Readily known by its pale-green foliage, and yellow capsule with a red operculum. (Eu.)

3. **B. convolùta,** Hedw. Stems short, crowded; leaves spreading, oblong-lanceolate, rather obtuse, the margins plane; costa ceasing at or below the apex; perichætial leaves oblong, almost truncate, convolute, the upper ones ecostate; capsule cylindrical, oblique; annulus distinct; pedicel (1' high) yellow; inflorescence diœcious. — Raccoon Mts., Alabama, *Lesquereux.* (Eu.)

4. **B. tortuòsa,** Web. & Mohr. Stems 1'–3' high, dichotomously branched; leaves very long, linear-lanceolate, spreading, flexuose, undulated on the margins, crisped when dry, costa slightly excurrent; capsule cylindrical, inclined: diœcious. — On rocks, Alleghany Mountains. — One of the largest species of the genus. (Eu.)

5. **B. squarròsa,** Notaris. Stems loosely cæspitose, 1'–2' long, branched; leaves long, from a broad sheathing base, squarrose-recurved, narrowly lanceolate, denticulate above, undulate, crisped when dry, longer and crowded at the apex of the stem, the margins below diaphanous; costa slightly excurrent. (Capsule cylindrical, slightly inclined; annulus simple: diœcious. *Bryol. Eur.*) — On trees, in a cedar swamp, a quarter of a mile south of Lebanon, Wilson County, Tennessee, *Robinson,* 1842. Without fruit. (Eu.)

* * *Teeth of the peristome arising from a long tubular and tessellated membrane.*

6. **B. mucronifòlia,** Br. & Sch. Stems short and thick; leaves condensed, oblong or obovate-oblong, mucronate by the excurrent costa; capsule cylindrical, regular or slightly curved; annulus double; operculum rather short: inflorescence as in No. 2. — Rocky banks of streams, &c.; frequent. (Eu.)

7. **B. rurális,** Hedw. Stems 1'–3' high, branched, loose; leaves squarrose-recurved, oblong or obovate, very obtuse, concave-carinate, reflexed on the margins; costa excurrent into a long, spinulose-dentate, white, capillary point; capsule subcylindrical, erect or slightly arcuate, annulate: diœcious. — On rocks, Nahant, Massachusetts, *D. Murray:* Texas, *Wright.* (Eu.)

* * * *Inflorescence and fruit unknown.*

8. **B. papillòsa,** Wils. Stems short (3″–4″ high), thick, crowded; leaves close, recurved-spreading, oblong-spatulate, very concave above, shortly hair-pointed, papillose on the back; areolæ rather large, quadrate, granulose, those at the base larger, oblong, pellucid; costa percurrent, bearing crowded slightly pedicellate gemmæ on its papillose upper surface, each composed of 2 to 5 clustered roundish green cellules. — (Pottia Russellii, *Sulliv. mss.,* 1848.) — Trunks of Elm trees, Mass., *J. L. Russell,* 1843; common. — Until lately considered a gemmiparous state of the last species. (Eu.)

21. DESMÁTODON, Brid.   (Tab. 16.)

Calyptra cuculliform. Operculum conic, obtusely rostrate. Capsule oval-oblong or cylindrical, annulate, long-pedicellate. Peristome single : teeth 16, subulate, 2 – 3-cleft, united by a basilar membrane. Inflorescence monœcious or diœcious. — Plants of rather low stature, growing on the ground or on rocks, in general habit, ramification, and structure of leaves having much in common with Trichostomum and Barbula. — (Name from δέσμα, -ατος, a *band*, and ὀδών, a *tooth*, in allusion to the membrane uniting the teeth.)

1. **D. arenáceus**, Sulliv. & Lesqx. (Musc. Bor.-Amer., No. 93.) Stems 2″ – 3″ high, gregarious ; leaves oblong, linguæform, very obtuse, slightly denticulate at the apex ; apiculate by the excurrent costa ; capsule cylindrical, tapering into the pedicel (4″ – 5″ long) ; annulus simple, persistent ; teeth of the peristome 2-cleft, straight, white. — Sandstone rocks, Ohio. — Near D. flavicans.

2. **D. plinthòbius**, Sulliv. & Lesqx. (Musc. Bor.-Amer., No. 94.) Stems 2″ – 5″ high, fastigiately branched ; leaves erect, elongated-oblong, very obtuse, carinate-concave, narrowly reflexed on the margins ; areolation minute, opaque, dot-like above, larger oblong and pellucid below ; costa excurrent into a smooth white hair-point nearly as long as the leaf ; capsule elliptic-cylindrical, its mouth orange-red ; operculum ⅓ the length of the capsule ; teeth of the peristome pale yellow, more or less cloven along the medial line ; annulus large : diœcious. (Barbula muralis, *James* ; not of *Hedw*.) — Grows in hoary or pale-green and dense patches, on brick pavements, Charleston, S. Carolina, *Ravenel* : on the walls of the College at Nashville, Tennessee, *Lesquereux*. (Tab. 16.)

22. DIDÝMODON, Br. & Sch.   (Tab. 16.)

Calyptra cuculliform. Operculum conic, shortly and obtusely rostrate. Capsule subcylindrical, annulate, long-pedicellate. Peristome single : teeth 16, linear-lanceolate, entire, or more or less bifid, rather short, fugacious, and without a basilar membrane. Inflorescence various. — Very nearly allied to the last genus ; and it is questionable if either is entitled to rank higher than as a section of Trichostomum. (Name from δίδυμος, *twin*, and ὀδών, a *tooth*.) (Tab. 16.)

1. **D. rubéllus**, Br. & Sch. Stems ½′ – 1′ high, loosely cæspitose ; leaves spreading, oblong-lanceolate, recurved on the margins, costate to the apex, the upper ones dull-green, the lower reddish ; annulus simple ; antheridia naked in the axils of the perichætial leaves. — Pennsylvania, on the ground ; rare (Tab. 16.) (Eu.)

2. **D. lùridus**, Hornsch. Rather smaller than the last ; leaves lurid-green, rigid, ovate-lanceolate, with a reddish-brown costa, ceasing at the apex ; peristome minute, irregular : male flower terminal on a separate plant. — Falls of Niagara, *Drummond*. (Eu.)

TRIBE VIII. DISTICHIEÆ.

23. DISTÍCHIUM, Br. & Sch.   (Tab 16.)

Calyptra cuculliform, long-rostrate. Operculum conic, short. Capsule oval-oblong or cylindrical, annulate, long-pedicellate. Peristome single: teeth 16, linear-lanceolate, more or less cloven and perforated. Inflorescence monœcious. — Alpine species, growing upon moist rocks; stems densely cæspitose, dichotomously branched, with distichous and subulate-setaceous costate leaves, of an areolation dense roundish above, enlarged diaphanous below. (Name from δίστιχος, *two-ranked*, referring to the leaves.)

1. **D. capillåcenm,** Br. & Sch. Stems 1'-2' high; leaves abruptly long-subulate from a dilated sheathing base, spreading, flexuose, the costa percurrent; capsule subcylindrical, erect; antheridia axillary, naked. — Northern shore of Lake Superior, *Agassiz.* (Tab. 16.) (Eu.)

2. **D. inclinåtum,** Br. & Sch. Not so tall as the last; leaves more crowded and narrower, the perichætial ones 3-ranked; capsule cernuous, oval; antheridia with perigonial leaves. — Northern shore of Lake Superior, *Agassiz.* (Eu.)

24. EUSTÍCHIUM, Bryol. Europ. (Tab. 16.)

1. **E. Norvégicum,** Bryol. Europ. Stems frond-like, flat, mostly simple (about 1' long and 1'' broad), rooting only at the bulb-like base; leaves 2-ranked, complicate, closely imbricating, erect; those on the middle of the stem elongated-oblong, obliquely truncate, shortly acuminate, increasing in size as they ascend; the perichætial leaves attenuated into a long and linear, flexuous, pellucid, flat, equitant, and slightly serrulate point longer than the lamina; areolation above subrotund, below oblong, that of the point of the perichætial leaves linear; costa percurrent, its upper part narrowly winged: diœcious; flowers of both kinds terminal: fruit unknown. — Pendent on the perpendicular faces of sandstone rocks, six miles south of Lancaster, Fairfield County, Ohio. — The only other certain habitat recorded for this very interesting Moss is Iceland. That of Norway is apparently a mistake. — It is probably closely allied to Fissidens. (Sulliv. in Mem. Amer. Acad. n. ser. 3. p. 57. t. 1.) (Tab. 16.)

Tribe IX. POTTIEÆ.

25. PÓTTIA, Ehrh. (Tab. 16.)

Calyptra cuculliform. Operculum depressed-conic, more or less rostrate. Capsule obovate-truncate or oval-oblong, exserted or immersed. Peristome none. Inflorescence monœcious: male flower axillary. — Small annual or biennial plants, growing on newly exposed soil, with entire ovate-oblong or obovate-lanceolate and rather broadly costate leaves, of a quadrate or rectangular areolation, enlarged at the base. (Named in memory of *Professor J. F. Pott,* a German botanist.)

1. **P. truncåta,** Br. & Sch. Stems 2''-4'' high, gregarious, simple or branched; leaves obovate-lanceolate, mucronate by the excurrent costa; capsule obovate, truncate; operculum obliquely rostrate. — (P. eustoma, *Ehrh.* Gymnostomum truncatulum, *Hedw.*) — On the ground, New England and Pennsylvania. (Tab. 16.) (Eu.)

53 *

TRIBE X. TETRAPHÍDEÆ.

26. TÉTRAPHIS, Hedw. (Tab. 16)

Calyptra mitriform, large, irregularly plicate, lacerate at the base. Opercu-lum acutely conic. Capsule subcylindrical, long-pedicellate. Peristome single : teeth 4, three-sided, elongated-pyramidal, longitudinally striated on the back, not articulatel. Inflorescence monœcious : male flower gemmiform, terminal. —Perennial, growing on much decayed wood ; stems slender, simple or branched, often bearing at their apex leafy cup-shaped receptacles filled with lentiform pedicelled gemmæ ; leaves ovate-lanceolate, 3-ranked, costate, with an hexag-onal-rotund areolation. (Name from τέτρα, *four,* and φύς, *produced.*)

1. **T. pellúcida,** Hedw. Stems ½' - 1' high, closely tufted, reddish be low, light green above. — Woods ; common. (Tab. 16.) (Eu.)

27. TETRODÓNTIUM, Schwægr.

Calyptra large, mitriform, plicate, laciniate at the base, sometimes split on one side to the apex. Operculum conic. Capsule oval, exsertly pedicellate. Peristome as in Tetraphis, but the teeth shorter. Inflorescence monœcious : male flower gemmiform, terminal. —Minute bulb-like annuals, growing upon rocks (differing from Tetraphis chiefly in habit and structure of the foliage), with closely imbricated ovate-lanceolate scarcely costate leaves, rooting at the base and throwing out leafy flagelliform branchlets, or long linear-clavate frondose pro-cesses, sometimes trifid at the apex. — (Name from τέτρα, *four,* and ὀδών, *tooth.*)

1. **T. repándum,** Funk. Frondose processes very rare ; pedicel 3" - 5" high ; mouth of the capsule repand or notched between the teeth. — Damp shaded situations, on the ground near the " Glen House," Gorham, White Mountains of New Hampshire, *James.* (Eu.)

TRIBE XI. ENCALÝPTEÆ.

28. ENCALÝPTA, Schreber. (Tab. 16.)

Calyptra large, cylindrical-campanulate, longer than the capsule, subulate-rostrate, uneven or fringed at the base. Operculum conic, with a long slender subclavellate rostrum. Capsule elongated-ovate-cylindrical, long-pedicellate. Peristome variable, either absent, single or double. Inflorescence monœcious or diœcious. — A well-marked genus, approaching in habit and mode of growth the larger species of Barbula. — (Name from ἐνκαλυπτός, *covered with a veil,* in allusion to the remarkably large calyptra.)

1. **E. ciliáta,** Hedw. Stems ½' - 1' high, thick, radiculose, simple or sparingly branched ; leaves rather large, crowded, recurved-spreading, oblong-ovate or ligulate, shortly acuminate, slightly concave, rather undulate on the margin, somewhat crenulate near the apex ; areolation dot-like, granulose above, enlarged oblong and diaphanous below ; costa excurrent into a short point ; per-istome single, with 16 lanceolate distantly articulated teeth, without a medial

line, capsule smooth; annulus none; calyptra fringed at the base: monœcious; male flower gemmiform, axillary. — Rocks, Lake Superior, *Agassiz:* Jefferson County, New York. (Eu.)

2. **E. rhabdocárpa,** Schwægr. Differs from the last by its longer-pointed or piliferous leaves, and longitudinally ribbed capsule; annulus present; calyptra not fringed at the base; peristome and inflorescence the same. — British America, *Drummond.* (Tab. 16) (Eu.)

3. **E. commutáta,** Nees & Hornsch. Stems more slender than in No. 1; leaves subsquarrose, ovate-lanceolate, gradually long-acuminate, concave, undulate on the margin; areolæ very small; costa excurrent; capsule smooth; peristome none; annulus simple; base of the calyptra uneven, not fringed: monœcious. — British America, *Drummond.* (Eu.)

4. **E. streptocárpa,** Hedw. Stems more elongated than in No. 1; leaves not so spreading, ligulate, costate to the obtuse or cucullate apex; capsule spirally ribbed; peristome double; teeth 16, filiform, nodose; annulus compound; calyptra spinulose at the apex, crenate at the base; inflorescence diœcious. — British America, *Drummond.* — The Alleghany specimens usually referred to this species are without fruit, and hence doubtful. (Eu.)

29. SYRRHÓPODON, Schwægr. (Tab. 16.)

Calyptra large, campanulate-conic, rostrate, cloven on one side. Operculum conic, with a long-subulate rostrum. Capsule elliptic-cylindrical, exannulate, exsertly pedicellate. Peristome single: teeth 16, linear-lanceolate, articulated, without a medial line, short, nearly horizontal, inserted below the mouth of the capsule. Inflorescence diœcious or monœcious. — Perennial plants (the tropical representatives of Encalypteæ), with densely cæspitose simple or dichotomously branched stems, and costate elongated-ligulate leaves, from a whitish sheathing base composed of large pellucid rectangular areolæ, which elsewhere are minute, opaque, and granulose. (Name from σύρροπος, *connivent,* and ὀδών, *a tooth,* alluding to the horizontal position of the teeth of the peristome.)

1. **S. Floridánus,** Sulliv. Stems about 1' high; leaves erect-patent from an amplexicaul base; the margins convolute, thickened, more or less narrowly bilamellate, undulated, serrated; costa ceasing at or below the obtuse apex. (Syr. albovaginatus, *Hook. & Wils. in Drum. 2d coll , No.* 37.) — Northern shore of the Gulf of Mexico; also Florida: frequent. (Tab. 16.)

Tribe XII. ZYGODÓNTEÆ.

30. ZYGODON, Hook & Tayl. (Tab. 16.)

Calyptra small, cuculliform, smooth, oblique. Operculum obliquely rostrate from a conic base. Capsule pyriform, apophysate, striated, on a rather short pedicel, immersed or exserted. Peristome either double, single, or absent; when present, constructed as in (the nearly related genus) Orthotrichum. — Perennial species, growing on trees or on rocks, in large patches; stems with fastigiate branches, fertile at the apex; leaves linear-lanceolate, carinate, continuously

G. M.   3

costate, plane on the margins ; areolæ above guttulate ; below, enlarged oblong. (Name from ζυγός, *a pair*, and ὀδών, *teeth*, in allusion to the paired teeth.)

1. **Z. Lappónicus,** Br. & Sch. Stems ½'-1' high, radiculose ; leaves spreading, crisped when dry ; capsule scarcely exserted, 8-ribbed ; peristome none : monœcious ; male flower gemmiform. — Rocks, on the White Mountains of New Hampshire, *Oakes :* Alleghany Mountains of Pennsylvania, *Lesquereux.* (Tab. 16.) (Eu.)

2. **Z. Mougeótii,** Br. & Sch. More elongated and branched than No. 1 ; differing chiefly in its narrower and less concave perichætial leaves twice as long, the longer rostrum to the operculum, and the diœcious inflorescence. — With No. 1, in similar places, according to *Mr. Th. P. James.* (Eu.)

3. **Z. Sullivántii,** Mull. Stems 1'- 2' high, slender, with long filiform branches ; leaves subsquarrose from an erect half-clasping base, complicate-concave ; the margins below recurved, above plane and strongly serrate ; fruit unknown. — (Syrrhopodon excelsus, *Sulliv. Musc. Alleghan., No.* 170.) — North Carolina ; on rocks, top of Grandfather Mountain, *Gray & Sullivant :* Black Mountain, *Lesquereux.*

31. DRUMMÓNDIA, Hook.   (Tab. 16.)

Calyptra large, cuculliform, rostrate, slightly plicate at the base, and papillose at the apex. Operculum obliquely long-rostrate from a convex base. Capsule globose-oval or slightly obovate, exsertly pedicellate. Peristome single : teeth 16, very short, truncate. Inflorescence diœcious : male flower gemmiform. — Perennial, growing on trees ; stems prostrate, throwing up numerous short branches, bearing fruit on their summit ; leaves oblong, costate ; areolæ minute, roundish. — (Named after the late *Thomas Drummond*, who made extensive and very valuable collections of North American Mosses.)

1. **D. clavellàta,** Hook. Stems 2'- 4' long, creeping, densely covered with radicels ; branches crowded, erect, 2''- 3'' high ; leaves close, erect-patent, shortly acuminate ; costa ceasing with the apex. — Grows in deep-green and close thin mats (3'- 10' in diameter), on the bark of trees (particularly the Beech), Northern, Middle, and Western States. (Tab. 16.)

Tribe XIII. ORTHOTRÍCHEÆ.

32. ORTHÓTRICHUM, Hedw.   (Tab. 16.)

Calyptra large, campanulate, longitudinally plaited, crenate-lacerate at the base, hairy or glabrous. Operculum short, conic, rostellate. Capsule pyriform, more or less elongated, apophysate, pedicellate, immersed or exserted, 8 or 16 striated, ribbed when dry. Peristome single or double, rarely wanting ; the outer 16 teeth, with a medial line, mostly in pairs (often reflexed when dry) ; the inner 8 or 16 cilia. Inflorescence monœcious or diœcious : male flower gemmiform. — Perennial plants, growing in roundish cushion-like tufts, on trees or rocks, never on soil ; stems usually erect, simple or branched by innovations, fertile at their summit ; leaves crowded, elongated, costate nearly to the point, spreading, entire, usually revolute on the margins, of a minute dot-like areolation, except at the marginal base, the areolæ there being larger, rectangular, and pellucid. (Name from ὀρθός, *straight*, and θρίξ, τριχός, *a hair*, in allusion to the straight hairs on the calyptra.)

§ 1. *Capsule immersed or slightly exserted.* *Monœcious (except in No. 5 and 6).*

* *Peristome single: cilia wanting.*

1. **O. cupulàtum**, Hoffm. Stems nearly 1' high; leaves lanceolate, keeled; capsule immersed, with 16 striæ; teeth of the peristome nearly equidistant; calyptra sparsely hairy; male flower terminal. — On rocks, Niagara Falls, *Drummond:* Lake Superior, *Agassiz.* (Eu.)

2. **O. Stùrmii**, Hoppe & Hornsch. Very like the last species; but its immersed and obovate capsule is indistinctly 8-striated; the male flower axillary. — Texas, *Wright.* (Eu.)

3. **O. anómalum**, Hedw. Separated from the preceding (to which it approaches closely) mainly by its exserted and distinctly 8-striated capsule. — Rocks, near Salem, Mass., *Lesquereux:* Lake Superior, *Agassiz.* (Eu.)

4. **O. Texànum**, Sulliv. Larger than No. 2, which it resembles, but its immersed capsule is oblong-pyriform and distinctly 8-striated; teeth of the peristome in pairs; calyptra very hairy; leaves longer, narrower, and more re-curved-spreading. — Texas, *Wright:* Santa Fé, New Mexico, *Fendler.*

* * *Peristome double.*

5. **O. obtusifòlium**, Schrad. Stems 6″–10″ high; leaves when moist erect-patent, not recurved, ligulate from an oblong base, obtuse, concave, somewhat convolute on the margins, strongly papillose, the costa vanishing much below the point; capsule immersed, oblong-pyriform, the long apophysis gradually tapering into the very short pedicel; cilia of the peristome 8, composed of two rows of cellules half as wide as the teeth; calyptra glabrous. — Trees, Cambridge, Massachusetts, *Lesquereux.* (Eu.)

6. **O. exiguum**, Sulliv. Nearly related to No. 5, but much smaller; stems 3″–5″ high; leaves more acute, scarcely papillose: costa stouter, extending to the point; the areolæ at the base not so enlarged; capsule oval; the apophysis rather short; pedicel longer; cilia of the peristome 8, carinate, composed of two rows of cellules fully as broad as the teeth; operculum convex, apiculate. — Base of trees, Santee Canal, South Carolina, *Ravenel.* — The smallest of our Orthotricha. — This and the related species have, scattered on the surface of their leaves, a few articulated excrescences (*Conferva Orthotrichi*).

7. **O. Rógeri**, Brid. Leaves spreading-recurved, when moist narrowly ligulate from a ventricose concave base, canaliculate, plane on the margins above, revolute below, somewhat acute at the apex; capsule and calyptra as in No. 5; cilia 8, simple, filiform. — Trees, Lake Superior, *Agassiz.* (Eu.)

8. **O. strangulàtum**, Beauv. Stems short, compact; leaves broadly ovate-lanceolate, carinate, somewhat obtuse, the margins strongly reflexed; capsule oblong, somewhat pyriform, immersed, very much constricted below the mouth when dry; cilia of the peristome as in the last; calyptra hairy. — On trees; very common.

9. **O. Canadénse,** Br. & Sch. Differs from the preceding species in its more acute leaves, its shortly-exserted capsule smaller and not so constricted under the mouth, and in the 16 cilia of the inner peristome. — Central Ohio: rare; on trees.

10. **O. affíne,** Schrad. Larger and coarser than any of the foregoing; leaves oblong-lanceolate, rather obtuse, revolute (the upper ones rather undulate) on the margins, strongly papillose on both surfaces; capsule elliptic-oblong with a tapering apophysis, emersed; cilia as in No. 7; calyptra slightly hairy, greenish. — On rocks, Lake Superior, *Agassiz.* (Eu.)

11. **O. speciòsum,** Nees. Stems elongated, 1' - 2' high, loosely cæspitose; leaves lanceolate, keeled, with recurved margins; capsule shortly exserted, tapering into the pedicel, indistinctly striated, when dry ribbed near the mouth only; cilia of peristome 8; calyptra large, very hairy. — Trees; on banks of the St. Lawrence River. (Eu.)

12. **O. leiocárpum,** Br. & Sch. Size and mode of growth much as in the last; readily distinguished by its capsule without striæ, and entirely smooth when dry; and by the 16 large erose-articulate cilia of the peristome. — Trees, Lake Superior, *Agassiz.* (Eu.)

§ 2. *Capsule much exserted. Monœcious.*

13. **O. Ludwìgii,** Schwægr. Stems mostly decumbent; leaves linear-lanceolate, somewhat fasciculate, when dry slightly twisted, the margins plane or slightly undulate; capsule pyriform, when dry very much contracted and plicate at the mouth; inner peristome absent; calyptra moderately hairy, laciniate at the base. — On trees, Alleghany Mountains. (Eu.)

14. **O. Hutchinsiæ,** Smith. Stems aggregated in rather loose tufts; leaves lanceolate, carinate, scarcely reflexed on the margins, when dry erect-appressed, not twisted; capsule subclavate, with 8 broad striæ, the apophysis gradually tapering into the long pedicel; cilia of the peristome 8; calyptra large, copiously hairy. — Rocks; common in mountainous districts. (Tab. 16.) (Eu.)

15. **O. crispum,** Hedw. Stems closely tufted; leaves linear-lanceolate from a dilated base, much contorted and crisped when dry, slightly undulated; capsule clavate, when dry constricted under the mouth, with 8 strong ribs continued down the very long tapering apophysis; peristome with 8 cilia of a double row of cellules; calyptra very hairy; sporules brown. — Trees, Alleghany Mountains. (Eu.)

16. **O. crispulum,** Hornsch. More delicate than the last; leaves narrower and less crisped when dry; capsule shorter, pale, of thin texture, when dry not contracted below the mouth, its ribs less distinct; apophysis shorter, passing more abruptly into the pedicel; sporules green. — Trees, Alleghany Mountains. (Eu.)

17. **O. Bruchii,** Brid. Very closely allied to the last two species; from No. 15 it differs in its less crisped leaves, and deeper-colored larger capsule; from No. 16, by the narrowed mouth of the capsule and the much longer apophysis; from both by its longer pedicel, and the cilia of the peristome of but one row of cellules. — White Mountains, N. Hampshire, *Oakes:* rare. (Eu.)

33. MACROMÍTRIUM, Brid. (Tab. 16.)

Calyptra large, conic-mitriform, longitudinally plicate or sulcate, more or less laciniate at the base, hairy or glabrous. Operculum subulate-rostrate from a conic base. Capsule erect-ovate, oval or oblong, long-pedicellate. Peristome double or single, sometimes wanting ; the exterior 16 teeth lanceolate, usually in pairs ; the interior a more or less exserted membrane, truncate or cut to the base into 16 or more cilia. — Stems creeping ; branches erect, crowded, fertile at their summit ; leaves lanceolate-oblong, continuously costate, with a dense and minute dot-like areolation above, enlarged rectangular and pellucid below. (Name from μακρός, long, and μιτρίον, a veil, referring to the very large calyptra.)

1. **M. Drégei**, Hochstetter ! Stems slender, 1'-2' long, creeping, sub-pinnately branched ; branches short, erect ; leaves crowded, erect-patent, ovate-lanceolate, papillose, recurved on the margins, ventricose-concave at base, cana-liculate above ; capsule oval-oblong ; peristome single (the exterior wanting), a short truncate membrane ; calyptra hairy. — Top of Jonah Mountain, Georgia, *Lesquereux;* on the bark of old pine-trees. — We have seen Cape of Good Hope specimens apparently identical with ours, referred doubtfully to M. tenue and M. Dregei. (Tab. 16.)

34. SCHLOTHEÌMIA, Brid. (Tab. 16.)

Calyptra large, conic-mitriform, scabrous at the apex, with 4 or more inflexed lobes or appendages at the base. Operculum conic-subulate. Capsule subcy-lindrical, erect, pedicellate. Peristome double ; the exterior 16 teeth in pairs, linear-lanceolate (when dry revolute) ; the interior 16 or more irregular cilia. — Mode of growth, habit, and structure of leaves very much as in the last genus : both genera being the tropical analogues of Orthotrichum, and remarkable for the ferruginous or reddish-brown color usually predominant in their foliage. — (Named for *Count Schlotheim.*)

1. **S. Sullivántii**, C. Mull. Monœcious ; branches short ; leaves very crowded, ovate-oblong, obtuse, apiculate, rugose-undulate above, the costa ceas-ing below the point. — Grows in compact, rigid, dark-brown mats, on trees. — Lower portion of the Southern States. (Tab. 16.)

TRIBE XIV. PTYCHOMITRIÈÆ.

35. PTYCHOMÍTRIUM, Br. & Sch. (Tab. 16.)

Calyptra campanulate, plicate, deeply laciniate at the base. Operculum conic-subulate. Capsule oval, erect, annulate, pedicellate. Peristome single : teeth 16, perforated or fissile into two unequal filiform segments. Inflorescence mo-nœcious. — Perennial plants, growing on rocks and trees : in habit and aspect intermediate between Orthotrichum and Grimmia. — (Name from πτύξ, πτίχου, a fold, and μιτρίον, a veil, referring to the plicate calyptra.)

1. **P. incúrvum**, Schwægr. Stems 2''-3'' high, aggregated ; leaves crowded, oblong, ligulate, spreading, slightly incurved at the obtuse and some-what cucullate apex, concave, costate nearly to the point, of a rather thick tex

ture, composed of minute and somewhat quadrate cellules; capsule rotund-oval, its mouth small; teeth of the peristome often divided to the base; annulus large, unrolling. — (Musc. Alleghan., No. 135.) — On rocks, Pennsylvania and southward. (Tab. 16.)

2. **P. Drummóndii,** Hook. & Wils. Somewhat larger than the preceding; leaves linear-lanceolate, acute, crisped when dry; teeth of the peristome more or less perforated, inserted below the mouth of the oblong-oval capsule; annulus none. — On trees, Southern States.

Tribe XV. GRIMMIÈÆ.

36. SCHISTÍDIUM, Br. & Sch. (Tab. 16.)

Calyptra small, not extending to the mouth of the capsule, conic-mitriform and lacerate at the base, or cuculliform and entire at the base. Operculum depressed-convex, papillate or shortly rostellate, deciduous with the columella attached. Capsule roundish-oval, oval-oblong, or obovate, wide-mouthed, immersed, with a short erect pedicel. Peristome single : teeth 16, lanceolate, cribrose. Inflorescence monœcious : male flower gemmiform. — Growing in circular more or less compact tufts, on rocks (chiefly mountainous); stems simple, or dichotomously branched and fastigiate; leaves of a rigid and rather brittle texture, crowded, spreading, ovate-lanceolate, acuminate, concave below, channelled above, usually reflexed on the margins, continuously costate, mostly tipped with a pellucid hair-point; areolæ minute and nearly quadrate, those at the base larger, oblong and diaphanous. — (Name from σχίζω, to split, the base of the calyptra being laciniated.)

1. **S. apocárpum,** Br. & Sch. Loosely cæspitose; stems ½' - 1' long, upper leaves usually with white points; capsule elliptical, firm; teeth of peristome sometimes entire, purplish-red; annulus none; calyptra 5-lobed at the base. — On rocks, very common. — Foliage blackish-green : subject to numerous forms, dependent on locality. (Tab. 16.) (Eu.)

2. **S. maritimum,** Br. & Sch. More robust than the last, densely tufted; leaves longer, narrower, more rigid, never hair-pointed, the margins plane, the costa stouter and shortly excurrent; capsule obovate, truncate; sporules twice as large; calyptra the same. — On rocks near the sea, Eastport, Maine, J. L. Russell. (Eu.)

3. **S. confértum,** Br. & Sch. Resembles No. 1 exceedingly; tufts more compact; leaves less lurid, their margins not so recurved; capsule oval or roundish, of a thinner texture, paler-colored, almost pellucid; teeth of the peristome more cribrose and lacerated, and of an orange color; calyptra the same. — New England, Oakes. — A variety with obtuse leaves occurs on the White Mountains. (Eu.)

4. **S. ambíguum,** Sulliv. Near the preceding, but has larger and elliptic-lanceolate perichætial leaves, with a long, flexuous, dentate, pellucid hair-point; capsule oval-oblong; calyptra cuculliform. — (Mem. Amer. Acad. Art. and Sci. n. ser. 4, p. 170.) — Dry rocks, Santa Fè, N. Mexico, Fendler.

37. GRÍMMIA, Ehrh. (Tab. 16.)

Calyptra as in Schistidium, but larger and extending below the mouth of the capsule. Operculum conic-obtuse, or conic-rostrate, deciduous without the columella. Capsule ovate, oval, or nearly cylindrical, with an erect and curved or flexuous pedicel. Peristome single: teeth 16, lanceolate, cribrose, and 2-3-fid above. Inflorescence monœcious or diœcious. — Habit and mode of growth strongly resembling Schistidium and Racomitrium. Habitat, on rocks. — (Named after *Grimm*, a German botanist.)

1. **G. leucophæa,** Grev. Diœcious; stems 6″-10″ high, compactly cæspitose; leaves widely spreading, ovate or ovate-oblong, concave, plane on the margins, suddenly tapering into a very long pellucid dentate hair-point; capsule oval or oblong, erect, exserted; teeth of the peristome deeply 2-3-cleft; annulus large, unrolling; operculum short or long conic-rostellate; calyptra mitriform, 5-lobed at the base. — Sandstone rocks, S. Ohio. (Tab. 16.) (Eu.)

2. **G. Ólneyi,** Sulliv. Diœcious; tufts loose, stems 5″-10″ high, yellowish-green, linear-lanceolate, gradually tapering into a long diaphanous serrated hair-point; capsule oval or ovate-oval, not ribbed when dry, oblique or horizontal on an exserted curved pedicel; teeth of the peristome perforated above; annulus compound; operculum with a conic base and an oblique rostrum; calyptra cuculliform, 2-3-fid at the base. — Rocks, Rhode Island, *S. T. Olney.* — Approaches closely to G. trichophylla, *Grev.;* but that is a rather more slender plant; its leaves longer and more flexuous, with a smooth hair-point; capsule regularly and strongly ribbed when dry, pendulous on a longer and more curved pedicel; teeth of the peristome bifid; rostrum of the operculum straight; calyptra mitriform; annulus larger.

3. **G. Pennsylvánica,** Schwægr. Diœcious; loosely cæspitose; stem 1′ or more long; leaves much as in No. 2, but dark green, and with a stouter costa; capsule immersed, erect on a short pedicel, oval-oblong, smooth when dry; operculum conic-rostellate; calyptra mitriform, lobed. — On rocks, Alleghany Mountains; common: fruit rare. — Larger than any of the preceding.

4. **G. Donniàna,** Smith. Monœcious; tufts compact, small, hemispherical, hoary; stems 3″-4″ high; leaves linear-lanceolate, with a long and rough hair-point, their margins plane; capsule oval-oblong, shortly exserted on an erect pedicel; annulus rather narrow; operculum conic-obtuse; calyptra mitriform, lobed. — (G. obtusa, *Schwægr.*) — White Mountains of New Hampshire, *Oakes.* (Eu.)

38. COSCÍNODON, Spreng. (Tab. 18.)

Capsule large, campanulate, plicate, crenate at the base. Operculum conic, acute or shortly rostellate. Capsule obovate or oval-oblong, immersed, erect, short-pedicellate, annulate. Peristome single: teeth 16, equidistant, lanceolate, very much cribrose, reflexed when dry. Inflorescence monœcious or diœcious: male flower gemmiform. — Combines the characters of Orthotrichum and Grimmia; the habit and structure of the foliage being that of the last-named genus.

(Name from κόσκινον, a *sieve*, and ὁδών, a *tooth*, in allusion to the perforated teeth of the peristome.)

1. **C. Wrightii,** Sulliv. Monœcious; tufts compact, hoary; stems 3″- 4″ high, clavate; leaves closely imbricating (the lower smaller, oval, the upper larger, obovate), very concave, serrate above, suddenly produced into a long hyaline denticulate hair-point, costate half-way; areolæ at the base oblong, those near the apex oval, both pellucid, the central ones roundish and chlorophyllose; capsule oblong-oval, truncate at the base, on a very short curved pedicel; operculum conic-acute; annulus large, compound. — Rocks, near San Marcos, Texas, *Wright.* — C. pulvinatus, its only congener, has a straight and longer pedicel, obovate capsule, lanceolate leaves, and is diœcious. (Tab. 18.)

39. RACOMÍTRIUM, Br. & Sch.   (Tab. 16.)

Calyptra conic-mitriform, subulately rostrate, solid and papillose at the apex, membranous and multifid at the base. Operculum conic, with a short or long subulate rostrum. Capsule elliptical, nearly cylindrical or ovate-oblong, erect, smooth, long-pedicellate. Peristome single: teeth 16, 2 – 3-fid, the segments free or somewhat cohering. Inflorescence diœcious. — Tall, striking species, the largest among the Grimmioid Mosses; stems dichotomously or irregularly branched; leaves oblong-lanceolate, with or without a diaphanous hair-point, costate-carinate; areolæ above mostly quadrate, below enlarged, linear, with a sinuous outline. (Name from ῥάκος, *a shred*, and μιτρίον, *a veil*, referring to the lacerate base of the calyptra.)

§ 1. DRÝPTODON, Br. & Sch. — *Ramification dichotomous; the innovations simple, fastigiate.*

1. **R. aciculàre,** Brid. Loosely cæspitose, dull green; stems procumbent and leafless below, ascending, 1′ – 3′ long; leaves crowded, spreading every way or secund, ovate-oblong, the costa vanishing below the toothed or entire obtuse point; capsule elliptic-oblong, its mouth small; teeth of peristome deeply 2 – 3-fid; operculum long, subulate-rostrate. — On wet rocks, Alleghany Mountains. (Eu.)

2. **R. Sudéticum,** Br. & Sch. Patches loose, grayish or lurid; stems as in the last; leaves from an erect base, spreading, recurved or incurved, linearlanceolate, with a rather short denticulate pellucid hair-point; capsule small, oval or elliptic-oblong on a short erect or curved pedicel; operculum shortly rostrate. — Exposed rocks, Alleghany Mountains. (Eu.)

§ 2. RACOMITRIUM PROPER. — *Ramification irregular; branches ramulose; the innovations not fastigiate.*

3. **R. fasciculàre,** Brid. Patches loose, of a light green color; stems 1′ – 2′ long, assurgent, branched; branches with numerous fasciculate short branchlets; leaves crowded, spreading, linear-lanceolate, tapering, without a pellucid hair-point, margins reflexed, the areolæ above and below elongated and sinuous; capsule elliptical; rostrum of the calyptra strongly papillose its whole length; teeth of the peristome bifid to the base, slender, nodulose. — Moist rocks, Alleghany Mountains. (Tab. 16.) (Eu.)

4. **R. microcárpum,** Brid. Tufts rather compact, stems slender, fasciculately branched, with numerous short branchlets ; leaves yellowish, spreading, recurved or fulcate-secund, lanceolate, tapering, with a short diaphanous remotely serrated hair-point ; areolæ everywhere elongated and sinuous ; capsule small, oblong ; teeth of the peristome short. — Dry rocks, Alleghany Mountains. (Eu.)

5. **R. lanuginòsum,** Brid. Patches loose, extensive, hoary ; stems much elongated (4' – 10'), slender, flexuose, fragile, with fasciculate branches ; leaves crowded, erect-patent, rather flexuous, linear-lanceolate, tapering into a long diaphanous erose-dentate hair-point ; areolæ elongated and sinuous ; capsule small, ovate-oval, on a short scabrous pedicel ; teeth of peristome very long, 2-cleft, filiform. — Rocks, White Mountains, New Hampshire, *Oakes*. (Eu.)

6. **R. canéscens,** Brid. Patches loose, large, yellowish-green or hoary ; stems 2' – 4' long, more or less fasciculately branched ; leaves spreading, recurved, ovate-lanceolate, with a short erose-denticulate hair-point, papillose on both surfaces, the margins recurved ; areolation as in No. 5 ; capsule ovate-oblong, on a long smooth pedicel ; teeth of the peristome as long as the capsule, very slender, 2-parted, nodulose. — With the last, *Oakes*. (Eu.)

TRIBE XVI. HEDWIGIÈÆ.

40. HEDWÍGIA, Ehrh. (Tab. 16.)

Calyptra small, conic, smooth, sometimes hairy. Operculum plano-convex, with or without a central papilla. Capsule globose, erect, entirely immersed, very short-pedicellate. Peristome none. Inflorescence monœcious : male flower gemmiform, axillary. — Habit and mode of growth like Schistidium : stems dichotomously or irregularly branched ; leaves spreading, ovate-lanceolate, papillose, not costate, the apex diaphanous, erose-denticulate or fringed on the margins ; cellules at the central base elongated and subflexuous, elsewhere small and quadrate. (Dedicated to the distinguished cryptogamist, *J. G. Hedwig.*)

1. **H. ciliàta,** Ehrh. Stems 1' – 4' long, rooting at the base only ; leaves sometimes secund, with a longer or shorter diaphanous point. — On rocks and bowlders ; very common, forming large and hoary glaucous-green patches. (Tab. 16.) (Eu.)

TRIBE XVII. BUXBAUMIÈÆ.

41. BUXBAÙMIA, Haller. (Tab. 17.)

Calyptra cylindrical-campanulate, small, covering the operculum only. Operculum small, conic, obtuse. Capsule large, elongated-ovate, oblique, flat on the upper side, convex and gibbous underneath, apophysate, long-pedicellate. Peristome double (?) ; the exterior an irregularly incised membrane, composed of 3 or 4 layers of elongated cellular tissue, or 16 linear moniliform papillose teeth ; the interior a whitish and conic plaited membrane. Inflorescence monœcious : male flower gemmiform ; antheridium solitary, roundish. — Minute annuals or biennials ; stems scarcely any, partly buried in the soil : leaves few (5 or 6), scale-like, broad-ovate, deeply cut and long-ciliated on the margins, not costate, loosely reticulated. (Named after *J. C. Buxbaum*, an early German botanist.)

1. **B. aphýlla,** Haller. Stem and leaves having the appearance of a minute hairy bulb, many times smaller than the capsule with its short cylindrical apophysis; pedicel rather stout, 7″–10″ high, tuberculate.—New England and New York; rare. (Tab. 17.) (Eu.)

42. DIPHÝSCIUM, Weber & Mohr. (Tab. 17.)

Calyptra small, conic, entire at the base, scarcely covering the elongated-conic operculum. Capsule large, ovate, oblique, gibbous, subsessile, immersed. Peristome double (?); the exterior a very narrow slightly dentate ring, quite rudimentary; the interior as in Buxbaumia. Inflorescence diœcious: male flower terminal, gemmiform; antheridia numerous, paraphysated.—Small bulb-like mosses, annual or biennial, the sessile capsule forming the principal part; stem very short, its leaves lingulate, spreading, entire, costate, thick and fleshy; the perichætial leaves much larger, membranous, erect, lanceolate, ciliate-lacerate at the point, the costa excurrent into a long serrulate awn. (Name from δίς, *twice*, and φυσκίον, *a vesicle*; the wide separation of the thecal and sporangial membranes giving the appearance of one vesicle within another.)

1. **D. foliòsum,** Web. & Mohr. Whole plant 3″–4″ high.—Clayey or barren soil; not unfrequent in hilly districts. (Tab. 17.) (Eu.)

TRIBE XVIII. POLYTRÌCHEÆ.

43. ÁTRICHUM, Beauv. (Tab. 17.)

Calyptra narrowly cuculliform, naked, spinulose at the apex. Operculum hemispherical at the base, with a long slender rostrum. Capsule cylindrical or oblong, nearly erect, slightly arcuate, long-pedicellate. Peristome single: teeth 32, short, ligulate, obtuse, incurved and adhering by their summits to the margin of the disk-like apex of the columella. Inflorescence monœcious or diœcious: male flower cup-shaped. — Intermediate in habit between Polytrichum and Mnium; the flowering stems erect, simple or branched, from a creeping rhizoma; leaves small below, much larger and elongated above, crisped when dry, of a minute firm hexagonal areolation, the percurrent costa bearing on its upper surface 2 or 3 narrow lamellæ. — (Name from *a* privative, and θρίξ, τριχός, *a hair*, in allusion to the naked calyptra.)

1. **A. undulàtum,** Beauv. Stems erect, mostly simple; leaves long ligulate-lanceolate, undulate, spinulose-toothed, narrowly margined, the costa with 2–4 narrow lamellæ. (Catherinea undulata, *Brid.*) — Moist clay-banks, in hilly districts; rare. — Monœcious: fertile flower terminal on a prolongation of the axis of the sterile flowers. (Eu.)

2. **A. angustàtum,** Beauv. More slender than the preceding: leaves narrower, more densely reticulated, not denticulate below the middle, the costa with more numerous and broader lamellæ. — Shady woods, and margins of swamps; common. — Diœcious: male flower terminal. (Tab. 17.) Eu.)

3. **A. crispum,** T. P. James.   More robust than either of the foregoing ; stems simple, lower leaves small, somewhat spatulate ; the upper much larger, oblong-lanceolate, inclining to spatulate, slightly undulate, with a thickened dentate border, the costa percurrent, scarcely lamellate ; areolæ rather large, hexagonal-rotund ; capsule obovate-oblong, erect-cernuous, its mouth ample ; teeth of the peristome very short, somewhat irregular ; pedicel stout, red : diœcious. — Banks of small streams, New Jersey, *James.* — A very distinct species.

44. POGONÀTUM, Beauv.   Hair-cap Moss.   (Tab. 17.)

Calyptra cuculliform, very hairy ; the hairs forming a dense mat, covering the whole capsule. Operculum rostellate from a convex base. Inflorescence diœcious : male flower cup-shaped. — Mode of growth as in Atrichum ; leaves more rigid, spreading from a sheathing base, lanceolate, the costa below narrow, above very broad and covered with numerous crowded lamellæ. — (Name from πώγων, *a beard;* from the hairy calyptra.)

* *Stems extremely short.*

1. **P. brevicaûle,** Brid.   Stems 2″–3″ high ; leaves few, erect-appressed, the lower ovate-acute, the upper narrowly lanceolate from a broad base, erose-denticulate above ; capsule cylindrical, erect ; operculum shortly rostellate ; calyptra whitish. — Moist clayey banks, Eastern States and westward. — The ground around is always covered by a green stratum of confervoid filaments.

2. **P. brachyphyllum,** Michx.   Much like the last; stems shorter ; leaves oval-oblong, obtuse, entire ; capsule oblong, cernuous ; calyptra brownish. — On the ground, road-sides, &c., Southern States.

* * *Stems elongated.*   (*Alpine species.*)

3. **P. urnigerum,** Brid.   Stems divided above ; leaves lanceolate from a short sheathing base, pointed, serrate, the lamellæ of the costa abruptly thickened on their borders ; capsule cylindrical, the surface granulated. — White Mountains, New Hampshire. — Plant 2′–4′ high. (Tab. 17.) (Eu.)

4. **P. capillâre,** Brid.   Very like the preceding, but a smaller plant ; leaves oblong, approaching to spatulate, pointed, more loosely placed on the stem ; pedicels more slender ; rostrum of the operculum rather flexuous ; teeth of the peristome more linear, their basal membrane conspicuously emergent. — White Mountains, New Hampshire.

5. **P. alpinum,** Brid.   Stems much elongated, fastigiately branched above ; leaves linear-lanceolate from a long sheathing base, serrate ; lamellæ of the costa gradually thickened at their margins ; capsule erect or oblique, ovaloblong, the surface smooth. — White Mountains, New Hampshire. — Larger than any of the above. (Eu.)

45. POLÝTRICHUM, Brid.   Hair-cap Moss.   (Tab. 17.)

Calyptra and operculum as in the last. Capsule 4–6-sided, oblong or ovate, with a discoid apophysis, erect (when dry horizontal), long-pedicellate. Peristome single : teeth 64 : — otherwise as in Atrichum ; with the inflorescence and mode of growth of Pogonatum. — Tall showy Mosses, among the largest of the

Acrocarpi ; stems firm from a suberect rhizoma (hence forming more compact tufts), almost woody, triangular, dark purple, shining ; leaves rigid and coriaceous, linear-lanceolate, below sheathing, above spreading, and mostly occupied by the broad lamelligerous costa. (Name from σολύς, *many,* and θρίξ, τριχός, *a hair ;* from the hairy covering of the calyptra.)

1. **P. commúne,** Linn. Stems erect, mostly simple ; leaves spreading or recurved, flat, serrate on the margins and back ; the lamellæ somewhat 2-cleft at their margins ; capsule oblong, 4-sided, the angles acute ; operculum shortly rostrate from a convex base. — Shady moist places ; common. — Plant 6′–12′ high. (Tab. 17.) (Eu.)

2. **P. formôsum,** Hedw. Differs from the preceding by its longer and slightly curved capsule with obtuse angles, a smaller obconic apophysis tapering into the pedicel, and the conical operculum. — Woods, around the base of trees, &c. (Eu.)

3. **P. grácile,** Menzies. Usually somewhat smaller than No. 1 or 2 ; capsule ovate, 4–6-sided, obtuse-angled ; operculum long-rostrate ; the hairy covering of the calyptra shorter than the capsule ; spores larger ; basal membrane of the peristome not emergent. — Boggy places, Ipswich, Massachusetts, *Oakes.* (Eu.)

4. **P. juniperinum,** Hedw. Stem simple or divided ; leaves linear-lanceolate, awn-pointed, denticulate on the back, the margins inflexed, entire ; capsule and operculum as in No. 1. — Var. STRICTUM. Stems elongated, slender ; leaves appressed ; capsule cubical. — Margins of woods, in exposed places, &c. — Plant 4′–7′ high ; the variety subalpine. (Eu.)

5. **P. piliferum,** Schreb. Stems simple ; leaves clustered at the summit, lanceolate, the margins inflexed, entire ; costa excurrent into a long diaphanous and spinulose awn ; capsule ovate-oblong, 4-sided ; operculum conical, rostrate. — Rocky places, in mountainous districts. — Plant 2′–4′ high. (Eu.)

TRIBE XIX. BRÝEÆ.

46. TÍMMIA, Hedw.   (Tab. 17.)

Calyptra large, cuculliform. Operculum hemispherical, papillate or with a central depression. Capsule oblong, subpyriform, erect-cernuous, broadly annulate, long-pedicellate. Peristome double ; the exterior of 16 lanceolate geniculate-incurved teeth ; the interior, a membrane divided half-way into 64 cilia coherent in fours at their apices. Inflorescence monœcious : male flower gemmiform, axillary. — Partaking more or less of the characters of Mnium, Aulacomnion, and Polytrichum ; stems cæspitose, ascending from a decumbent radiculose base, innovating sparingly above ; leaves of a firm and rather rigid texture, sheathing at the base, elongated-lanceolate, spreading, strongly dentate, with a stout and terete percurrent costa ; areolæ rotund above, elongated-hexagonal below. (Named after *J. C. Timm,* a German botanist.)

1. **T. megapolitàna,** Hedw. — The calyptra is often arrested in its growth, and found attached to the pedicel, having given egress to the capsule by

a lateral fissure not extending through its tubular base. — Shady banks of water-courses; not uncommon. (Tab. 17.) (Eu.)

47. AULACÓMNION, Schwægr. (Tab. 17.)

Calyptra cuculliform. Operculum shortly and obtusely rostellate from a convex base. Capsule oblong, cernuous, striate (ribbed when dry), long-pedicellate, annulate. Peristome as in Bryum, but with ciliolæ (2 or 3 together) always present. Inflorescence monœcious or diœcious. — Plants having, besides a peculiar habit of their own, a mixed resemblance to species of Mnium, Bartramia, and Meesia; stems erect, tomentose; upper portion of the branches in some species elongated, leafless, pedicel-like, and terminated by capitula of rudimentary leaves (pseudopodia); leaves oblong or linear-lanceolate, costate nearly to the apex, with a granular dot-like areolation. (Name from αὐλαξ, -ακος, *a furrow*, and μνίον, *a moss*, in allusion to the furrowed or ribbed capsule.)

1. **A. heteróstichum,** Br. & Sch. Leaves obovate-oblong, strongly serrate, turned to one side; capsule cylindrical-oblong, slightly curved; operculum obliquely rostellate. — Woods, moist shady banks, &c.; common. — Monœcious; sterile flower gemmiform, axillary: pseudopodia wanting. (Tab. 17.)

2. **A. túrgidum,** Schwægr. Leaves ovate-oblong, obtuse, entire; capsule curved, somewhat gibbous. — White Mountains of New Hampshire. — Diœcious: sterile flower discoid: presence of pseudopodia doubtful.

3. **A. palústre,** Schwægr. Leaves elongated-lanceolate, denticulate at the apex; capsule cernuous, ovate-oblong, gibbous at the back. — Borders of swamps; not unfrequent. — Inflorescence as in No. 2: pseudopodia less frequent than in the next species. (Eu.)

4. **A. andrógynum,** Schwægr. Diœcious; a miniature resemblance of the preceding species; distinguished by its gemmiform male flower and oblong, regular, inclined capsule: pseudopodia more abundant and fruit more rare. — Chimney Rocks, on the French Broad River, Tennessee. (Eu.)

48. BRYUM, Br. & Sch. (Tab. 18.)

Calyptra small, cuculliform, fugacious. Operculum convex, apiculate or shortly rostellate. Capsule pyriform, clavate or oblong, with a tapering neck or apophysis, inclined or pendulous, long-pedicellate, mostly annulate. Peristome double; the exterior 16 lanceolate teeth, with a flexuous medial line, hygroscopic; articulation close, internally prominent: the interior a membrane divided half-way into 16 carinate processes or cilia, alternating with the teeth; intermediate ciliolæ (1-3 together) mostly present. Inflorescence various: male flower with filiform paraphyses. — A very natural genus, containing numerous species, growing on the ground or on rocks, seldom on trees; stems closely cæspitose, erect, sparingly branched by innovations from the floral apex; leaves enlarged as they ascend, usually of an ovate or lanceolate outline, with a percurrent costa, smooth texture, and rather large rhomboidal areolation. (Βρύον, an ancient name for Moss.)

Leaves narrow, elongated; the costa ceasing below the apex.

← Inflorescence hermaphrodite.

1. **B. pyrifórme,** Hedw. Stems short (3″-4′), simple; leaves bright shining green, spreading, linear-setaceous, subflexuous, slightly serrate at the apex; capsule pyriform, pendulous, glossy, yellowish-brown, of a thin texture; operculum convex, mammillate; pedicel long.—Mostly on the ground in burnt woods, &c.; frequent. (Eu.)

2. **B. crúdum,** Schreb. Patches glaucous-green, somewhat loose; stems 1′-2′ high; lower leaves oval-lanceolate, the terminal linear-lanceolate, subflexuous, serrated at the apex; capsule oval-pyriform or oblong, suberect or horizontal; operculum as in No. 1.—White Mountains, New Hampshire, *Oakes*—Sometimes dioecious. (Eu.)

← ← Inflorescence dioecious: male flower gemmiform, terminal.

3. **B. Lescuriànum,** Sulliv. Loosely cæspitose, greenish-yellow, without any tinge of red; stems 4″-6″ long, subdecumbent; lower leaves oblong-lanceolate, the terminal much longer, linear, acuminate, serrate at the apex, the margins reflexed at the middle; capsule short, pyriform, pendulous, when dry wide-mouthed; annulus compound, unrolling; operculum hemispherical, apiculate; pedicel erect from a geniculate base, 7″-8″ long.—(*Mem. Amer. Acad.,* n. ser. 4, p. 171.)—Clay-banks, Ohio and Pennsylvania: rare.

4. **B. annótinum,** Hedw. Plant considerably larger than the preceding; capsule oblong-pyriform, with a long, tapering, reddish neck, and constricted under the mouth when dry.—Mountains of New England, *Oakes*—The sterile shoots have numerous axillary, deciduous, bulb-like gemmæ. (Eu.)

← ← ← Inflorescence monoecious: antheridia axillary.

5. **B. elongàtum,** Dicks. Stems simple, 4″-10″ high; upper leaves linear-lanceolate, crowded, spreading, recurved on their lower margin, serrated at the apex; capsule inclined or horizontal, elongated, narrowly clavate, the collum very long; operculum subrostellate; pedicel 1′-2′ long.—Crevices of rocks, tops of high mountains in the Southern States.—Ciliolæ of the inner peristome often rudimentary. (Eu.)

6. **B. nútans,** Schreb. Stems about 1′ long; upper leaves linear-lanceolate, serrulate at the apex, the margins below recurved; capsule pendulous, oval-pyriform or elliptical, short-necked; operculum apiculate; ciliolæ of the inner peristome in twos or threes, large, appendiculate; pedicel 1′-2′ high, pale above. —Moist sandy soil, in hilly or mountainous districts. (Eu.)

7. **B. cucullàtum,** Schwægr. An alpine species, often confounded with alpine forms of the last species; its most reliable distinctive characters are the larger obovate capsule, with a small operculum, and the absence of the ciliolæ of the inner peristome.—White Mountains of New Hampshire, *Gray, Oakes.* (Eu.)

** *Leaves broad; costa ceasing below the apex. (Dioecious: male flower terminal.)*

8. **B. róseum,** Schreb. Stems 1′-2′ long, decumbent at the base; lower leaves small, appressed, the upper very large, serrated, spatulate, apiculate, forming terminal stellate clusters; capsule pendulous, clavate-oblong or sub-

cylindrical, slightly curved, short-necked; pedicels 1 - 5 from the same perichæth; male flower somewhat discoid. — Shaded woods, at the base of trees: common. — Among the largest of the genus. (Eu.)

9. **B. Wahlenbérgii,** Schwægr. Patches extensive, pale glaucous-green; stems erect, or decumbent at the base, 1' - 2' long; leaves serrate, the lower ones ovate-acuminate, the uppermost lanceolate, serrate at the apex, with a rather loose areolation; capsule short-pyriform, pendulous, short-necked, when dry wide-mouthed; annulus none; male flower somewhat discoid, conspicuous, on a slender stem. — Springy and gravelly places; not uncommon: but the fruit rare. (Eu.)

10. **B. argénteum,** Linn. Patches silvery-white; stems 4" - 10' high, divided; branches julaceous; leaves very concave, entire, loosely areolated; the lower distant, broadly ovate; the upper ovate-lanceolate, imbricating; capsule abruptly pendulous, oval-oblong, deep purple when ripe. — On exposed ground, roofs, pavements, &c.: extremely common. — A small species. (Eu.)

＊ ＊ ＊ *Leaves mostly ovate ; the costa extending to the apex.* (*Diœcious.*)

11. **B. pseudo-triquètrum,** Schwægr. Patches large, deep green, inclining to blackish or purplish; stems 1' - 3' high, radiculose; leaves ovate and ovate-lanceolate, slightly bordered, the margins recurved, slightly serrulate at the apex; capsule pendulous, oblong-pyriform, with a tapering neck. — Wet rocks, in hilly districts, Southern Ohio. — Resembles B. bimum, but is more robust, and with a different inflorescence. (Eu.)

12. **B. turbinátum,** Hedw. Patches pale green, sometimes with a reddish tinge; stems 1' - 2' long; leaves ovate-acuminate and oblong-lanceolate, subdecurrent, slightly recurved on the margins, the marginal cellules long and narrow; capsule ventricose-pyriform, very much constricted under the mouth when dry. — Wet rocks, below Niagara Falls. (Eu.)

13. **B. Duválii,** Voit. Distinguished from the preceding (some forms of which it much resembles) by its more slender stems; its remote, spreading, very much decurrent, less elongated leaves, of a looser areolation and with plane margins; capsule less constricted under the mouth when dry. — Mountains of New England, *Oakes.* (Eu.)

14. **B. alpìnum,** L. Tufts dense, deep red, shining; stems ($\frac{1}{2}$' - 2' high) stiff; leaves lanceolate, nearly erect, closely imbricating, straight, recurved on the margins; costa strong, rigid; capsule oblong-pyriform, pendulous, deep red. — Alpine region of the White Mountains, New Hampshire, *Oakes.* (Eu.)

＊ ＊ ＊ ＊ *Leaves ovate ; the costa excurrent.*

← *Inflorescence hermaphrodite.*

15. **B. cérnuum,** Hedw. Closely cæspitose; stems branched, radiculose; leaves ovate-acuminate, concave, with recurved margins; capsule pendulous, oblong-pyriform, the mouth and operculum very small; inner peristome imperfect, adherent to the teeth. — Wet woods, Northern Ohio. (Eu.)

16. **B. bìmum,** Schreb. Stems 1' - 2' long, matted by the purplish radicels; leaves above yellowish or lurid-green, below reddish-brown, ovate-

lanceolate, spreading, subdecurrent, somewhat margined, slightly serrated at the apex ; capsule pendulous, oblong-pyriform, mouth and operculum rather large ; inner peristome perfect. — About the roots of trees, on the borders of swamps ; Ohio. (Tab. 18.) (Ea.)

17. **B. intermèdium,** Brid. Densely cæspitose ; stems short (3''–6'' high); leaves ovate-acuminate and ovate-lanceolate, imbricated, erect, their margins reflexed, the excurrent portion of the costa sometimes denticulate; capsule somewhat pendulous, oblong-pyriform ; inner peristome perfect. — Crevices of shaded limestone cliffs, Ohio ; and on brick walls, near the Santee Canal, South Carolina. (Eu.)

18. **B. torquéscens,** Br. & Sch. Much like the last ; but distinguished by its leaves contorted when dry, and its larger, clavate-obconic, somewhat pendulous capsule, usually incurved. — Texas, Wright. (Eu.)

← ← *Inflorescence diœcious : male flower gemmiform, terminal.*

19. **B. capillàre,** Hedw. Stems ¼'–1 long, rather closely tufted ; leaves strongly contorted when dry, narrowly margined, the lower ovate-oblong, apiculate ; the upper obovate-oblong with slender points ; capsule rather pendulous, variable, oval-pyriform, oblong-clavate, or short-obovate ; operculum red. — On rocks, road-sides, mountains of Pennsylvania, Lesquereux : rare. A variable species. (Eu.)

20. **B. cæspiticium,** L. Tufts compact; stems ¼'–1' long ; leaves straight when dry, ovate-acuminate and ovate-lanceolate, the margins reflexed ; capsule usually oblong-obovate or pyriform, pendulous ; operculum yellow. — On the ground, rocks, &c., in dry places : frequent. (Eu.)

21. **B. atropurpùreum,** Web. & Mohr. Smaller than the last ; stems densely crowded ; leaves ovate-acute and ovate-lanceolate, erect-patent, concave, reflexed on the margins ; capsule pendulous, dark purple, oval-oblong, not pyriform, the neck abruptly passing into the pedicel ; operculum wider than the mouth of the capsule. — Sandy soil, among the Lookout Mountains, Alabama, Lesquereux. (Eu.)

22. **B. sanguineum,** Ludwig. Distinguished from the last species, which it much resembles, by its leaves more elongated, longer-cuspidate, plane on the margins, and serrate at the apex ; capsule deep blood-red, oblong-pyriform, the neck gradually tapering into the pedicel ; the operculum more pointed. — With No. 21. (Ea.)

← ← ← *Inflorescence monœcious : male flower gemmiform, terminal on proper branches.*

23. **B. uliginòsum,** Br. & Sch. Cæspitose ; stems short (3''–7'' high), radiculose ; leaves oval-lanceolate, the margins plane above and with narrow cellules ; capsule pendulous, clavate, not pyriform, irregular, gibbous on the back near the small oblique mouth ; cilia of the inner peristome wanting or rudimentary. — Wet woods, Northern Ohio, Lesquereux. — Foliage green. (Eu.)

24. **B. palléscens,** Schwægr. Stems 1'–2' high, compactly tufted ; leaves ovate-lanceolate, the margins reflexed ; capsule oblong-pyriform, symmetrical, pendulous ; cilia of the inner peristome present and appendiculate. — Central Ohio : very rare — Lower leaves with a reddish tint. (Eu.)

49. MNÌUM, Br. & Sch. (Tab. 17.)

Calyptra small, cuculliform, fugacious. Operculum convex at the base, apiculate or rostellate. Capsule oval or oblong, not pyriform, mostly pendulous, long-pedicellate, annulate. Peristome as in Bryum. Inflorescence diœcious or hermaphrodite : male flower with clavate paraphyses. — Nearly allied to the preceding genus, its species however larger and more showy, conspicuous for their broad, smooth, glossy leaves, with a spinulose-serrated thickened border, a percurrent costa, and large roundish-hexagonal areolæ ; stems innovating from near their base, stoloniferous ; growing on the ground or on rocks in shady situations. (Mνίον, an ancient name for Moss.)

* *Inflorescence diœcious : male flower terminal, discoid.*

1. **M. affìne,** Bland. Stems radiculose, 1'-3' high ; upper leaves large, elliptic-oblong or ligulate-obovate, crowded, spreading, undulated or crisped when dry, their thickened border simply spinulose-serrate ; leaves of the procumbent or arched shoots roundish, 2-ranked ; capsule oblong, large ; operculum apiculate ; pedicels often 2-4 from the same perichæth. — On the ground, shaded banks in woods : frequent. (Eu.)

2. **M. hórnum,** Hedw. Stems and barren shoots erect, 1'-3' high ; leaves erect-patent, narrowly lanceolate, their thickened border doubly spinulose-serrate ; capsule oblong, tapering into the pedicel, horizontal ; operculum apiculate. — White Mountains of New Hampshire, *Oakes.* (Eu.)

3. **M. orthorhýnchum,** Brid. Stems simple, 1'-1½' high ; upper leaves ovate-lanceolate, subspatulate, the border as in the last species ; areolæ unusually small and opaque for the genus ; capsule horizontal, oblong, slightly incurved ; operculum conic-rostellate. — Wet pine-woods, near Montreal, Canada East. (Eu.)

4. **M. stellàre,** Hedw. Stems closely cæspitose, 1'-2' high ; leaves oval-oblong, inclining to spatulate, without a thickened border, strongly serrate above, very brittle when dry ; areolæ roundish, rather small ; capsule oblong, horizontal, slightly incurved ; operculum simply hemispherical. — Margins of woodland brooks : fruit rare. — Foliage dark green with an indigo tinge, and acid to the taste. (Eu.)

5. **M. punctàtum,** Hedw. Stems ½'-4' high, radiculose ; leaves large, spreading, roundish-obovate, narrowed at the base, scarcely pointed, with a thickened firm border, not serrate ; capsule rather pendulous, oval ; operculum conic-rostellate. — Wet places, on the ground, Alleghany Mountains. — Foliage with a reddish tinge. (Eu.)

** *Inflorescence hermaphrodite.*

6. **M. serràtum,** Brid. Stems ½'-1' high, loosely cæspitose ; leaves ovate-lanceolate, the thickened border doubly spinulose-dentate ; capsule nearly horizontal, oval, gradually tapering into the pedicel ; operculum short-rostellate. — Margins of rivulets, in woods. — Among the smallest species. (Eu.)

7. **M. Drummóndii,** Br. & Sch. Densely cæspitose ; stems about 1' high ; leaves erect from an oblong narrow base, broad-ovate, shortly acuminate, scarcely crisped when dry, with a narrow, thickened, and simply spinulose-den-

G. M. 4

tate border; capsule short, oval, pendulous; operculum short, conic-acute.— White Mountains, New Hampshire, *Oakes*.

8. **M. rostràtum,** Schwægr. Stems $\frac{1}{2}'-1'$ high; the sterile branches longer, decumbent or somewhat creeping; leaves oval-oblong, obtuse, very short-apiculate, the thickened border obtusely dentate; operculum rostrate, half as long as the capsule; pedicels often 2–5 together.— Along woodland rivulets. (Eu.)

9. **M. cuspidàtum,** Hedw. Stems $\frac{1}{2}'-1'$ high, closely tufted, radiculose, the sterile branches arcuate or decumbent; lower leaves obovate-acuminate, the upper oval-acuminate with a narrowed base, the thickened border simply serrate; capsule somewhat pendulous, solitary; operculum convex, scarcely apiculate.— Woods, about the roots of trees: frequent. (Tab. 17.) (Eu.)

Tribe XX. MEESIÈÆ.

50. MEÉSIA, Hedw.   (Tab. 17.)

Calyptra small, cuculliform, fugacious. Operculum conic. Capsule apophysated, erect-cernuous, clavate, with a small oblique mouth, very long-pedicellate, narrowly annulate. Peristome double; the exterior of 16 short obtuse teeth, with a medial line; the interior of 16 carinate cilia, much longer than the teeth, with a narrow basal membrane. Inflorescence various: male flower with clavate paraphyses.— Tall and striking species, inhabiting bogs and swamps, remarkable for their slender stems and long pedicels, in habit Bryoid, in shape of capsule allied to the Funarieæ; leaves of a lanceolate outline, with a semiamplexicaul and decurrent base; the costa percurrent; areolæ small, compact, oblong. — (Named for *D. Meese*, a Dutch botanist.)

1. **M. longisèta,** Hedw. Hermaphrodite; stems 3'–5' high, tomentose; leaves ovate-lanceolate, spreading, plane and entire on the margins, serrate, twisted when dry; capsule clavate-pyriform, incurved, the apophysis constituting half its length (as in the other species); the exterior peristome more or less adherent to the interior; annulus rather persistent; operculum obtuse; pedicels 4'–5' long.— Cranberry marshes, Northern Ohio. — A variety, smaller in all its parts, occurs among the mountains of New England. (Tab. 17.) (Eu.)

2. **M. tristicha,** Br. & Sch. Distinguished from the preceding by its 3-ranked, wider, squarrose and denticulate leaves, and the diœcious inflorescence, with a terminal discoid male flower. — Grows in similar places. (Eu.)

3. **M. uliginòsa,** Hedw. Smaller than No. 1 and 2, monœcious and hermaphrodite on the same plant; leaves linear-lanceolate or linear, obtuse, with entire recurved margins and a heavy costa; operculum truncate. — White Mountains, New Hampshire, *Oakes*: St. Paul, Minnesota, *Lesquereux*. (Eu.)

Tribe XXI. BARTRAMIÈÆ.

51. BARTRÀMIA, Hedw.   (Tab. 17.)

Calyptra small, dimidiate, fugacious. Operculum small, conic-convex. Capsule globular, cernuous, seldom erect or pendulous, exannulate, striated,

when dry furrowed, with a long and erect (rarely short and arcuate) pedicel.
Peristome usually double, sometimes single or none; the exterior of 16 teeth
like those of Bryum; the interior a plicated membrane divided half-way into 16
cilia, splitting along their middle; their segments divergent; rudimentary ciliolæ
often present. Inflorescence various.—Plants remarkable for their globose
capsule; growing in extensive tufts on the ground, and on rocks, rarely on
trees; stems covered with a dense radicular tomentum; leaves lanceolate, more
or less elongated, serrate, papillose on both surfaces, of a firm texture; areolæ
dense, quadrate or oblong; costa percurrent or excurrent. (Named in honor of
John Bartram, the earliest native American botanist.)—In the following species
the capsule is cernuous: peristome double: pedicel long and erect.

§ 1. BARTRAMIA Proper.—*Stems dichotomously branched.*

1. **B. ithyphylla,** Brid. Hermaphrodite; tufts compact, bright yellowish-green; stems ½'-2' high; leaves erect-patent, lanceolate, subulate from a
broad, sheathing, whitish base; costa large, excurrent, with a scabrous point —
Alpine and subalpine rocks, White Mountains, New Hampshire. (Eu.)

2. **B. Œderi,** Swartz. Hermaphrodite; tufts loose, extensive, dark-green;
stems slender, 1'-3' high; leaves remote, patent-recurved from an erect (not
sheathing) base, lanceolate, carinate, scarcely papillose, recurved on the margins.
costate to the apex.—Mountains of New England. (Eu.)

3. **B. pomiformis,** Hedw. Monœcious; tufts large, rather dense,
glaucous-green; stems 1'-3' high; leaves crowded, spreading, lanceolate-subulate or linear-subulate, crisped when dry, flattish, the costa excurrent; male
flower gemmiform, contiguous to the female. —Shady banks, either dry or
moist: common. (Tab. 17.) (Eu.)

§ 2. PHILONÒTIS, Brid. — *Stems fasciculately branched.*

4. **B. fontàna,** Brid. Diœcious; tufts extensive, dense, yellowish or
glaucous-green; stems elongated (3'-7' high); branches interruptedly verticil-
late; leaves of two forms, either short, ovate-acuminate and appressed, or longer,
lanceolate and spreading or secund, both reflexed on the margins below and obscurely plicate at the base; inner leaves of the discoid male flower obtuse, not
costate.— Wet springy places, in mountain districts. (Eu.)

5. **B. calcàrea,** Br. & Sch. Diœcious; compared with the last species
(which it very closely resembles), its leaves are longer, more rigid and gradually
tapering, less papillose, with a larger areolation and a stronger costa; perigonial leaves costate to the acuminated apex; teeth of the peristome not so closely
articulated.— Specimens intermediate between this species (as above described
from European specimens) and No. 4, were gathered by *Lesquereux*, on wet
rocks, in the mountains of North Carolina. (Eu.)

6. **B. Màrchica,** Brid. Diœcious; resembles reduced forms of B. fon-
tana; leaves uniform in shape, spreading or secund, narrow, lanceolate, not plicate, mucronate by the excurrent costa; capsule thin-walled; male flower gemmiform; perigonial leaves erect, lanceolate, acute, costate. — (B. Muhlenbergii,
Schwægr ? — Gravelly and springy places. (Eu.)

7. **B. radicàlis,** Beauv. Monœcious; stems short; leaves linear-lanceolate, erect, cuspidate by the long-excurrent scabrous costa; male flower gemmiform, close to the female. — Wet clay-banks, Ohio and southward.

52. CONÓSTOMUM, Swartz.   (Tab. 17.)

Calyptra cuculliform. Operculum conic-rostellate. Capsule globular, cernuous, exannulate, with a long erect pedicel. Peristome single: teeth 16, linear-lanceolate, prominently articulated, with a medial line, united at their apices. Inflorescence diœcious: male flower subdiscoid, with clavate paraphyses. — A genus scarcely distinguishable from Bartramia, differing only in the structure of the peristome, the rostellate operculum, and the larger and less fugacious calyptra. (Name from κῶνος, *a cone*, and στόμα, *a mouth*, in allusion to the cone-like appearance of the peristome.)

1. **C. boreàle,** Swartz. Stems compactly cæspitose, ½'–2' high, glaucous-green above, brownish below; leaves erect, imbricated in 5 rows, lanceolate-acuminate, serrate, sharply carinate, mucronate by the excurrent costa. — On rocks, in bleak alpine situations, White Mountains of New Hampshire. (Tab. 17.) (Eu.)

Tribe XXII. FUNARIÈÆ.

53. FUNÀRIA, Schreb.   (Tab. 17.)

Calyptra cuculliform, inflated below, subulate above. Operculum conic or convex-obtuse. Capsule obliquely pyriform, rather ventricose, cernuous, with a small oblique mouth, long-pedicellate. Peristome double: the exterior of 16 teeth, oblique, lanceolate-attenuated, and connected at their apices by a small reticulated disk; the interior a membrane divided to the base into 16 lanceolate cilia, opposite the teeth. Inflorescence monœcious: male flower subdiscoid, its paraphyses much enlarged at their apex. — Annual or biennial gregarious plants, growing on the ground; stems at first simple, terminated by a male flower, afterwards branched, the branches producing fertile flowers; lower leaves remote; upper ones clustered, larger, broad-lanceolate, of a thin and loose texture; the areolæ large, hexagonal-oblong; costa loosely cellular, ceasing below the apex. (Name from *funis,* a rope, from the twisted pedicel.)

1. **F. hygrométrica,** Hedw. Stems 3''–10'' high; upper and perichætial leaves connivent, crowded into a bud-like cluster, broadly ovate-lanceolate, very concave, entire, costate nearly to the apex; the perigonial leaves serrate; capsule furrowed when dry, the border of its mouth corrugated; annulus large, spirally unrolling; pedicel (2'–3' long) arcuate and flexuous — Var. CALVÉSCENS has the pedicel more elongated and straight, the capsule more slender, and almost erect. — Very common, on the ground (particularly when lately burnt over), and on walls; the variety occurs mostly in the Southern States. (Tab. 17.) (Eu.)

2. **F. flávicans,** Michx. In general appearance very much like the last, but the color paler; leaves not so connivent and with a long cuspidate point, the

costa excurrent; pedicels not arcuate nor so flexuous; capsule less obovate, very slightly furrowed when dry; mouth larger, not so oblique, and its border smooth. — Southern States.

3. **F. Muhlenbérgii,** Schwægr. Very much smaller than No. 1 or 2; stems 1″–3″ high; upper leaves erect-patent, oblong-obovate, suddenly acuminate, obtusely serrate, the costa ceasing below the point; capsule shortly pyriform, not furrowed when dry; operculum convex, apiculate; annulus none; pedicels 6″–8″ high, twisted to the right when dry; spores more than twice the diameter of those of No. 1, granular on the surface. — Pennsylvania. (Eu.)

4. **F. serráta,** Beauv. Intermediate in size between Nos. 1 and 3; compared with the last, the leaves are longer, spatulate-lanceolate, distantly and sharply serrated above, the costa excurrent; operculum convex, not apiculate; the pedicel 1′–1½′ high, when dry twisted to the left its whole length; spores larger. — Pennsylvania and southward.

54. ENTÓSTHODON, Schwægr. (Tab. 18.)

Calyptra rostrate, cuculliform, inflated below. Operculum depressed-convex. Capsule erect, pyriform, symmetrical, smooth, long-pedicellate. Peristome single: teeth 16, short, somewhat fissile, linear-lanceolate, inserted below the orifice of the capsule, horizontal. — Inflorescence, ramification, and structure of leaves as in Funaria. — (Name formed of ἐντοσθεν, *from within,* and ὀδών, *tooth,* alluding to the insertion of the teeth.)

1. **E. Drummóndii,** Sulliv. Stems 1″–2″ high; leaves connivent, elliptic-oblong, rather obtuse, slightly crenate on the margin, concave, costate to the apex, areolation large; capsule globose-pyriform, operculum flattish; pedicels 5″–7″ high; calyptra erect, with a straight subulate rostrum as long as the capsule. — (E. obtusifolius, *Hook. & Wils. in Drum. 2d coll.* No. 36.) — Wet, clayey soil, Southern States. — The short-pyriform capsule and the long-subulate rostrum of the calyptra, readily distinguish this species from the nearly allied E. Templetoni, *Schwægr.* and E. obtusifolius, *J. D. Hook.* (Tab. 18.)

55. PHYSCOMÍTRIUM, Brid. (Tab. 18.)

Calyptra long-rostrate, mitriform and lobed at the base, or inflated-cuculliform. Operculum flattish-convex, with or without an apiculus. Capsule pyriform, symmetrical, exannulate, its pedicel mostly erect. Peristome wanting. — Annual and biennial plants, with the inflorescence, ramification, and structure of leaves as in Funaria. (Name from φύσκος, *something inflated,* and μιτρίον, *a little cap.*)

1. **P. pyrifórme,** Br. & Sch. Stems 2″–5″ high; leaves spatulate-lanceolate, serrate, spreading, the costa nearly percurrent, capsule globose-pyriform, on an erect exserted pedicel 5″–8″ long; calyptra mitriform, lobed. — On the ground; extremely common. (Eu.)

2. **P. immérsum,** Sulliv. Leaves obovate-lanceolate, serrate, the costa percurrent; capsule immersed, hemispherical without the operculum, which is

short-pointed from a convex base, and deciduous with the columella attached ; calyptra small, mitriform, 4 – 5-lobed at the base. — (P. sphæricum, *Musc. Alleghan.*, No. 196.) — Banks of the Ohio River subject to inundation. — A minute annual : length of the whole plant 2″ – 3″. (Tab. 18.)

3. **P. tetrágonum,** Br. & Sch. Stems gregarious, scarcely 1″ high ; leaves connivent, ovate-lanceolate, acuminate, the costa ceasing at the apex or excurrent ; capsule globose-pyriform, on an erect pedicel (1″ high), wide-mouthed when dry ; operculum convex, apiculate ; calyptra very large, twice as long as the capsule, fusiform, 4-sided, splitting on one side. — On the ground, San Marcos, Texas, *Wright :* Vincennes, Indiana, *Lesquereux.* (Eu.)

56. APHANORHÉGMA, Sulliv.   (Tab. 18.)

Calyptra small, campanulate-mitriform, lobed at the base. Operculum hemispherical, apiculate. Capsule immersed (including the operculum), spherical, nearly sessile, exannulate. Peristome none. Inflorescence monœcious or hermaphrodite : paraphyses globosely distended at the apex. — A genus, by its feeble dehiscence, globose capsule, and the characters of vegetation, forming an intermediate link between Physcomitrella among Cleistocarpous, and Physcomitrium among Stegocarpous Mosses. (Name from ἀφανής, *unapparent*, and ῥῆγμα, *rupture*, or *suture;* i. e. dehiscence obscure.)

1. **A. serráta,** Sulliv. Stems 2″ – 3″ high, simple or innovating from below the apex ; leaves oblong-lanceolate, serrate, costate nearly to the point of a large and loose hexagonal areolation ; capsule (when mature) separating under pressure along an indistinct transverse suture (not visible at an early stage) into two equal portions ; antheridia (occasionally intermixed with a few archegonia) in the axils of the perichætial leaves, usually naked, sometimes with 1 or 2 small perigonial leaves. — (*Sulliv. in Mem. Amer. Acad.*, n. ser. 4, p 60, t. 2.) — Damp soil, New England to Ohio. — Strikingly like Physcomitrella patens ; distinguished mainly by its feeble operculation, and the denser texture of the outer wall of the capsule. (Tab. 18.)

Tribe XXIII. SPLACHNEÆ.

57. SPLÁCHNUM, L., Br. & Sch. Umbrella-Moss. (Tab. 18.)

Calyptra small, conic, entire or uneven at the base : operculum convex or mammillate. Capsule erect, obovate-oblong or subcylindrical, with a very large spongy and differently colored obovate, globose or umbraculiform apophysis, long-pedicellate. Peristome single, of 16 double teeth in pairs, reflexed when dry. Columella emergent, capitate. Inflorescence mostly diœcious : male flower capituliform, terminal. — Plants of a peculiar structure, readily recognized by the exceedingly large apophysis of the capsule ; perennial, cæspitose, growing only on the dung of herbivorous animals ; stems innovating from below the floral apex, dichotomous, of a succulent soft texture ; leaves lanceolate, taper-pointed, thin and delicate, with large loose, oblong, hexagonal areolæ ; costa slight, ceasing below the point. (Σπλάγχνον, a name used by Dioscorides for some cryptogamous plant.)

1. **S. ampullàceum,** L. Stems $\frac{1}{2}'-2'$ long; leaves oblong- or obovate-lanceolate, acuminate, entire or irregularly dentate; apophysis violet-purple, obovate, tapering into the purplish pedicel, and twice or thrice the width of the yellow capsule. — New England to Pennsylvania: rare. (Tab. 18.) (Eu.)

2. **S. rùbrum,** L. Stems short $(3''-6'')$; leaves spatulate-obovate, long-pointed, serrate, somewhat complicate and undulate on the margins; apophysis deep red, very large, umbrella-shaped, 7 - 10 times as wide as the minute capsule; pedicels $4'-5'$ long. — Maine, *A. Young.* (Eu.)

58. TETRÀPLODON, Br. & Sch. (Tab. 18.)

Calyptra small, conic, entire, or split on one side and somewhat cuculliform. Operculum conical-convex, obtuse. Capsule erect, small, oval-oblong, with a solid clavate apophysis tapering into an exserted pedicel. Peristome single, of 16 double teeth, at first in fours, afterwards in pairs, reflexed when dry. Columella not emergent. Inflorescence monœcious: male flower gemmiform or capitulæform, axillary or terminal. — A genus scarcely separable from the last; besides the above characters, the stems are more compactly cæspitose; the apophysis does not increase in size after the maturity of the capsule, and the color and consistence of the two is uniform; the cellular tissue of the leaves not so lax; and the habitat is on animal substances, or on the dung of carnivorous animals. — (Name from τετραπλόος. *fourfold*, and ὀδών, *tooth*; the teeth of the peristome being at first in fours.)

1. **T. angustàtus,** Br. & Sch. Stems $\frac{1}{2}'-3$ long, radiculose; leaves erect-patent, remote, oblong-lanceolate, produced into a long flexuous point, obsoletely or distinctly dentate; apophysis oblong-obconic, somewhat wider than the capsule; calyptra whitish, conic, cuculliform, descending to the top of the apophysis. — White Mountains of New Hampshire, *B. D. Greene, Oakes:* Lake Superior, *Loring.* — A northern species. (Eu.)

2. **T. austràlis,** Sulliv. & Lesqx. (Musc. Bor.-Amer., No.151.) Resembling very closely the last species; leaves often with 3 - 5 large tooth-like lobes on each side, sometimes almost pinnatifid, rarely simply dentate or nearly entire; apophysis much longer and more tapering; teeth of the peristome less deeply inserted within the capsule's mouth, the rim of which has angular-rotund (not transversely oblong) cellules; calyptra yellowish, elongated-conic, (not split on one side,) descending scarcely to the base of the hemispherical apiculate operculum. — (Splachnum setaceum, *Hook. & Wils. in Drum. 2d coll. No.* 27; — not of *Michx.*, whose plant was from Canada, and most probably belongs to the preceding species.) — Swamps, near the sea-coast, New Jersey to Florida. — It is doubtful whether this species belongs to the present, or to the last genus. (Tab. 18.)

3. **T. mnioìdes,** Br. & Sch. Stems $\frac{1}{2}'-2'$ high; leaves erect-patent, rather close, elliptic-oblong or obovate, concave, suddenly attenuated into a long flexuous point; capsule and its clavate apophysis of about the same width, both dark red. — Catskill Mountains, New York, *Olney.* (Eu.)

Div. II. **Pleurocárpi.**

Fruit lateral on the stem or branches.   (Peristome mostly double.)

TRIBE XXIV.   FONTINÀLEÆ.

59. FONTINÀLIS, Dill.   FOUNTAIN-MOSS.   (Tab. 18.)

Calyptra small, conic, crenate or somewhat lacerate at the base.   Operculum conic.   Capsule ovate, oval, or cylindrical, subsessile.   Peristome double; the exterior 16 linear-lanceolate teeth cohering at their apices in pairs; the interior 16 cilia connected by cross-bars, forming a more or less complete tessellated cone. Inflorescence diœcious. — Large Mosses, floating in water, and rooting at their base only; leaves 3-ranked, ecostate, with a minute linear areolation; capsule immersed in the perichætial leaves, and terminal on short, lateral, supra-axillary branches.   (Name from *fontinalis*, a fountain, in allusion to its place of growth.)

1. **F. antipyrética,** L.   Stems 8'–12' long, very much divided, flexile; leaves broadly ovate-acuminate, complicate-carinate, the margin on one side reflexed; perichætial leaves oblong, obtuse, eroded at the apex, closely embracing the oval capsule; inner peristome a complete tessellated cone. — Mountain rivulets, New England. — Variable in size and color.   (Tab. 18.)   (Eu.)

2. **F. squamòsa,** L.?   Smaller than No. 1; ramification more fasciculate; leaves concave, not complicate-carinate. — Mountain streams, Southern States: without fruit. — Perhaps a different species.   (Eu.)

3. **F. bifórmis,** Sulliv.   Leaves of two forms, those appearing in the spring large, broad, ovate-lanceolate, concave, flaccid, disappearing in the summer, and succeeded by others much smaller, narrowly linear-lanceolate, convolute, and clothing new branches; both kinds denticulate at the apex, their basal angles auriculate, and composed of large oblong pellucid cellules; capsule oval or oblong-cylindrical; perichætial leaves as in No 1; operculum more elongated; teeth of the exterior peristome with 18–20 articulations; cilia of the interior peristome connected at their tips only by a few cross-bars, elsewhere appendiculate.   (F. disticha, var. *Musc. Alleghan., No.* 191, and Pilotrichum sphagnifolium, *Mull. Synop.* 2. *p.* 150, are the spring state of the plant; F. disticha, var *Musc. Alleghan., No.* 192, and Pilotrichum distichum, *Mull. l. c.,* are the summer state.) — Woodland rivulets, near Columbus, Ohio: New Haven, Conn., D. E. Eaton. — Fruit rare: male flowers terminal on short club-shaped branches

4. **F. dísticha,** Hook. & Wils. (in Drum. S. Mosses, No. 151.)   A stiff, elastic species, much more slender than any of the preceding; stems reddish; branches short and widely spreading; leaves erect-patent or rather appressed, linear-lanceolate, convolute, attenuated, dentate at the extreme point; capsule cylindrical, its length 5 times its diameter; operculum narrowly conic, one third as long as the capsule; teeth of the peristome more or less cleft along the medial line between the 12–15 articulations; cilia granulated and connected as in No. 3. — Rivulets near Mobile, Alabama.

5. **F. Lescúrii,** Sulliv.   (Musc. Bor.-Amer., No. 228.)   Near the last, but a soft, flaccid, and somewhat larger species; leaves broader, shorter, not

so attenuated, nor the areolation so linear; capsule cylindrical, its length only 2½ times its diameter, and with a perichætial branch much longer; teeth of the peristome not cleft along the centre, articulations 20-25; cilia not so granulated, more connected from their apices downwards by cross-bars: antheridia 3-5, large, projecting beyond the perigonial leaves, with long paraphyses. — Falls of Little River, Lookout Mountains, Alabama, *Lesquereux.* — Fruit rare.

6. **F. Dalecárlica,** Bryol. Europ. Slender and much divided; branches numerous, elongated, somewhat julaceous; leaves narrowly-lanceolate, sinvolute; perichætial leaves acute, the 3 inner ones recurved at the apex and longer than the ovate capsule; operculum short; teeth of the peristome perforated between the 10-12 articulations; cilia as in No. 3, but not granulated. — (F. squamosa, *Drum. Musc. Amer.,* No. 233; *Musc. Alleghan.,* No. 168.) — White Mountains, *Oakes, James;* Fulton County, New York, *D. C. Eaton.* (Eu.)

60. DICHELÝMA, Myrin. BROOK-MOSS. (Tab. 18.)

Calyptra dimidiate or cuculliform, entire at the base. Operculum conic-rostrate. Capsule oval or oblong, pedicellate. Peristome double; the exterior 16 linear teeth perforated along the medial line; the interior 16 cilia longer than the teeth, and more or less connected by cross-bars. Inflorescence diœcious. — Stems slender, floating in water, sparingly divided and branched; leaves 3-ranked, much elongated, with a percurrent costa, those of the perichæth very conspicuous and ecostate. (Name from διχάω, to divide, and ἔλυμα, a veil, in allusion to the cleft or cuculliform calyptra.)

1. **D. falcàtum,** Myrin. Leaves lanceolate-subulate, complicate-carinate, falcate-secund; the inner perichætial leaves very much elongated, closely wrapped around the lower half of the long pedicel; capsule oval-oblong; inner peristome a tessellated truncated cone; calyptra dimidiate, elongated, clasping the pedicel. — Head-waters of the Saco River, White Mountains, New Hampshire, *James;* Brattleborough, Vermont, *C. C. Frost.* (Eu.)

2. **D. capilláceum,** Bryol. Europ. Branches few, widely spreading; leaves dark or yellowish-green, subulate from a narrow lanceolate base by the long-excurrent costa, secund-falcate, denticulate at the apex; those of the perichæth convolute, overtopping the oval capsule which emerges laterally; calyptra dimidiate, extending below the capsule, and spirally convolute; cilia of the inner peristome connected at their apices only. — Rivulets, Pennsylvania and northward. (Tab. 18.) (Eu.)

3. **D. palléscens,** Bryol. Europ. Much like No. 2, but smaller; leaves pale green, shorter, wider, more complicate-carinate, and more falcate, with a larger areolation; cilia of the inner peristome not connected by cross-bars. - - (D. capillacea, *Drum. Musc. Amer.,* No. 234.) — British America, *Drummond.*

4. **D. subulàtum,** Myrin. Stems elongated, subpinnate; branches short, widely spreading; leaves erect-patent, lanceolate, complicate-carinate, the costa ceasing at the denticulate apex: capsule ovate-oval, short-pedicelled, concealed by the broad and straight perichætial leaves; calyptra cuculliform, not descending below the convex-rostellate operculum; cilia of the inner peristome free, except at their apices. — Louisiana, *Drummond.*

Tribe XXV. CRYPHÆÈÆ.

61. CRYPHÈA, Mohr.   (Tab. 19.)

Calyptra conic-mitriform, papillose at the apex, small. Operculum conic. Capsule immersed, ovate-oblong, short-pedicellate, annulate. Peristome double; the exterior 16 lanceolate-subulate teeth remotely articulated, granulated; the interior 16 subulate cilia, the basilar membrane nearly obsolete. Inflorescence monœcious: antheridia oval, with long pedicels and short paraphyses. — Rather slender Mosses, growing on trees, with leafless creeping stems and ascending or pendulous and subsimple densely leafy branches, bearing in lines or clusters numerous perichætia enveloping the capsule. (Name from κρυφαῖος, *hidden*, in allusion to the concealed capsule.)

1. **C. glomeràta,** W. P. Sch. The ascending branches nearly simple, 1' long; leaves crowded, when dry appressed, when moist recurved-spreading, ovate-acuminate, minutely-serrulate at the apex, semi-costate, with a minute oval areolation; annulus broad; perichætial leaves obovate-oblong, suddenly cuspidate. — (Daltonia heteromalla, var. *Hook. & Wils. in Drum. Musc. 2d coll. No.* 99.) — Southern States: common. — Larger than the European C. heteromalla, *Brid.*, with more crowded spreading leaves, much shorter peristome, and larger spores. (Tab. 19.)

2. **C. nervòsa,** Hook & Wils. Has the aspect of No. 1; leaves when dry erect, not appressed, with recurved margins; costa extending to the point; calyptra split on one side; annulus narrow; perichætial leaves longer-lanceolate and papillose on the back. — Grows with the last.

3. **C. inundàta,** Nees. (in Neuvied Trav.) Stems pendulous, loosely pinnately-branched; branchlets recurved at the apex; leaves distant, oblong-lanceolate, carinate, the lower ones complicate, oblique; costa heavy, excurrent, capsules oval, unilateral on the stems, immersed in the long ecostate perichætial leaves; cilia of the interior peristome red, persistent, incurved at the apex, as long as the teeth. — Floating in water, and attached to the immersed branches of trees, Wabash, Fox, and Black Rivers, Illinois. — Scarcely a Cryphæa: very probably Dichelyma subulatum, or a closely allied species.

Tribe XXVI. LEUCODÓNTEÆ.

62. LEÙCODON, Schwægr.   (Tab. 18.)

Calyptra dimidiate, large, clasping the pedicel. Operculum conic-rostrate. Capsule broadly oval, its pedicel enclosed by the long sheathing perichæth. Peristome double; the exterior 16 linear-acuminate, whitish, granulated teeth more or less perforated along the medial line; the interior (when present) a simple annular membrane extending ½ the length of the teeth. Inflorescence diœcious. — Species of moderate size, with a filiform and leafless creeping primary stem, and numerous terete nearly simple branches, densely clothed with ovate-acuminate ecostate leaves. (Name composed of λευκός, *white*, and ὀδών, *tooth*, from the color of the outer peristome.)

1. **L. juláceus,** Sulliv. Branches 8″-10″ high; leaves appressed, when dry recurved, horizontal when moist, ecostate, revolute on the margins; areolation minute, oval-rotund; perichætial leaves as long as the pedicel. — Trees, Middle States, in districts not mountainous. (Tab. 18.)

2. **L. bráchypus,** Brid. Very like the preceding; branches more elongated (1½′-2′ long), recurved; leaves longer, when dry second; operculum longer-rostrate; pedicel shorter; perichætial leaves overtopping the capsule. — Alleghany Mountains.

63. LÉPTODON, Mohr. (Tab. 18.)

Calyptra dimidiate, large, hairy. Operculum conic-rostellate. Capsule ovate-oblong, its pedicel concealed by the large perichæth. Peristome double; the exterior 16 linear acuminate whitish teeth, more or less fissile along the medial line; the interior a membrane lining and bordering the teeth. Inflorescence diœcious. — Rather stiff Mosses, with prostrate filiform naked stems, and crowded mostly simple and pinnated branches, densely clothed with oblong-ovate leaves, having a dot-like areolation. (Name composed of λεπτός, narrow, and ὀδών, a tooth.)

1. **L. trichomitrion,** Mohr. Main branches 1½′-2′ long; leaves when moist erect-patent, ecostate, reflexed on the margins; the perichætial leaves long as the pedicel. — In woods; forming elastic masses on the trunks of trees, sometimes on rocks; Northern and Middle States.

2. **L. immérsum,** Sulliv. & Lesqx. (Musc. Bor.-Amer., No. 234.) Somewhat smaller than the preceding; leaves not so crowded, more suddenly acuminate; capsule urceolate-oblong, its mouth larger; articulations of the teeth of the peristome closer; perichætial leaves concealing (besides the pedicel) the larger portion of the capsule. — Trees, Southern States.

3. **L. Ohioénse,** Sulliv. Much like No. 1; but stems more slender and elongated, less regularly pinnate; leaves when moist spreading horizontally, the costa extending to the middle. — Trees, Central Ohio. (Tab. 18.)

64. ANTITRÍCHIA, Brid. (Tab. 18.)

Calyptra cuculliform. Operculum conic. Capsule oval, exannulate, with a flexuose-arcuate pedicel. Peristome double; the exterior 16 lanceolate-subulate teeth; the interior 16 subulate fugacious cilia. Spores large. Inflorescence diœcious. — A large Moss with distantly subpinnate and flexuous ascending or pendulous stems, and crowded broadly ovate-acuminate semi-costate leaves; the perichætial elongated and sheathing. (Name from ἀντί, opposite, and τρίχιον a little hair, the cilia erroneously supposed to be opposite the teeth.)

1. **A. curtipéndula,** Brid. Leaves ciliate-serrate at the apex, recurved on the margins, plicate with 4-5 short costæ at the base, the central one extending beyond the middle; cellules minute, those at the basal angles oval, disposed in oblique lines, elsewhere oblong. — Summit of Black Mountain, North Carolina, Lesquereux. (Tab. 18.) (Eu.)

Tribe XXVII. LÉSKEÆ.

65. ANÓMODON, Hook & Tayl.   (Tab. 19.)

Calyptra cucullate. Operculum conic-rostrate. Capsule cylindrical, erect, long-pedicellate. Peristome double; the exterior 16 subulate-lanceolate teeth; the interior 16 cilia shorter than the teeth, and connected at base by a narrow membrane.   Inflorescence dioecious. — Stems prostrate, stoloniferous, microphyllous: the branches ascending, simple, 2–3 divided or fasciculately ramulose, with elongated, costate, opaque, granulated leaves; their areolation minute and dot-like. (Name, ἄνομος, *irregular*, and ὀδών, *tooth*, from a supposed abnormal construction of the peristome.)

1. **A. viticulòsus,** Hook. & Tayl. Branches 2′–2½′ high, often geniculate; leaves secund, larger as they ascend, linear-lanceolate from an oblong-ovate base, obtuse, of a thick compact structure, minutely papillose on both surfaces; costa pellucid, ceasing near the apex; annulus double, persistent. — Shaded rocks, Niagara Falls; without fruit. (Eu.)

2. **A. apiculàtus,** Br. & Sch. Very near the preceding, rather smaller; leaves linear-oblong from a cordate-ovate base, apiculate; cellules with longer papillæ, those of the basal margins slightly ciliate; costa shorter, often forked. — On old logs, Alleghany Mountains.

3. **A. obtusifòlius,** Br. & Sch. Branches compressed, shorter than in No. 1, less divided; leaves 2-ranked, of a more uniform width throughout, linear-oblong, very obtuse, the costa shorter; capsule elliptical; inner peristome wanting or rudimentary; annulus large. — Trunks of trees, near watercourses, in low grounds. (Tab. 19.)

4. **A. attenuàtus,** Hub. Branches 1′–2′ long, fasciculately ramulose; the ramuli incurved, attenuate; leaves ovate-lanceolate, somewhat obtuse, subsecund; annulus none; peristome well developed, the cilia nearly as long as the teeth, and with 1–2 interposed ciliolæ. — On rocks and roots of trees, near streams; common. (Eu.)

5. **A. longifòlius,** Hartm. Distinguished from the last by its more attenuated branches, straighter and longer acuminate leaves, smaller capsule, shorter pedicel, and much less complete peristome. — Habitat similar: said to be North American by Schimper. (Eu.)

6. **A. ? Toccòæ,** Sulliv. & Lesqx. (Musc. Bor.-Amer.) Branches 1′–2 long, rather stout, simple or sparingly divided, when dry circinate; leaves lanceolate from an oblong base, reflexed on the lower margins, concave below, concave-carinate above, very strongly and irregularly serrate at the point; cellules very minute, quadrate-rotund, protuberant (not papillose), arranged in lines; costa nearly percurrent and flexuous at its upper end. — Toccoa Falls, Georgia, *Lesquereux:* with perichætia only. — In the Herbarium of the late Dr. Taylor are specimens marked "Neckera Nepalensis, *T. T. mss.*, Nepal," apparently the same as those from Toccoa Falls, with imperfect fruit like that of No. 4.

7. **A. ? tristis,** Cesati. Much smaller than any of the foregoing; branches filiform, rigid, sparingly divided; leaves brittle, usually broken, when moist

squarrose, somewhat l.gulate-acuminate from a broad suberect amplexicaul base, crenulate on the margins by the large protuberent cellules; costa indistinct, seldom extending half-way. — Leskea fragilis, *Hook. & Wils. in Drum. Mosses*, 2d *coll. No.* 101. — Hypnum triste, *Mull. Synop. Musc.* 2. *p.* 473.) — Very common throughout the United States; on trees, particularly the Hornbeam. Fruit unknown. (Eu.)

66. LÉSKEA, Hedw.; Bryol. Europ. (Tab. 19.)

Calyptra cuculliform. Operculum conic, acuminate or rostrate. Capsule oval or cylindrical, pedicellate. Peristome double; the exterior 16 lanceolate-subulate teeth; the interior 16 narrow cilia, as long as the teeth, arising from a carinate membrane. Annulus persistent. Inflorescence monœcious or diœcious. Stems prostrate, irregularly or subpinnately branched; leaves of the stem and branches uniform, ovate-lanceolate, more or less acuminate, mostly costate, smooth or papillose, with close subrotund or oval areolation. (Named for *N. G Leske*, an early German botanist.)

1. **L. polycárpa**, Hedw. Monœcious; stem 2' long or more, irregularly branched; branches ascending, ½'-1' high; leaves ovate-lanceolate, patent or secund, recurved on the margins below, strongly costate to near the apex; capsule cylindrical, slightly curved; operculum conic, acute; perichætial leaves striate. — Roots of trees, in wet places. (Eu.)

2 **L. obscúra**, Hedw. Monœcious; smaller than No. 1; ramification the same; leaves ovate or oblong-ovate, rather obtuse, opaque, the margins below recurved; costa reaching to the apex; capsule erect, oblong-elliptical; operculum short, conic; cilia of the inner peristome perforated. — On trees, within reach of floods: fruits copiously. (Tab. 19.)

3. **L. microcárpa**, W. P. Sch. in litt. Monœcious; stems subpinnately branched; leaves ovate or oval, concave, long and slenderly acuminate, spreading, rather lax; costa reaching nearly to the point; capsule oval-oblong. — (L. nervosa, *Musc. Alleghan*, No. 69.) On roots of trees, in wet woods, near Montgomery, Alabama. — Very near the European L. nervosa, but a more flaccid plant, its leaves more spreading, not so recurved on the margins, nor so attenuated at the point; the costa extending higher up; capsule not cylindrical; peristome smaller and lighter-colored, the interior more imperfect; and mainly the inflorescence different.

4. **L. rostráta**, Hedw. Diœcious; branches erect, crowded, fasciculate, terete; leaves closely imbricating, ovate-lanceolate, long and slenderly acuminate, papillose on both surfaces, the margins broadly recurved below; costa pellucid, vanishing below the apex; capsule oval-oblong; operculum rostrate. — Woods, in dense and extensive mats, on the base of trees: frequent. (Eu.)

5. **L.? denticuláta**, Sulliv. Diœcious; branches ascending, crowded, somewhat compressed; leaves closely imbricating, slightly secund, concave, ovate, suddenly and rather long acuminate, denticulate, ecostate; areolation oval; capsule oblong; operculum obliquely rostrate. (Musc. Alleghan., No 62.) — Base of trees; not uncommon in the Western States: fruit very rare, found only in Southern Alleghany specimens. — A small species.

67. CLASMÁTODON, Hook. & Wils.   (Tab. 19.)

Calyptra cuculliform. Operculum conic-rostellate. Capsule oval, erect, pedicellate. Peristome single : teeth 16, short, 1-2-divided into irregular segments, remotely articulated. Annulus large, imperfect, somewhat persistent. Spores large. Inflorescence monœcious. — Very small species, with creeping, entangled, irregularly branched stems, and broadly ovate-acuminate semi-costate leaves, of an oval-elliptical areolation. — (Name from κλάσμα, *a fragment*, and ὀδών, *tooth*, descriptive of the peristome.)

1. **C. párvulus,** (Hampe,) Hook. & Wils. Leaves concave, patent, reflexed on the margins below, acute or obtuse ; areolation of the basal angles quadrate ; mouth of the capsule small ; operculum variable in the length of the rostrum. — (Ptcrigonium marginatum, *Schweinitz* (not *Michaux*). Leskea parvula, *Hampe. L. Sullivantii, Bryol. Europ.?* Anisodon tenuirostris, *Bryol. Europ.* Clasmatodon pusillus, *Hook. & Wils.*) — On the bark of trees, in dry places, or on their roots in localities subject to inundations : very common in the Southern States. — A variable species. (Tab. 19.)

TRIBE XXVIII. THELIÈÆ.

68. THÈLIA, Sulliv.

Calyptra cuculliform, narrow. Operculum conic, rostrate. Capsule ovate-cylindrical, erect, pedicellate. Peristome double ; the exterior 16 long, linear-subulate, white, granulated, distantly articulated teeth ; the interior a carinate membrane extending to ⅓ the length of the teeth, with or without rudimentary cilia. — Growing in compact glaucous- or yellowish-green mats ; stems villous, with a radicular tomentum, creeping, throwing up densely crowded short and terete branches, clothed with deeply concave closely imbricating deltoid-ovate slenderly pointed leaves, composed of pellucid elliptical and conspicuously uni-papillate cellules. (Name from θηλή, *a papilla*, referring to the prominent papillæ of the leaf.)

1. **T. hirtélla,** (Hedw.) Sulliv. — Leaves inclining to a dark yellowish-green, obsoletely semi-costate, ciliate-dentate on the margins, strongly papillose on the back, the papillæ elongated, curved, simple ; perichætial leaves fringed. (Pterigynandrum hirtellum, *Hedw.*) — Roots and trunks of trees in woods ; common.

2. **T. asprélla.** (Schimp.) Sulliv. — Growing with No. 1, formerly confounded with it ; distinguished by the glaucous-green color of its leaves, their papillæ 2-lobed at the apex ; and by the narrower, longer, and nodose teeth of the peristome, and smaller sporules. — (Leskea asprella, *W. P. Sch.*) — Northern and Middle States, and westward.

3. **T. Lescúrii.** Sulliv. (Musc. Bor.-Amer., No. 249.) Near the last species ; ramification more fasciculate, not so condensed ; the branches longer ; leaves glaucous-green, with a bluish tinge, shorter, broader, not so acuminate, the areolation much smaller, not so pellucid, the papillæ 3-lobed at the apex ; pedicel twice as long ; capsule longer, often slightly curved, the mouth with a

broad reddish rim; teeth of the peristome not nodose; inner peristome better developed, the short carinate cilia quite evident; perichætial leaves yellowish. — Dry, sandy and hilly ground, in thin woods, never on trees. — Southern States, *Lesquereux*.

69. MYURÉLLA, Bryol. Europ. (Tab. 19.)

Calyptra cuculliform, narrow. Operculum convex-conic, obtuse, large. Capsule oval or obovate-oval, with a short and tumid erect collum, pedicellate, annulate. Peristome large, constructed as in Hypnum; the ciliolæ, however, very short, often absent. Inflorescence diœcious. — Small, subalpine, glaucous green, densely tufted species; with erect, sparingly divided, julaceous, stoloniferous stems; and closely imbricating, subrotund, ecostate, more or less papillose leaves, composed of pellucid rhombic cellules.

1. **M. Careyàna,** Sulliv. Stems slender, branched by innovations, leaves very concave, with a short filiform point, strongly papillose on the back, and ciliate-dentate on the margins; perichætia orange-red, leaves smooth, narrowly lanceolate, filiformly acuminate, the margins at the upper end of the lamina fringed. — High mountain-tops, New England, *J. Carey:* Pennsylvania, *Lesquereux:* North Carolina (Negro Mountain), *Gray & Sullivant.* — The two other species of this genus, M. julacea and M. apiculata, were collected in British America by *Drummond.* (Tab. 19.)

TRIBE XXIX. FABRONIÈÆ.

70. FABRÒNIA, Raddi. (Tab. 18.)

Calyptra cuculliform. Operculum conic, acuminate. Capsule pyriform, erect, pedicellate; its mouth wide. Peristome single (in No. 4 absent); the exterior 16 linear-lanceolate teeth approximated in pairs, when dry reflexed. Inflorescence monœcious. — Minute species, uniform in habit and size, with prostrate stems, and erect crowded subfasciculate branches; leaves shining, ovato-lanceolate, filiformly acuminate, dentate or ciliate, semi-costate; the areolation lax, pellucid, the cellules at the basal angles quadrate, elsewhere larger and rhomboidal, with conspicuous primordial utricles: reticulation of the capsule-wall quadrate, flexuous. (Named after *Fabroni*, an Italian botanist.)

1. **F. Wrightii,** Sulliv. (Musc. Bor.-Amer., No. 251.) Capsule oblong-pyriform; operculum conic-rostellate; teeth of the peristome light golden-yellow; the vaginula concealed by the gradually acuminated perichætial leaves. — San Marcos, Texas, *Wright.* — Near the European F. octoblepharis; but that species has a mamellate operculum, dark brownish-red peristomial teeth, leaves with more numerous quadrate alar cellules, and an emergent vaginula.

2. **F. Ravenélii,** Sulliv. (Musc. Bor.-Amer., No. 252.) Leaves of a clear deep-green color, closely imbricating, entire on the margins, or occasionally with a few teeth; costa distinct, extending beyond the middle; perichætial leaves numerous, dentate, gradually acuminate; vaginula as in No. 1; teeth of the peristome rather short, dusky yellow; sporules large. — On dry rocks, South Carolina, *Ravenel.* (Tab. 18.)

3. **F. Carolìnìàna,** Sulliv. & Lesqx. (Musc. Bor.-Amer., No. 253.) Capsule, operculum, peristome, and perichætium nearly as in the last species; leaves yellowish-green, dentate on the margin, with a less conspicuous costa; sporules smaller. — On decayed logs, near the Santee Canal, South Carolina, *Ravenel.*

4 **F. gymnóstoma,** Sulliv. & Lesqx. (Musc. Bor.-Amer., No. 254.) Leaves whitish-green, elliptical-lanceolate, dentate-ciliate; costa reaching half-way or obsolete; perichætial leaves few, short, obovate, suddenly subulate-acuminate; capsule broad-oval, shortly apophysated; peristome none. — Santa Fé, New Mexico, *Fendler.*

71. ANACÁMPTODON, Brid.   (Tab. 18.)

Calyptra conic-cuculliform.   Operculum conic-subrostellate.   Capsule oval, erect, pedicellate.   Peristome double; the exterior 16 narrowly lanceolate teeth smooth on both surfaces, approximated in pairs, when dry reflexed (hence the name); the interior 16 slender cilia, without a basilar membrane.   Inflorescence monœcious. — Low, cæspitose, with irregularly branched stems, and spreading ovate-lanceolate semi-costate leaves, of a rather loose and pellucid rhombic areolation.   (Name from ἀνακάμπτω, *to bend back,* and ὀδών, *a tooth.*)

1. **A. splachnoìdes,** Brid.   Cilia of the inner peristome always erect, capsule when dry much constricted below the mouth; foliage deep green. — In the forks and open hollow knots of partly decayed trees: rare, though its range is extensive. (Tab. 18.)   (Eu.)

Tribe XXX. PYLAISÈÈÆ.

72. PYLAÌSÆA, Bryol. Europ.   (Tab. 18.)

Calyptra cuculliform, rostrate.   Operculum conic, more or less rostellate. Capsule oblong, erect, pedicellate.   Annulus narrow, simple.   Peristome double: the exterior 16 linear-lanceolate teeth inserted below the mouth of the capsule; the interior as in Leskea, but with the cilia more or less ruptured along their keel, or a membrane adherent to and bordering the teeth; ciliolæ rudimentary or none.   Inflorescence monœcious: male flower gemmiform, axillary. — Small species, fruiting abundantly, with glossy, concave, elongated, closely linear-areolated and ecostate leaves, their alar cellules numerous, small, quadrate, and opaque.   (Named for *B. de la Pylaie,* a French botanist.)

1. **P. denticulàta,** W. P. Sch.   Grows in closely entangled mats; branches crowded, short, ascending; leaves lanceolate, acuminate, slightly denticulate at the apex; capsule oblong-cylindrical; pedicels 3″-5″ high; operculum with a rostrum about as long as the conic base; inner peristome firm, yellow, much as in Leskea, the cilia or processes often split along the keel, the basilar membrane broad; sporules bright yellow, smooth, about ᵥₒₒ of a line in diameter. — Bark of trees, Columbus, Ohio; very rare.

2. **P. intricàta,** Bryol. Europ.   Size and mode of growth much as in the last; branches short, recurved; leaves ovate-lanceolate, acuminate, nearly

entire, more or less secund; capsule oval or ovate-oblong, its mouth small; pedicels 5″-7″ high; operculum conic, scarcely rostellate; inner peristome a granulated grayish membrane, adherent to and bordering the lower half of each tooth, free above, and split into two linear-lanceolate divergent segments, as in Bartramia; sporules light greenish-yellow, their diameter one half greater than in No. 1.—(Pterigynandrum intricatum, *Hedw.*)—Trees and logs; common. (Tab. 18.)

3. **P. velutina,** W. P. Sch. Exceedingly like and formerly confounded with No. 2; leaves with fewer quadrate alar cells; capsule cylindrical, its mouth larger; operculum decidedly rostellate; teeth of the peristome more closely articulated, narrowly bordered their whole length by the adherent inner peristome; sporules dark yellowish-green, granulated, with a diameter twice as great as in the first species.—Bark of trees, Columbus, Ohio.

(P. POLYÁNTHA, a common European species, and found in British America by Drummond, has the peristome of No. 1, with the capsule and short-conic operculum of No. 2.)

73. HOMALOTHÈCIUM, Bryol. Europ. (partly.) (Tab. 19.)

Calyptra cuculliform, hairy. Operculum conic, subrostellate. Capsule ovate-cylindrical, regular and erect, or oblique and incurved, pedicellate, annulate. Peristome double; the exterior 16 linear-lanceolate teeth, with close articulations conspicuous on the margins; the interior 16 short cilia from a plicate base; or a membrane lining the teeth. Inflorescence monœcious or diœcious.—Stems prostrate, closely and pinnately branched; leaves shining, costate, serrulate, with an oblong-rhomboidal areolation.—(Name from ὁμαλός, *equal,* and θήκη, *a capsule;* applicable to the type of the genus, Leskea sericea, *Hedw.*)

1. **H. subcapillàtum,** Bryol. Europ. Monœcious; leaves elliptical or obovate-elliptical, suddenly acuminated, not striate, serrulate; costa single or forked, extending half-way; pedicel rough; capsule inclined, slightly incurved; teeth of the peristome dark-red, with a broad pellucid central stripe marked by a delicate zigzag medial line; inner peristome a membrane lining the teeth.— (Pterigonium ascendens, *Schwægr. Suppl. t.* 243. Pt. decumbens, *Schwægr. l. c. t.* 110. Pterigynandrum brachycladon, *Brid. Bryol. Univ.* 2. *p.* 185.)—A small species resembling Pylaisæa intricata, and growing with it on trees: common. (Tab. V.)

74. PLATYGÝRIUM, Bryol. Europ. (Tab. 19.)

Calyptra cuculliform, elongated, slightly spiral. Operculum conic, short-rostrate. Capsule oval-oblong, erect, pedicellate. Peristome double; the exterior 16 linear-lanceolate broadly margined teeth; the interior 16 filiform cilia, the basilar membrane obsolete. Annulus very large. Inflorescence diœcious.— Rather small species, with prostrate closely entangled subpinnate stems; and oblong-lanceolate ecostate leaves, with a linear areolation.—(Name composed of πλατύς, *large,* and γυρός, *ring,* referring to the annulus.)

1. **P. rèpens,** Bryol. Europ. Branches short, rather julaceous, ascend-

G. M.   5

ing; pedicels 5' - 6" high; leaves reflexed on the margins. — (Neckera brachy-
clada, *Mull. Synop.* 2. *p.* 88.) — Old fences, logs, &c., forming dense brownish-
yellow patches. Fruits abundantly. (Tab. 19.) (Eu.)

TRIBE XXXI. CYLINDROTHECIÈÆ.

75. CYLINDROTHÈCIUM, Bryol. Europ.   (Tab. 19.)

Calyptra dimidiate, narrow, elongated. Operculum conic-rostellate. Capsule
cylindrical, erect, pedicellate, annulate. Peristome double ; the exterior 16 linear distantly articulated teeth ; the interior 16 narrow carinate cilia, connected at
the base by a very narrow membrane. Columella usually exserted. Inflorescence monœcious. — A very natural genus, with prostrate and usually compressed
stems, and closely imbricating ecostate polished leaves, with a minute linear transparent areolation. (Name from κύλινδρος, *a cylinder*, and θήκη, *a little case*,
referring to the shape of the capsule.)

* Pedicels reddish.

1. **C. cladorrhizans,** Bryol. Europ. Stems 2' - 3' long; sparingly
and subpinnately branched ; leaves oblong-ovate, acute, slightly serrulate at the
apex, concave, indistinctly bicostate at the base ; operculum conic, with a thick
obtuse rostrum. — Woods, on old bogs, in large mats. Conspicuous by the broad
flat branches, and greenish-yellow foliage, dashed with bright brown ; very common. (Tab. 19.) (Eu.)

2. **C. sedúctrix,** Bryol. Europ. Separated from No. 1 by its less compressed, almost cylindrical stems and branches. (Fruits much more abundantly,
and affects humid situations.) — Margins of swamps, on old logs and roots of
trees. — Its numerous dark-red pedicels give it a striking character.

3. **C. compréssum,** Bryol. Europ. Near No. 1, but distinguished by
its smaller size ; more compressed branches ; the leaves loosely imbricating, more
concave, with an obtuse entire apex, and a more lax areolation ; shorter ovate-
oval capsule ; and substriate perichætial leaves. — (Leskea compressa, *Hedw.*) —
Trunks of trees, on river-banks, subject to inundation, Central Ohio : rare.

4. **C. Sullivántii,** (C. Mull.) Bryol. Europ. A more slender species than
any of the preceding ; stems and branches elongated, narrow, and quite flat ;
leaves laxly imbricating, oblong-ovate, short-pointed ; annulus conspicuous ;
operculum with a slender acute rostrum. — (Neckera Sullivantii, *Mull. Synop.* 2.
p. 65, 1850. C. gracilescens, *W. P. Schimper, Bryol. Europ. fasc.* 46, 47, 1851.)
— On stones, near the surface of the ground ; banks of the French Broad River,
North Carolina.

* * Pedicels yellowish.

5. **C. Drummóndii,** W. P. Sch. About the size of No. 1, which it
much resembles ; but its stems and branches are more complanate ; leaves not
so closely imbricating ; teeth of the peristome perforated along the medial line,
more distantly articulated ; sporules half the size ; annulus nearly obsolete. —
(N. cladorrhizans, *Hook. & Wils. in Drum.* 2d *coll. No.* 96   C. Rugelianum,
W. P. Sch.?) — North Carolina, *Ravenel*: Texas, *Wright.*

6. C. brevisètum, Bryol. Europ. Ramification subfasciculate; branches nearly terete, acuminate; leaves crowded, ovate and oblong-ovate, the point extended and subserrulate, the margins slightly reflexed; annulus large; inner peristome abortive, or a membrane lining the teeth. — Dry places, on trees, &c., Western and Southern States; not common. Fruits sparingly.

TRIBE XXXII. NECKÈREÆ.

76. NÉCKERA, Hedw.; Bryol. Europ.   (Tab. 19.)

Calyptra cuculliform. Operculum conic, rostellate. Capsule oval, erect, pedicellate, immersed or exserted. Peristome double; the exterior 16 long linear-acuminate teeth; the interior 16 subulate cilia, more or less developed, the basilar membrane very narrow. Inflorescence monœcious or diœcious. — Rather large species, conspicuous for their flat broad stems, and shining, complanate, ovate-lanceolate, scarcely costate, and mostly transversely undulate leaves, of a thin, smooth texture, and a minute elongated-rhomboidal areolation. (Named for *N. J. Necker.*)

1. **N. pennàta,** Hedw. Monœcious; branchlets obtuse; leaves acuminate; capsule immersed in the long perichætial leaves; cilia of the inner peristome obsolete or rudimentary. — Trunks of trees; common in mountainous districts. (Tab. 19.) (Eu.)

2. **N. complanàta,** Bryol. Europ. Diœcious; branches often attenuated, flagelliform; leaves ovate-oblong, obtuse, apiculate, not undulate; capsule long-pedicelled, exserted; peristome with cilia half as long as the teeth. — (Leskea complanata, *Hedw.*) — On rocks, New England, Alleghany Mountains, and Tennessee. (Eu.)

77. OMÁLIA, (Brid.) Bryol. Europ.   (Tab. 19.)

Calyptra cuculliform. Operculum conic, rostellate. Capsule oblong, erect, or slightly cernuous, pedicellate. Peristome as in Hypnum. Inflorescence monœcious. — Ramification irregular; stems and branches flat, interruptedly leafy; leaves complanate, ovate-oblong, semi-costate, obtuse, apiculate, shining, with a minute rhombic areolation. (Name from ὁμαλός, *flat*, referring to the stems and branches.) (Tab. 19.)

1. **O. trichomanoìdes,** (Brid.) Bryol. Europ. Main branches ascending, arcuate-incurved, irregularly ramulose; leaves often somewhat falciform, lax, pale-green, serrulate above; capsule oval-oblong; ciliolæ of the inner peristome rudimentary or absent. — On rocks, about Lake Superior, but rare, *Drummond.* (Eu.)

2. **O. Jamesiàna,** W. P. Sch. mss. Found by Mr. Thomas P. James on the White Mountains, New Hampshire, and on the Catskill Mountains, New York. — (Hypnum trichomanoides, *James, Enum.*) — We have seen no description of this species, and our specimens are too imperfect (being without fruit) to exhibit the distinctive characters.

3. **O.? Wrightii,** Sulliv. (Musc. Bor.-Amer. No. 269.) Stems pro-

trate, rooting copiously from the under side ; leaves dark-green, somewhat close, serrulate at the apex ; costa extending more than half-way ; capsule cylindrical ; ciliolæ of the inner peristome long ; operculum conic, shortly rostrate. — On the roots of trees, San Antonio, Texas, *Wright:* also Santa Fé, New Mexico, *Fendler.* (Tab. 19.)

Tribe XXXIII. HOOKERIÈÆ.

78. HOOKÈRIA, Smith.   (Tab. 19.)

Calyptra conic-mitriform, shortly lobed at the base.   Operculum conic-rostrate. Capsule oval, horizontal, pedicellate.   Peristome double ; the exterior 16 linear-lanceolate and closely articulated teeth ; the interior 16 carinate lanceolate-subulate cilia, arising from a broad plicate membrane.   Inflorescence monœcious. — Large and handsome species, with an irregular sparse ramification, broad and flat stems and branches, and complanate shining membranaceous leaves, of a very loose areolation, formed by large oval-hexagonal hyaline cellules. — (Named after *Sir Wm. J. Hooker.*) — (Tab. V. contains a figure of the type of the genus, Hookeria lucens, with ecostate and obtuse leaves, which has not been detected on this continent, except in Oregon.)

1. **H. acutifòlia**, Hook.? Grows on the ground, beneath dripping rocks, Southern Ohio, and Alleghany Mountains, in Pennsylvania and North Carolina. — Our specimens, as far as we are able to determine, (being without fruit,) agree well with H. acutifolia, *Hook.*, an East-Indian species, which appears to differ from H. lucens, *Smith*, only in its acute leaves.

Tribe XXXIV. CLIMACIÈÆ

79. CLIMÀCIUM, Web. & Mohr.   (Tab. 19.)

Calyptra dimidiate, somewhat twisted, long, embracing the top of the pedicel. Operculum conic-rostellate.   Capsule oval-oblong or cylindrical, erect, long-pedicelled.   Peristome double ; the exterior 16 linear-lanceolate, closely articulated teeth ; the interior 16 linear-lanceolate, carinate, lacunose cilia, connected at the base by a very narrow membrane.   Columella emergent.   Inflorescence diœcions. — Large and striking Mosses, of a tree-like aspect. — (Name from κλιμάκιον, *a little ladder*, from the appearance of the cilia of the inner peristome.)

1. **C. Americànum**, Brid.   Main stems rhizoma-like, subterraneous ; primary branches erect ($2\frac{1}{2}'-3'$ high), below simple, furnished with small and appressed scale-like leaves, above fasciculately branched ; leaves ovate-lanceolate, auriculate at the base, concave, plicate, costate nearly to the apex, serrate above, with a minute elliptical areolation ; capsule cylindrical. — On the ground, or on very much decayed logs, in moist shady woods. (Tab. 19.) (Eu.)

C. DENDROÌDES, Web. & Mohr., (common in Europe,) with a shorter and oval-oblong capsule, obtuse branchlets, and leaves not dilated at the base, occurs in British America, *Drummond;* and probably on the White Mountains, New Hampshire, *Oakes.*

Tribe XXXV. HYPNEÆ.

80. HÝPNUM, Dill. (Tab. 19.)

Calyptra dimidiate, small, fugacious. Operculum between hemispherical-apiculate and conic-rostrate. Capsule ovate or cylindrical, more or less unequal, usually arcuate-cernuous. Peristome double; the exterior 16 linear-lanceolate articulate teeth, marked on the back by a medial line, and cristate on the inner face by projecting cross-bars; the interior 16 carinate processes or cilia, arising from a plicate membrane, with 1–3 ciliolæ between each pair. Inflorescence monœcious, diœcious, or polygamous.—A genus, as generally received, embracing a very large number of species, which, presenting in habit and structure great diversity, may for the most part be combined into natural groups, many of them seemingly of generic value. (Ύπνος, an ancient Greek name for some sort of Moss.)

§ 1. THUÍDIUM, Bryol. Europ.—*Stems profusely villous, prostrate or ascending, 1–3-pinnate; branchlets mostly short, slender, crowded: stem-leaves broadly ovate, long-acuminate; those of the branchlets much smaller, ovate, and ovate-lanceolate; all papillose; areolation dot-like, granulated, opaque; costa subcontinuous, translucent: capsule oblong-oval, or cylindrical, more or less cernuous: operculum hemispherical-apiculate or conic-rostrate.*

1. **H. tamariscinum**, Hedw. Diœcious; stems prostrate; ramification closely 3-pinnate; stem-leaves with reflexed and crenulate-denticulate margins; branch-leaves ovate-lanceolate; perichætial leaves fringed on the margin; operculum conic-rostrate.—On the ground and old logs.—A large and very common species. (Eu.)

2. **H. delicátulum**, L. Diœcious; very much like the preceding, but its ramification only 2-pinnate; operculum conic, acuminate, not rostrate; perichætial leaves not fringed.—On the ground, in dry places.—Mountains of Pennsylvania: rare. (Eu.)

3. **H. minútulum**, Hedw. Monœcious; smaller than the preceding, with a simply pinnate ramification; capsule horizontal, oval, nearly regular; operculum large, convex-conic, with a long slender beak.—On decayed logs, in woods; not rare. (Eu.)

4. **H. pygmǽum**, Bryol. Europ. (Musc. Bor.-Amer. No. 275.) Much smaller than the last; ramification 2-pinnate; leaves more suddenly acuminated; perichætial leaves elongated, with a more lax reticulation.—Shaded ravines, on limestone rocks, Central Ohio; growing with H. minutissimum.—Among the smallest of the Hypna.

5. **H. scitum**, Beauv. Monœcious; intermediate in size between No. 2 and 3; ramification pinnate; easily recognized by its cylindrical, nearly regular, and erect capsule, with a conical, shortly rostrate operculum.—Hilly districts, on the base of trees, particularly the Beech.

6. **H. grácile**, Br. & Sch. Monœcious; size and ramification as in the last; capsule oblong, incurved-cernuous; operculum convex-conic, apiculate.—

On decayed logs, in deep woods. — Varies in the papilloseness of the leaves and the shape of the operculum. — Var. RAVENELII, which occurs in South Carolina on brick walls, is smaller in size; leaves more papillose; capsule more slender, and with a longer conic, acute operculum, borne on a strikingly cygneus pedicel : perhaps a distinct species.

7. **H. abietinum,** L. Diœcious; stems erect, sparingly and dichotomously divided, simply pinnate; branchlets attenuated; capsule cylindrical, suberect, slightly incurved; operculum conic. — Mts. of New England. (Eu.)

§ 2. ELODIUM, Sulliv. — *Stems villous, ascending,* 1 - 2-*divided, distantly pinnate: branchlets subcompressed: leaves lanceolate, acuminate, not papillose, striate; areolation elongated-rhomboidal: costa continuous: capsule oblong, cernuous: operculum convex-conic.*

8. **H. paludosum,** Sulliv. Diœcious; stems 3' - 4' long; leaves yellowish-green, with a cordate-concave base, the margins recurved, entire. — Swamps, Northern and Middle States.

§ 3. HYLOCOMIUM, Bryol. Europ. — *Stems villous, arcuate-ascending: divisions few, irregularly pinnate; leaves broadly lanceolate, more or less acuminate, squarrose or reflexed, shortly bicostate; areolation linear: capsule short, turgid, horizontal, annulate: operculum short-conic or conic-rostellate: large and robust species.*

9. **H. squarrosum,** L. Diœcious; leaves pale green, shining, long-lanceolate from an ovate concave loosely imbricating base, acuminate, subdenticulate; capsule ovate-globose; operculum convex-conic, apiculate. — Wet, grassy places, woodlands of Pennsylvania. — Seldom fruits. (Eu.)

10. **H. triquetrum,** L. Diœcious; divisions of the stem somewhat fastigiate; the branchlets elongated, deflexed, acute; leaves bright green, shining, from a broadly triangular-lanceolate narrow base, sulcate, sparsely papillulose on the back, dentate at the apex.; capsule oval, gibbous; operculum conic-mammillate. — On the ground, in woods. — The largest of our Hypna. (Eu.)

11. **H. brevirostre,** Ehrh. Diœcious; the branches subfasciculately arranged; stem-leaves broadly cordate, suddenly acuminate, decurrent, sulcate; branch-leaves ovate-lanceolate, not squarrose; capsule ventricose-ovate; operculum conic-rostellate. — Rocks, and base of trees, Alleghany Mountains. — Foliage greenish-yellow : smaller than the last two species. (Eu.)

§ 4. PLEUROZIUM, Sulliv. — *Stems villous, arcuate-prostrate, increasing by annual, lateral, simple or 2 - 3-pinnate prolifications: leaves concave, patent, broadly ovate or oblong-ovate, more or less acuminate, membranous, shining, shortly bicostate, or semicostate; areolation linear-flexuous: capsule roundish-ovate: operculum conic, or conic-acuminate.*

12. **H. splendens,** Hedw. Diœcious; stems 3' - 6' long, composed of 3 - 5 distinct, closely bipinnate, frond-like growths or innovations; stem-leaves broadly ovate-oblong, cirrhose-acuminate, shortly 2-costate, serrulate; operculum rostrate. — On the ground, in woods. (Eu.)

13. **H. umbratum,** Ehrh. Diœcious; stems fasciculately and bipinnately branched; branchlets incurved; leaves cordate, acuminate, plicate, bicos-

tate at the base, serrate; operculum short-conic.—Shaded rocks; Alleghany Mountains. (Eu.)

14. **H. Oakèsii,** Sulliv. (1848, and Mem. Amer. Acad. n. ser. 4, p. 173, t. 5.) Diœcious; stems with elongated, arcuate, subcompressed, distantly ramuloso innovations; branchlets incurved; leaves ovate-oblong, acuminate, plicate, semicostate, the upper half sharply and irregularly dentate; capsule gibbose-ovate, drooping; operculum conical, acute; pedicels long. (H. fimbri atum, *Hartm. Skand. Flora,* 1849. H. Pyrenaicum, *Spruce, in Ann. Nat. Hist.* 1849.)—White Mountains of New Hampshire, *Oakes.*—Intermediate between H. umbratum and H. brevirostre; larger than either. (Eu.)

§ 5. THÁMNIUM, Bryol. Europ.—*Primary stems rhizoma-like; secondary ones arcuate-erect, below leafless, above simple, flat-branched, somewhat dendroid: leaves ovate-lanceolate; areolation minute, elliptical; costa stout, subcontinuous: capsule turgid, suboval, unequal, cernuous: operculum rostrate: pedicels short, aggregated.*

15. **H. Alleghaniénse,** C. Mull. Hermaphrodite; leaves dark green, strongly serrated above, as is the costa on the back.—Rocky margins of mountain rivulets.

§ 6. ISOTHÈCIUM, Bryol. Europ.—*Main stem prostrate, small-leaved; the principal branches ascending, below simple, above with an irregular fasciculate ramification: leaves ovate-lanceolate, acuminate, semicostate; areolation minute, linear, flexuous: capsule oblong, nearly erect, subequal: operculum rostrate.*

16. **H. myosuroídes,** L. Diœcious; branchlets filiform, arcuate; leaves ovate-acuminate, serrulate.—Trunks of trees, and rocks, in hilly districts: rare. (Eu.)

§ 7. EURHÝNCHIUM, Bryol. Europ.—*Stems prostrate, extended, irregularly subpinnately or fasciculately branched: leaves loose or imbricating, ovate or oblong, acuminate, unicostate; areolation oval-rhomboidal or elongated: capsule oval, unequal, cernuous: operculum conic, usually long-rostrate: pedicel smooth or scabrous.*

＊ *Pedicel rough.*

17. **H. hians,** Hedw. Diœcious; grows in thin loose patches; stems prostrate, elongated, distantly pinnated; branchlets short, subcompressed; leaves roundish-ovate, serrulate, spreading, loose; costa suddenly ceasing more than half-way.—On the ground, in woods.

18. **H. Sullivántii,** Spruce. Diœcious; smaller than the last, with a condensed and subfasciculate mode of growth; stems somewhat firm, stoloniferous; branches ascending, subterete; stem-leaves elongated-ovate, those of the branches linear-lanceolate, all long-acuminate, decurrent, denticulate, more or less papillose, costate beyond the middle, margins reflexed below; rostrum of the operculum rather short. (H. graminicolor (*Brid. ?*), *Wils. & Hook. in Drum. S. Mosses, No.* 133.)—Woods, on the banks of rivulets, Ohio and Pennsylvania.

＊ ＊ *Pedicels smooth.*

19. **H. strigòsum,** Hoffm. Pseudo-monoecious; stem creeping, stoloniferous; main branches arcuate-ascending, distichously or subfasciculately ramulose; branchlets attenuated; leaves crowded, spreading, cordate, oblong-ovate,

somewhat obtuse, serrulate; costa ceasing near the apex. — Wooded hill-sides, on the ground. (Eu.)

20. **H. diversifòlium,** Bryol. Europ. Diœcious; very near the preceding, but has a more simple ramification, obtuse turgid branchlets, and leaves more densely imbricating; those of the stem and branches deltoid-ovate, acuminate, sulcate; those of the branchlets ovate-obtuse. — Sandy soil; hilly portions of Southern Ohio, *Lesquereux*. (Eu.)

21. **H. Bóscii,** Schwægr. Diœcious; stems prostrate, with a somewhat fasciculate ramification; branches elongated, turgid, terete, obtuse, flaccid; leaves densely imbricated, ovate from a broad auriculate base, apiculate, very concave, serrate; costa extending more than half-way. — On the ground, mostly in hilly and wooded districts. — A large species, with golden yellow foliage: does not well associate with the four preceding species in a natural arrangement.

§ 8. RHYNCOSTÈGIUM, Bryol. Europ. — *Stems prostrate, irregularly branched, more or less compressed: leaves ovate and ovate-lanceolate, unicostate or shortly bicostate; areolation somewhat loose, elongated-rhomboidal: capsule oval and inclined, or oblong and cernuous: operculum rostrate.*

22. **H. serrulàtum,** Hedw. Monœcious; leaves pale green, membranous, lax, bifariously directed, spreading, ovate-lanceolate, acuminate, serrulate, costate beyond the middle; capsule oblong, cernuous. — On the ground, in dry woods, forming thin strata; occasionally condensed, the branches becoming cylindrical.

23. **H. deplanàtum,** W. P. Sch. Diœcious; stems and obtuse branches very flat, profusely rooting underneath their whole length; leaves bright green, shining, crowded, distichously imbricating, broadly ovate-lanceolate, serrulate, shortly bicostate; capsule gibbose-oblong; annulus narrow. (H. depressum, *James, in Proceed. Amer. Acad.* 1855.) — Dry woods, in close, thin mats, near the ground, on stones and roots of trees. — Fruit rare.

24. **H. ruscifórme,** Weis. Monœcious; branches somewhat arcuate, fasciculate, elongated, very slightly compressed; leaves oblong-ovate, shortly acuminate, sharply serrate, sometimes subsecund, costate nearly to the apex; capsule oval, rather incurved; annulus large. — Mountain rivulets: frequent. — A rather rigid species, with lurid green foliage of a firm texture. (Eu.)

§ 9. RAPHIDOSTÈGIUM, Bryol. Europ. — *Stems prostrate, subcompressed: ramification irregular: leaves subsecund, oblong-lanceolate, ecostate or shortly bicostate; the margins reflexed: areolation minute, linear, flexuous; the 3 - 5 cellules at each of the basal angles large, oblong, inflated: capsule oblong, suberect or cernuous: operculum subulate: small species.*

25. **H. demissum,** Wils. Monœcious; stems filiform, elongated, sparingly branched; leaves yellowish, shining, rather lax, narrowly acuminate, ecostate; capsule narrowly elliptical, horizontal, cernuous. (H. Rngelianum, *Bryol. Europ.*) — Mountainous districts. — Usually grows in thin flakes, on the inclined faces of moist exposed rocks: variable. When much shaded, and on

horizontal surfaces, it assumes an upright and larger growth, and becomes H. Marylandicum and H. Carolinianum, *Mull. Synop.* (Eu.)

26. **H. microcárpum,** C. Mull. Monœcious; growth close and entangled; branches short, recurved; leaves shining, bright green or yellowish, narrowly oblong-lanceolate, concave, obsoletely short-costate; capsule more or less symmetrical, erect or inclined; ciliolæ of the peristome often absent. (Leskea adnuta, *Michx.*) — Trunks of trees, in the Southern States.

27. **H. cylindricárpum,** Mull. Synop. (1851). Diœcious; stems prostrate, subpinnately branched; leaves narrowly lanceolate, with a long-attenuated serrate point, bifariously imbricated, falcate-secund, ecostate; capsule elongated-cylindrical, regular and erect, or slightly unequal and curved; ciliolæ of the inner peristome rudimentary. (Musc. Alleghan. No. 60. Leskea tenuirostris, *W. P. Sch.; Ed.* 1, 1848.) — Grows in close, yellowish, shining mats on logs, in woods, Alleghany Mountains and Central Ohio.

28. **H. recúrvans,** Schwægr. Monœcious; forms palish-green shining mats, fruiting abundantly; leaves bifariously imbricating, ovate-lanceolate from a constricted base, secund-falcate, strongly serrate near the point, with two faint costæ at the base; capsule short-oval, horizontal-incurved. — Decayed logs, Alleghany Mountains. Very common, and variable in size.

29. **H. álbulum,** C. Mull. Monœcious; stems and branches flat; leaves lax, spreading, bifarious, oblong-lanceolate, slightly serrulate and subsecund, with two very short costæ at the base; capsule oblong, cernuous. (H. subsimplex, *Hook. & Wils.; Musc. Alleghan.*) — Moist places, on the ground and on decayed wood. — A small Moss, with delicate pellucid foliage, varying from dark to pale-whitish green: difficult to distinguish from small forms of H. recurvans: the alar cellules less distinct and inflated.

′ 10. LIMNÓBIUM, Bryol. Europ. — *Main stems prostrate, irregularly branched, ascending: leaves varying from orbicular to elongated-lanceolate, shortly unicostate or obsoletely bicostate; cellules oblong or linear: capsule turgid-ovate or oblong, cernuous: operculum hemispherical, apiculate, or short-conic.*

30. **H. eugýrium,** Bryol. Europ. (Musc. Bor.-Amer. No. 303.) Monœcious; main-stems leafless below, rigid; branches irregularly divided; leaves broadly ovate-lanceolate and oblong-lanceolate, shortly acuminate, concave, more or less complicate and contorted, secund, subfalcate, shortly bicostate, the excavated basal angles composed of large pellucid fulvous cellules; capsule oblong, cernuous-incurved; annulus very broad. (H. palustre, *James, in Proceed. Acad. Nat. Sci.* 1855. Limnobium rufescens, *Schimp. ined.*) — White Mountains, New Hampshire, *Oakes, James.* Smoky Mountains, Tennessee, *Rugel.* — H. palustre, L., Bryol. Europ., (common in British America, *Drummond,*) not yet found within our limits, has no annulus; and the basal angles of the leaves are different. (Eu.)

31. **H. mólle,** Dickson. Monœcious; somewhat larger than the preceding; branches thicker and more obtuse, not so divided; leaves flaccid, widely spreading, subsecund, roundish, apiculate, entire or erose-denticulate at the apex; capsule short, turgid. — Mountain rivulets, North Carolina, *Curtis, Lesquereux.* (Eu.)

32. **H. ochràceum,** Turner. (Musc. Bor.-Amer. No. 305.) Diœcious; stems and branches extended; leaves varying from ovate-lanceolate to elongated oblong-lanceolate, more or less contorted, concave, falcate, striated; costa single or forked, extending to the middle; capsule annulate, oval, incurved, with a short erect collum. (H. caulescens, *Sulliv. & Lesqx. ined.*) — Mountains of New England, *Oakes, Eaton, Frost, James.* (Eu.)

33. **H. montànum,** Wils. in James, Enum. l. c. (Musc. Bor.-Amer No. 306.) Not unlike the last in general aspect; but a smaller species, with monœcious inflorescence; differing from H. palustre by its broad annulus; and from H. alpestre by its leaves longer and more suddenly acuminated from a broad-ovate oase, subsquarrose, more or less falcate-secund, with reflexed and distinctly serrate margins, a shorter costa, and a looser reticulation. (H. rivulorum, *Sulliv. & Lesqx. ined.*) — White Mountains, New Hampshire, *Oakes, James.*

§ 11. CALLIÉRGON, Sulliv. — *Stems erect, ascending: the divisions few, simple or subpinnately branched, terete, turgid: leaves more or less closely imbricating, ovate and oblong, obtuse, deeply concave, not striate; membranous, shining; cellules minute, linear; costa variable: capsule oblong, unequal, horizontal: operculum convex-conic: rather large species, mostly found in wet places.*

34. **H. cuspidàtum,** L. Diœcious; stems 5'–7' long; main divisions simply pinnate, and, like the brunchlets, cuspidate; leaves pale yellowish-green, oblong-ovate or oblong, obtusely pointed, shortly bicostate; cellules at the basal angles large, subquadrate and pellucid; capsule gradually tapering into the pedicel, shortly operculate, and broadly annulate. — Grassy marshy places. (Eu.)

35. **H. Schrèberi,** Willd. Diœcious; much like the preceding, but easily known by its bright red stems, visible through the pale green or fulvous foliage, obtuse branches, perichætial leaves not striate, and the absence of an annulus. — On the ground, in moist woods. (Eu.)

36. **H. cordifòlium,** Hedw. Monœcious; stems 6'–8' long; divisions simple or very sparingly branched; leaves large, rather distant, spreading, ovate-oblong, obtuse, costate nearly to the apex, decurrent; basal cellules large, pellucid; capsule gibbous, oblong, exannulate. — Swamps. (Eu.)

37. **H. scorpioìdes,** L. Diœcious; stems robust, 7'–10' long, flexuous-erect or decumbent; the divisions remotely and irregularly ramulose; branchlets more or less falcate at the apex; leaves dark green or purplish-brown, broadly ovate, obtuse, flaccid, ecostate; the margins above usually inflexed. — Bogs and springy places. (Eu.)

38. **H. stramíneum,** Dickson. Diœcious; stems 6'–8' long, very slender, erect, mostly simple; leaves straw-colored, ovate-oblong, obtuse, not crowded, costate beyond the middle; annulus absent. — Sphagnous swamps, New England. (Eu.)

39. **H. trifàrium,** Web. & Mohr. Diœcious; closely resembling the last, but a larger species, very brittle when dry; leaves brownish-green, somewhat 3-ranked, more closely imbricated, not so long, broader and more obtuse, and only semicostate; capsule more turgid, and broadly annulate. — Cranberry marshes, Northern Ohio. (Eu.)

§ 12. HARPÍDIUM, Sulliv. — *Stems rootless, ascending, fastigiately divided ; divisions long, subpinnately branched ; branches more or less hooked-curved ; leaves filiformly attenuated, falcate-secund, subcontinuously costate ; texture membranaceous, firm ; areolation minute, linear : capsule oblong, cylindrical, erect-cernuous : pedicels long : operculum short, convex-conic : mostly marsh-species.*

40. **H. uncinâtum,** Hedw. Monœcious ; stems 2'-4' long, somewhat rigid ; leaves crowded, gradually lanceolate-subulate from a broad base, plicate-striate, serrulate, costate beyond the middle ; capsule cylindrical, erect-cernuous ; annulus broad. — Rocks and decayed logs, in moist places, White Mountains of New Hampshire, *Oakes.* — Forms large, loose, pale yellowish-green turfs. (Eu.)

41. **H. revólvens,** Swartz. Monœcious ; distinguished from the preceding by its softer, dark purple, larger, more linear leaves, when dry rather tortuous, not plicate, with a shorter costa ; and by its somewhat incurved oblong capsule. — Marshes and bogs, Northern Ohio. (Eu.)

42. **H. fluitans,** L. Monœcious ; stems longer than in the last two species ; stem-leaves elongated-lanceolate, remote, flaccid, often not falcate-secund, costate nearly to the point ; capsule turgid-oblong, incurved-horizontal, with a distinct erect collum ; annulus absent. — Swamps and stagnant water. — Color usually dark green. (Eu.)

43. **H. adúncum,** Hedw. Diœcious ; typical form slenderer than in the three species above ; leaves broadly ovate-lanceolate, acuminate, with a short compressed costa reaching nearly to the point, and a somewhat rectangular areolation ; alar cellules large, inflated, pellucid ; capsule turgid, incurved-oblong. — Swamps and bogs. — Var. GRACILÉSCENS, Bryol. Europ. Stems more delicate ; leaves shorter, with a looser areolation. — Limestone springs, Penn., *Lesquereux.* — Var.? GIGÁNTEUM, Bryol. Europ. "Ethans Pond," Willey Mountain, New Hampshire, *James.* St. Paul, Minnesota, *Lesquereux.* (Eu.)

§ 13. CRATONEÙRON, Sulliv. — *Stems prostrate or ascending, villous and densely radiculose : the divisions few, interruptedly pinnate : leaves lanceolate or lanceolate-attenuated from a cordate base, spreading or falcate-secund ; areolation dense, oblong ; costa stout, subcontinuous : capsule cylindrical, cernuous : operculum short-conic. — Mostly in wet places, on calcareous soil.*

44. **H. filicinum,** L. Diœcious ; leaves evenly concave ; annulus simple. — Wet places, on dripping rocks, Ohio. — H. commutatum, *Hedw.*, a closely related species found in British America, is a somewhat larger plant ; having the leaves softer, longer-attenuated, plicate, and more falcate, with a shorter costa, and a large compound annulus. (Eu.)

§ 14. PTÍLIUM, Sulliv. — *Stems erect, large, rigid, rootless, villous, simple or dichotomous, with one or two short innovations, densely cristate-pinnate, frond-like : leaves ovate-lanceolate, attenuated, circinnate-secund, obsoletely bicostate, sulcate, areolation minute, linear : capsule cylindrical, incurved-horizontal : operculum convex-conic : pedicels long.*

45. **H. Crista-Castrénsis,** L. Diœcious ; leaves yellowish or fulvous, shining. — On the ground in mountainous districts ; a striking, showy species, sometimes forming deep spongy beds, many rods in extent. (Eu.)

§ 15. HÝPNUM Proper. — *Stems procumbent or ascending, irregularly divided, with a more or less densely pinnate ramification, sparingly villous: leaves ovate-lanceolate, more or less long-acuminate, usually subsecund or falcate-secund, obsoletely bicostate, membranaceous, shining; cellules linear, compact: capsule annulate, mostly oblong and erect-cernuous: operculum conic, more or less rostellate.*

46. **H. mollúscum,** Hedw. Diœcious; grows in soft mats; stems procumbent or ascending, dichotomously divided; the divisions very closely and pinnately ramulose, much as in No. 45; branchlets incurved at their points; leaves suddenly lanceolate-attenuate from a broad base, falcate-secund, serrate; capsule horizontal, turgid-oval. — On rocks and on the ground, in dense woods; mostly in mountainous regions. (Eu.)

47. **H. cupressifórme,** L. Diœcious; stems creeping, irregularly or subpinnately ramulose; leaves broadly oblong-lanceolate, attenuated, often serrulate at the point, falcate-secund; capsule oblong or cylindrical, erect-cernuous; annulus broad; operculum convex-conic, more or less acutely rostellate. — Hilly districts, on the trunks of trees, rocks, or on the ground, in shaded places. — Very variable. (Eu.)

48. **H. impòneus,** Hedw. Diœcious; stems prostrate, extended, divided, regularly and closely pinnate; leaves broadly ovate-lanceolate, long-acuminate, falcate-secund, sharply serrate at the point, the margins below reflexed; capsule cylindrical, suberect, slightly incurved. — On the ground, and on decayed logs; forming extensive thin mats, in localities not mountainous. — One of our most common species. (Eu.)

49. **H. réptile,** Michx. Monœcious; stems slender, creeping, elongated, subpinnately ramulose; leaves ovate-oblong, moderately acuminated, subsecund, more or less falcate, strongly serrate at the point; capsule cylindrical, erect-cernuous; operculum large, rostellate from a tumid base. — Smaller than the last; occurs only in mountainous districts, where it is very common. (Eu.)

50. **H. curvifòlium,** Hedw. Diœcious; in general aspect like No. 47 and 48, but larger, and not so pinnately ramulose; readily recognized by its large, cernuous, and, when dry, sulcate capsule; and by the conspicuous whitish, plicate, perichætial leaves. — Grows with No. 48.

51. **H. Haldaniàuum,** Grev. Monœcious; stems creeping, irregularly branched; branches subcompressed; leaves ovate-lanceolate and broadly oblong-lanceolate, entire, spreading, more or less secund; capsule elongated, cylindrical, nearly erect, slightly incurved; operculum acutely conic or subrostellate. — Grows in same places as the last. (Eu.)

52. **H. nemoròsum,** Koch. Monœcious; stems creeping, elongated, with several main divisions, which are closely subpinnately and fasciculately ramulose; branchlets subcompressed; leaves ovate-lanceolate, with a long and narrow strongly serrate and subflexuous point, patent, more or less secund; capsule oblong, erect-incurved; operculum short-conic. — Decayed logs, on summits of the Alleghany Mountains. — About the size of No. 48. (Eu.)

53. **H. praténse,** Koch. Diœcious (in European specimens pseudomonœcious, *Bryol. Europ.*); stems ascending, divided, subfastigiately branched;

branches sparingly ramulose; cauline leaves subcomplanate, decurved at the apex (those of the branches secund-falcate), ovate-lanceolate, minutely serrulate above; capsule cernuous, incurved-oblong; operculum convex-conic. — Wet rocks on the ground, forming loose spongy masses, New York : rare. — Resembles No. 50, and large forms of No. 47; but its ramification and mode of growth are quite different. (Eu.)

§ 16. RHYTÍDIUM, Sulliv. — *Stems prostrate; the main divisions robust, rigid, arcuate-ascending, irregularly pinnate, with short subuncinate branchlets: leaves ovate-lanceolate, attenuated, often secund and subfalcate, undulate-rugose, semicostate; areolation compact, linear, flexuous: capsule cylindrical, arcuate-horizontal: operculum conic, shortly rostellate: calyptra large.*

54. **H. rugòsum,** Ehrh. Diœcious; stems erect, 2′-3′ high; foliage yellow or fulvous. — Grows in large elastic cushions, mostly in exposed places, on limestone rocks : not uncommon ; but extremely rare in fruit. (Eu.)

§ 17. BRACHYTHÈCIUM, Bryol. Europ. — *Stems prostrate, rarely suberect, ramification profuse, irregular, occasionally subpinnate: leaves erect-patent, usually ovate or ovate-lanceolate, more or less acuminate, the margins below recurved; areolation rhomboidal, more or less elongated ; costa ceasing half-way, or continuous : capsule ovate or oblong, cernuous or suberect : operculum convex-conic : pedicel smooth or scabrous.*

* *Pedicels smooth.*

55. **H. nìtens,** Schreb. Monœcious; stems tomentose, suberect, 3′-5′ long, interruptedly and subpinnately ramulose ; leaves yellowish-green, shining, elongated-lanceolate, attenuated, strongly sulcate-plicate ; costa light, subcontinuous ; capsule oblong, cernuous ; operculum short, convex-conic, apiculate; annulus large ; pedicels 1′-2′ long. — Sphagnous swamps, Northern and Middle States. (Eu.)

56. **H. salebròsum,** Hoffm. Monœcious ; stems 3′-4′ long, prostrate, irregularly branched ; leaves moderately acuminated from a rounded base, subserrulate, slightly striate ; areolation broader and more lax near the base ; costa slender, vanishing about midway ; capsule gibbose-ovate, turgid, cernuous ; annulus small ; pedicels 6″-10″ long ; perichætial leaves subsquarrose. — On the ground, decayed logs, rocks, &c.; common and variable. — Foliage yellowish-green and shining. (Tab. V.) (Eu.)

57. **H. lætum,** Brid. Very like (and often confounded with) No. 56 ; but more slender, with an erect-cernuous oblong-cylindrical capsule and diœcious inflorescence. — Similar situations.

58. **H. acumināum,** Beauv. Diœcious ; resembles the last species ; but is every way smaller; stems prostrate, closely entangled ; the branches crowded, ascending ; leaves slightly spreading, ovate-lanceolate, serrulate near the point, costate beyond the middle, the margins broadly recurved ; capsule cylindrical, nearly regular, erect, or slightly curved ; annulus none ; ciliolæ of the inner peristome present or absent. (Leskea acuminata, *Hedw.*) — On the ground and decayed logs, in moist, shady places. —Prominent among its many varieties are var. RUPÍNCOLUM : leaves shorter; branches subjulaceous ; capsule

shorter. — On dry rocks. Var. SETÒSUM : branches more elongated and slender, leaves attenuated, of a yellowish silky hue. — Base of trees, in dry places.

** Pedicels rough.*

59. **H. rutàbulum,** L. Monœcious; stems 3' - 5' long, prostrate or arcuate, with an irregular ramification ; branches ascending ; leaves pale green, broadly ovate and ovate-lanceolate, concave, serrulate, thin, shining, substriate only when dry, costate above half-way; capsule oval or oblong-cernuous; annulus large ; perichætial leaves recurved ; vaginula emergent, pilose : a large species. — On the ground, in wet and springy places. (Eu.)

60. **H. plumòsum,** L. (Bryol. Europ.) Monœcious ; stems 3' - 4' long, creeping branches ascending, ramulose ; leaves yellowish-green or reddish-brown, ovate and deltoid-ovate, with a short rather oblique point, serrulate above, semicostate, estriate; capsule gibbous, oval, inclined ; annulus narrow ; only the upper half of the pedicel scabrous. (H. pseudo-plumosum, *Brid., Mull. ;* also H. chrysostomum, *Michx.*) — Alleghany Mountains. (Eu.)

61. **H. populeum,** Hedw. Monœcious ; stems 2' - 3' long, irregularly branched ; branches ascending or arcuate ; leaves gradually and narrowly lance-olate, acuminate, serrulate above ; the costa continuous ; capsules numerous, small, roundish-ovate, suberect ; a small species, with yellowish silky foliage. (H. reflexum, *James in Proceed. Acad. Philad.,* 1855.) — Rocks and trunks of trees, in hilly districts. (Eu.)

62. **H. Féndleri,** Sulliv. (Musc. Bor.-Amer. No. 334.) Polygamous (staminate, pistillate, and hermaphrodite flowers on the same plant); stems 1 - 2' long, creeping ; branches erect, simple or ramulose ; leaves ovate-lanceolate, serrulate, semicostate ; capsule oval-oblong, suberect, rarely unequal and inclined ; ciliolæ of the peristome rudimentary or absent ; operculum conic, with a short obtuse rostrum ; pedicels slightly scabrous below, smooth above : resembles the European H. velutinum, *L.* (Leskea Fendleri, *Sulliv. in Mem. Amer. Acad. n. ser.* 4, *p.* 170, *t.* 1.) — Dry rocks, Santa Fè, New Mexico, *Fendler.*

63. **H. refléxum,** Starke. Monœcious ; stems procumbent, filiform, 2' - 3' long ; branches crowded, slender, arcuate ; leaves rather distant, decurrent, broadly or deltoid-ovate, suddenly and narrowly lanceolate, spreading at their point, serrulate, heavily costate to the apex ; capsule globose-ovate, horizontal. {H. subtenue, *James, l. c.*) — Rocks, and base of trees, White Mountains of New Hampshire, *Oakes, James.* (Eu.)

64. **H. Stárkii,** Web. & Mohr. Monœcious ; resembles the last species, but is much larger, and has a slenderer costa extending about half-way up the leaf. — White Mountains of New Hampshire, *Oakes.* (Eu.)

65. **H. rivulàre,** Bryol. Europ. Distinguished from H. rutabulum by its somewhat larger size, more rigid stems, firmer, wider, shorter, and more suddenly acuminated leaves, with a heavier costa, papillose pedicels (1' - 1½' long), and essentially by its diœcious inflorescence. — Wet rocks, mountains of New England and of Pennsylvania. (Eu.)

66. **H. Novæ-Ángliæ,** Sulliv. & Lesqx. (Musc. Bor.-Amer. No. 338.) Diœcious ; stems 1½' - 2' long, rather stiff ; main divisions arcuate-ascending,

irregularly pinnate and, like the branchlets, subjulaceous; leaves patent-in-curved, widely cordate-ovate, with a short abrupt point, decurrent, very concave, slightly striate, serrulate, the costa vanishing beyond the middle; capsule oblong, oblique, slightly incurved, narrowly annulate; operculum elongated-conic, scarcely rostrate; pedicels 6″ - 7″ long; perichætial leaves filiformly attenuated. — Mountains of New England, *Oakes, Frost, James, Eaton.* — Approaches the last species; but that is twice as large, and has more elongated, spreading, membranous, plicate, distant, and less concave leaves, with a more glossy surface. The growth, ramification, and operculum separate it from H. hians.

§ 18. CAMPÝLIUM, Sulliv. — *Stems prostrate, with an irregular, crowded ramification, or ascending and fastigiately branched: leaves suddenly long-acuminate from a broadly ovate base, subsquarrose, scarcely costate, scarious; areolation minute, linear, flexuous: capsule subcylindrical, erect-cernuous: operculum convex-conic.*

67. **H. stellàtum,** Schreb. Diœcious; stems ascending, fastigiately branched, 3′ - 4′ high, rather stout; leaves deltoid-ovate, long-acuminate, entire, ecostate, the margins reflexed below, the basal angles excavated and furnished with large diaphanous cellules. — Bogs and marshes: grows in compact turfs. — Fruit rare: foliage yellowish, shining. (Eu.)

68. **H. polymórphum,** Bryol. Europ. Diœcious; a more slender species than the preceding; stems procumbent, subpinnately ramulose; leaves cordate-ovate at the base, entire, less squarrose, unicostate half-way; without diaphanous cellules at the basal angles. — Moist and shaded clayey banks. (Eu.)

69. **H. hispidulum,** Brid. Monœcious, much smaller than the last; stems prostrate; leaves not so crowded, nor so long-acuminate, obscurely bicostate at the base; the margins minutely dentate. — Dry places, at the base of trees, or on the ground; rocky hill-sides: forming close bright-green mats.

§ 19. HETEROCLÀDIUM, Bryol. Europ. — *Stems prostrate, divided, radiculose, sparingly villous, irregularly and subpinnately ramulose: leaves of two forms; the cauline larger, ovate-lanceolate, squarrose; the ramuline roundish-ovate, obtuse, suberect; all denticulate and obscurely bicostate at the base, more or less papillose; central areolæ larger, oblong-hexagonal, the marginal subquadrate: capsule oblong, cernuous: operculum conic, obtuse or slightly rostellate.*

70. **H. dimórphum,** Brid. Diœcious; stems 1′ - 2′ long, filiform, rigid, fragile, with minute, opaque, dark green and lustreless leaves. — Dry shaded rocks, Ellis River, White Mountains of New Hampshire, *James.* (Eu.)

§ 20. AMBLYSTÈGIUM, Bryol. Europ. — *Stems creeping, much and irregularly branched: leaves erect-patent, rarely bifariously directed, ovate and ovate-lanceolate, mostly entire; areolation hexagonal-rhomboidal; costa variable: capsule oblong or cylindrical, more or less curved: operculum convex-conic.*

71. **H. súbtile,** Hoffm. Monœcious; branches crowded, erect; leaves distant, ovate-lanceolate, acuminate, ecostate, spreading or slightly secund, with a loose areolation; capsule oblong, suberect or slightly cernuous; operculum large, apiculate; the basal membrane of the internal peristome narrow; ciliola absent. — Trees, New England. — A very minute species. (Eu.)

72. H. minutíssimum, Sulliv. & Lesqx. (Musc. Bor.-Amer. No. 343.)
Monœcious; stems capillary, irregularly branched; leaves ecostate, subentire,
those of the stem narrowly lanceolate from a broadly ovate base, widely spreading; branch-leaves much smaller, linear-lanceolate, subappressed; capsule obovate, inclined, cernuous; operculum large, hemispherical-conic, apiculate; annulus simple, narrow; inner peristome ciliolate; perichætial leaves strongly
and irregularly serrate. (Musc. Alleghan. No. 31.) — Grows with H. pygmæ-
um, in close, thin, deep-green strata, on limestone rocks; in shaded ravines,
Penn. and Ohio. — The smallest of our Hypna. Closely allied to H. confer-
voides, *Schwægr.*, and H. Sprucei, *Bruch:* the first is twice as large, and has a
pinnate ramification, an oblong capsule, and entire perichætial leaves: the second
is diœcious, with ciliate-dentate perichætial leaves; but in all other. respects
(even in the capsule, which is erroneously described as erect and regular) it
approaches very near to this species.

73. H. adnátum, Hedw. Monœcious; leaves closely imbricated, ovate
and ovate-lanceolate, suddenly acuminated, concave, shortly bicostate, the margins nearly entire and reflexed below; capsule oblong, erect-cernuous; perichætial leaves irregularly denticulate. — A small species, growing in thin, close
mats, on stones near the surface of the ground; seldom on trees.

74. H. sérpens, Hedw. Monœcious; stems sparingly divided, closely
ramulose; branches simple, filiform, unequal, flexuous-erect; leaves spreading,
ovate-lanceolate, acuminate, entire or obsoletely serrulate, costate about half-
way; areolation rather large and pellucid; capsule elongated-cylindrical, cernuous-incurved, broadly annulate. — On rocks, decayed logs, and the ground. —
Subject to many varieties. (Eu.)

75. H. radicále, Brid. (Bryol. Europ.) Monœcious; closely related
to the preceding, but larger and more rigid; leaves entire, longer and more
suddenly acuminated from a broader and rounder base, with a stouter costa
extending to the apex; areolation closer. (H. varium *of authors.*) — Same
localities as the last; likewise very variable. — (In *Bryol. Europ.* a new species,
Amblystegium serratum, near this, is indicated, with smaller strongly serrated
leaves and a shorter costa: founded on specimens from Reading, Penn.) (Eu.)

76. H. orthócladon, Beauv. Monœcious; larger than H. radicale,
with longer, thicker, succulent, upright and straight branches (whence its spe-
cific name); leaves flaccid, entire, shorter-acuminate from a broad cordate
base; costa continuous; areolation smaller. — Wet springy places.

77. H. noteróphilum, Sulliv. & Lesqx. (Musc. Bor.-Amer. No. 348.)
Monœcious; divisions of the stem with an irregular pinnate ramification; leaves
of the fertile stems broadly ovate-lanceolate, shortly acuminate, erect-spreading,
with a strong excurrent costa; those of the thick and firm immersed sterile
stems erect, appressed, narrowly linear-lanceolate, gradually tapering from an
ovate base, long-cuspidate by the heavy costa, which occupies nearly ⅓ of the
lamina; capsule elongated-cylindrical, erect-incurved, narrowly annulate. (H.
fluviatile, *James, in Proceed. Acad. Nat. Sci. Phil.* 1855.) — Abounds in limestone springs, Franklin County, Penn., *Prof. Porter.* — A stout, rigid, dark-
green Moss, resembling Amblystegium irriguum, var. fallax, *Bryol. Europ. foss.*

55, 56, *emend.,* but is a larger plant, the leaves narrower and entire, with a much heavier costa. The true Swartzian *H.* fluviatile of *Wils. Bryol. Brit.; Bryol. Europ. fasc.* 62-64, is a soft and flaccid plant, the rumification not pinnate. H. uoterophilum appears not unlike H. filicinum, var. Vallisclausæ, *Bryol. Brit.* (H. Vallisclausæ, *Brid.*), but differs in the inflorescence.

78. **H. ripàrium,** Hedw. Monœcious; stems much elongated, the divisions distantly and subpinnately branched; leaves usually remote, bifariously directed, ovate and oblong-lanceolate, acuminate, entire, costate half-way; thin; areolation minute, linear-rhomboidal; capsule oblong, cernuous. — Common about swamps; also on stones in rivulets. — Quite variable. (En.)

79. **H. polygamum,** Bryol. Europ. Staminate, pistillate, and hermaphrodite flowers in clusters, and on the same stem; stems procumbent or ascending, irregularly and subpinnately branched; leaves entire, spreading, subsquarrose, long and subulately acuminated from a concave, cordate, or ovate-lanceolate base, the point variously directed, costate half-way, or more or less distinctly bicostate at the base, scarious; areolation minute, linear; the cellules at the decurrent angles enlarged, oblong; capsule oblong, cernuous, broadly annulate. — Swamps, British America, *Drummond.* — Very much like H. stellatum, but somewhat smaller, and not so harsh a species.

80. **H. Lescùrii,** Sulliv. (Musc. Bor.-Amer. No. 350) Monœcious; stems prostrate; branches erect, simple or divided; leaves lax, widely spreading, broadly ovate, very shortly acuminated, concave, with a thickened yellowish border composed of several lines of linear flexuous cellules, which elsewhere are rhombic-oval; costa stout, extending to the serrulate point; capsule oblong, cernuous, broadly annulate; operculum acutely conic. — On wet rocks, Tallulah Falls, Georgia, *Lesquereux.* Also Brattleborough, V rmont, *Frost.*

§ 21. PLAGIOTHÈCIUM, Bryol. Europ. — *Stems procumbent or erect, sparingly branched; branches usually subcompressed or complanate, elongated, assurgent, mostly simple: leaves ovate and ovate-lanceolate, more or less unsymmetrical, ecostate or shortly bicostate; areolation elongated-rhomboidal, or linear and flexuous: capsule oblique, cylindrical, moderately curved, sometimes oblong, erect, and equal.*

* *Inflorescence monœcious.*

81. **H. denticulàtum,** L. Stems prostrate, 2'-3' long, stoloniferous; leaves obliquely ovate-acuminate, shortly bicostate, decurrent, the margins narrowly reflexed; areolation narrow and elongated; capsule oblong inclined; operculum conic, acute; annulus large, compound: pedicel red. — In loose tufts, on tussocks, in swamps and crevices of moist rocks: variable. — On the White Mountains, N. Hampshire, occurs what may be a form of this species; but it is smaller, with an upright growth, and an erect regular and narrowly annulate capsule; according well with Plagiothecium lætum, as given in *Bryol. Europ.,* except that its inner peristome is ciliolate, and even in this respect not differing from specimens received from W. P. Schimper under that name. (En.)

82. **H. Muhlenbéckii,** Bryol. Europ. Stems scarcely 1' long, ascending; branches short, arcuate-erect, fasciculate; leaves complanate, ovate-lanceolate, long-acuminate, subsecund, serrulate, shortly bicostate, decurrent; cellules at the basal angles large and inflated, elsewhere much smaller, elongated-

G. M.   6

rhomboidal; capsule suberect or oblique, oblong, tapering at the base, slightly incurved, broadly annulate; operculum convex-conic. — Alleghany Mountains, on rocks and the ground. (Eu.)

83. **H. fúlvum,** Hook. & Wils. Habit, ramification, and size of No. 81, but the color is dark fulvous; leaves longer-acuminated, with a close, elongated, linear, flexuous areolation; the margins erect; capsule strikingly small for the size of the plant, short-oblong, oblique, moderately incurved; operculum short-conic. — Sphagnous marshes; Louisiana, *Drummond, S. Mosses, No.* 110 : Augusta, Georgia, *Gray.* — When immersed in warm water, it imparts to it a beautiful saffron color.

* * Inflorescence diœcious.

84. **H. sylváticum,** L. Resembles very much No. 81, but, besides its different inflorescence, distinguished by its somewhat larger size; leaves more elongated and less acuminated, with a wider and laxer areolation, the margins not reflexed; capsule cylindrical; annulus narrow and simple; pedicels pale; operculum much longer, and distinctly rostrate. — White Mountains of New Hampshire, *Oakes :* rare. — Subject to varieties. (Eu.)

85. **H. Sullivántiæ,** W. P. Sch. Mode of growth upright; branches slightly compressed; leaves closely imbricating, ovate, narrowly acuminate, with a minute flexuous-linear areolation; capsule erect, regular; annulus large; pedicels coral-red; operculum elongated-conic. — On rocks, in dense woods, Central and Southern Ohio.

86. **H. élegans,** Hook. Stems and branches prostrate, flat; leaves plane, ovate-lanceolate, with a slender and distantly serrulate point; areolation as in the last species; capsule oval, more or less pendulous; operculum conic-rostellate. — White Mountains of New Hampshire, *James.* — Foliage retaining its brilliancy when dried. (Eu.)

₊ ADDITIONS TO MUSCI
To page 618.

3. **Seligeria pusilla,** Br. & Sch. In size and general appearance very like S. tristicha and S. recurvata; distinguished from the first by its leaves spreading every way (not 3-ranked), and from the second by its erect (not curved) pedicel. — St. Louis, *Drummond, S. Mosses, No.* 35. (Eu.)

To p. 627.

9. **Barbula agrária,** Hedw. Stems short (1″ – 2″ high); leaves tufted, oblong, shortly acuminate, concave, the margins not reflexed; costa strong, ceasing at the apex; capsule cylindrical, slightly curved, annulate, ribbed when dry; pedicel 4″ – 6″ high. — Apalachicola, Florida, *Drummond, S. Mosses, No.* 64. — The striking feature of this species is the ribbed capsule.

10. **B. murális,** Timm. Monœcious; stems cæspitose, short; leaves oblong, obtuse, subspatulate, the margins narrowly recurved; costa excurrent into a long and smooth pellucid hair-point; capsule erect, oblong, symmetrical; teeth of the peristome much contorted, with a narrow basilar membrane. — New Orleans, *Drummond, S. Mosses, No.* 63. (Eu.)

To p. 628.

3. **Didymodon cylindricus,** Br. & Sch. Diœcious; stems cæspitose, 4″-10″ high, branched; leaves linear-acuminate, spreading, flexuous, more or less undulate on the plane margins, costate to the apex; capsule narrowly cylindrical, annulate, its walls thin; pedicel slender, yellowish; operculum rostrate from a conic base; teeth of the peristome remotely articulated.—Chester County, Pennsylvania, *James.* (Eu.)

To p. 648.

10. **Mnium spinulosum,** Bryol. Europ. Hermaphrodite, cæspitose, stems 1′-1½′ high, radiculose; lower leaves minute, remote, reddish, obovate; upper leaves large, crowded, bright green, decurrent, broadly obovate and oblong-spatulate, shortly acuminate, with a thickened, doubly spinulose-dentate border; capsule oval, rather pendulous; operculum conic, shortly rostrate; pedicels aggregated.—White Mountains of New Hampshire, *James.*—Very near M. spinosum, *Bryol. Europ.,* found in British America by Drummond, but that has a diœcious inflorescence. (Eu.)

To p. 655.

Pilótrichum cymbifólium, n. sp. Diœcious; main stems 2′-3′ long, rhizoma-like, creeping, filiform, sparingly radiculose, with distant minute triangular-lanceolate leaves, scarcely visible to the naked eye; primary branches rather slender, erect, 1′-1½′ long, simple or irregularly and pinnately ramulose; leaves pale green, closely imbricated in 5 distinct spiral rows, lanceolate, acuminate, strongly cymbiform-concave, their upper half with the margins serrulate, recurved or platter-edged, the point flat; costa percurrent; areolation close, linear-fusiform, flexuose; the cellules at the basal angles minute-quadrate, opaque; fertile flowers numerous, paraphysated.—"From a tree on a hummock, E. Florida," *ex herb. Gray.*

Meteòrium? péndulum, n. sp. Diœcious (?); stems 7′-8′ long, divided, divisions with distant branches, all filiform, pendulous and flexile; leaves at the base of the branches broader and 2-ranked, elsewhere narrower and erect-patent every way, all linear-lanceolate, tapering into a long and slender serrulate point, costate beyond the middle, papillose on the back; the areolation close, linear, with a small disk of minute quadrate cellules in each of the basal angles; capsule small, oblong-oval, on a short axillary pedicel (1″-2″ long); peristome double, the exterior 16 linear-lanceolate articulated teeth, more or less fissile along the medial line; the interior 16 perforated cilia, arising from a somewhat broad membrane; operculum conic-rostellate; spores large; perichæth small; vaginula emergent; calyptra not seen.—Western Louisiana, *Teinturier, Prof. Riddell.*—A pale-yellowish Moss, with thread-like stems and branches.

To p. 661.

Myurella Careyana, add:—Capsule oval, with a conspicuous collum, inclined, annulate; cilia of the inner peristome nodulose, operculum hemispherical-conic, pedicels 3″-4″ high.—Brattleborough, Vermont, *Frost.*

Hypnum palustre, L. (see p. 671) has also been found, with the last, by Mr. Frost.

ORDER 140. HEPÂTICÆ. (LIVERWORTS.*)

Moss-like plants, of a loose cellular texture, usually procumbent, and emitting rootlets from beneath; the calyptra not separating from the base, but usually rupturing at the apex; the capsule not opening by a lid, containing spores usually mixed with elaters (which are thin thread-like cells, containing one or two spiral fibres). — Vegetation sometimes *frondose*, i. e. the stem and leaves confluent into an expanded leaf-like mass; sometimes *foliaceous*, when the leaves are distinct from the stem as in true Mosses, entire or cleft, 2-ranked, and often with an imperfect or rudimentary row (*amphigastria*) on the under side of the stem. Reproductive organs of two kinds, viz. *antheridia* and *pistillidia*, much as in Mosses (p. 607), variously situated. The matured pistillidium forms the *capsule*, which is immersed in or sessile upon the frond, or borne on a long cellular pedicel, or attached to the under side of disk-like peduncled receptacles, and dehisces by irregular openings, by revolute segments at its apex, or lengthwise by 2 – 4 valves: a *columella* is rarely present. The *perianth* is a tubular organ (sometimes absent), enclosing the calyptra, which is always present, and directly includes the pistillidium. Surrounding the perianth is the *involucre* (occasionally wanting), also a tubular organ, or leaves of particular forms. The antheridia in the foliaceous species are situated in the axils of perigonial leaves; in the frondose species, scattered within the substance, or sessile upon the surface of the frond, or immersed in sessile or peduncled disk-like receptacles.

Artificial Analysis of the Genera.

I. Vegetation frondose (stem and leaves confluent in a frond).

* Elaters and columella wanting.

1. RICCIA. Capsule valveless, globular immersed in the frond   Involucre none.
2. SPHÆROCARPUS. Capsule valveless, globular, sessile on the frond. Involucre sessile.

* * Elaters none, or imperfect: columella present.

3. ANTHOCEROS. Capsule 2-valved, elongated linear, pedicelled.
4. NOTOTHYLAS. Capsule 2-valved half-way down, sessile on the frond.

* * * Elaters with 1 or 2 spiral fibres: columella none.

← Capsule opening irregularly, nearly sessile. Fertile receptacle peduncled.

5. MARCHANTIA. Fertile receptacle 8–10-rayed.
6. PREISSIA. Fertile receptacle 4 - 6 ribbed.
7. DUMORTIERA. Fertile receptacle convex, hairy.
8. FEGATELLA. Fertile receptacle conical.
9. REBOULIA Fertile receptacle hemispherical, 4-5 lobed; the lobes acute.
10. GRIMALDIA. Fertile receptacle conical-hemispherical, 4–5 lobed; the lobes truncate.
11. FIMBRIARIA Fertile receptacle conical, tuberculate: involucre fringed.
12. PLAGIOCHASMA. Fertile receptacle minute, 2 - 4 lobed, concealed by the ascending involucres.

← ← Capsule opening regularly by 4 valves, pedicelled.

13. METZGERIA. Frond with a midrib, which bears the fruit on its lower surface.

---

* By WILLIAM S. SULLIVANT, Esq.

14. ANEURA Frond without a midrib, bearing the fruit underneath near the margin.
15. STEETZIA. Frond with a midrib, bearing the fruit on its upper side.
16. PELLIA. Frond without a definite midrib. Fruit dorsal.
17. BLASIA. Frond with a midrib, bearing the fruit near its apex.

II. Vegetation foliaceous (leaves and stem distinct).

* Leaves succubous, i e. the apex of each leaf lying under the base of the succeeding leaf.
+ Amphigastria present (except in No. 18).

18. FOSSOMBRONIA. Perianth campanulate; its mouth wide, undulate.
19. GEOCALYX. Perianth none: involucre fleshy, becoming subterranean.
20. CHILOSCYPHUS. Perianth obovate, 2 - 3 lobed. Calyptra chartaceous.
21. PLEURANTHE. Perianth fusiform, concrete with the calyptra.
22. LOPHOCOLEA. Perianth 3-lobed, triangular; the lobes crest-toothed.
23. SPHAGNŒCETIS. Perianth triangular at the apex; its mouth denticulate.
24. JUNGERMANNIA. Perianth tubular; its mouth contracted, denticulate

+ + Amphigastria absent.

25. SCAPANIA. Perianth compressed parallel to the stem. truncate Leaves 2-lobed.
26. PLAGIOCHILA Perianth compressed contrary to the stem. Leaves not 2-lobed.
27. SARCOSCYPHUS. Perianth and involucre united Leaves 2-lobed.
28. GYMNOMITRIUM. Perianth wanting. Leaves 2-lobed.

* * Leaves incubous, i. e. the apex of each leaf lying on the base of the succeeding leaf Amphigastria present (except in No. 32).

+ Leaves complicate - 2-lobed.

29. FRULLANIA. Perianth keeled beneath. Lower lobe of the leaf auriculiform.
30. LEJEUNIA. Perianth terete or angular Lower lobe of the leaf plane.
31. MADOTHECA. Perianth compressed, 2-lipped
32. RADULA. Perianth compressed. Amphigastria absent.
33. PTILIDIUM. Perianth terete. Leaves and amphigastria ciliate.

+ + Leaves not complicate - 2-lobed.

34. SENDTNERA. Perianth 3- or 6-angular; its mouth many-cleft. Leaves 5 - 6-cleft.
35. TRICHOCOLEA Perianth none. Leaves capillary-many-cleft.
36. MASTIGOBRYUM. Perianth triangular Stems flagelliferous.
37. LEPIDOZIA. Perianth 3-plaited; its mouth denticulate.
38. CALYPOGEIA. Perianth none. Involucre fleshy, subterranean.

SUBORDER I. RICCIÀCEÆ.

Terrestrial or aquatic, frondose little annuals, with the fruit immersed in the frond, or sessile upon it. No perianth nor elaters. Capsule sessile, bursting irregularly.

1. RICCIA, Mich.   FLOATING LIVERWORT. (Tab. 20.)

Fruit immersed in the frond. Involucre none. Calyptra coherent with the globose capsule, and crowned with the persistent style. Spores angular. Inflorescence monœcious or diœcious: antheridia imbedded in the frond. (Named after *Ricci*, an Italian botanist.)

* *Frond without air-cavities: terrestrial.*

1. R. glauca, L. Frond somewhat stellate-lobed; its divisions linear-obovate, emarginate-lobed, channelled, dotted, glaucous, membranaceous along the margin. — On moist ground. (En.)

2. **R. Beyrichiàna,** Hampe. Frond oblong-linear, thickened and bifid at the apex, narrowly channelled above, dark purple beneath; the margins
entire, ascending. — Tennessee.

3. **R. bifúrca,** Hoffm. Frond suborbicular, pale-green; its divisions
wedge-shaped, 2-lobed at the apex; lobes spreading, dotted, broadly channelled
above, purplish beneath, the thickened margins ascending. — "North America."
(*G. L. & N. Syn. Hepat. p.* 600.) (Eu.)

  * * *Frond with large air-cavities: terrestrial or aquatic.*

4. **R. nàtans,** L. Frond inversely heart-shaped, channelled above (3″ –
5″ broad), clothed beneath with long pendent rootlets in the form of linear-lan
ceolate, serrate, purple fringes; capsules in two rows, lengthwise of the frond
— Floating on the surface of stagnant water. (Tab. 20.) (Eu.)

5. **R. flùitans,** L. Frond radiately expanding (1′ or more in diameter);
divisions narrowly linear, repeatedly forking, nearly membranaceous; at the
apex thickened, emarginate and cavernous; capsule protuberant from the lower
surface of the frond. — Floating on stagnant water. (Eu.)

6. **R. lutéscens,** Schwein. Frond light-green, orbicular, 1′ – 1½′ in diameter; the divisions 6 – 8, linear, 2 – 3 times forking, channelled above, obcordate at the extremity, thickened, with whitish obliquely-ovate and appressed
scales beneath. — On the ground, margins of ponds, &c. — Fruit unknown. —
(*Sulliv. in Mem. Amer. Acad. n. ser.* 4, *p.* 176, *t.* 4.)

7. **R. crystallìna,** L. Frond orbicular, 4″ – 6″ in diameter; its divisions obcordate or linear-bifid, the margins subcrenate, the surface broken up
by deep pits, communicating with the air-cavities. — Damp ground. — Fruits
abundantly. (R. velutina, *Hook. Ic. Pl. t.* 149, is founded on sterile fronds of
No. 6, and fertile fronds of No. 7.) (Eu.)

2. SPHÆROCÁRPUS, Mich.   Round-headed Liverwort.
(Tab. 20.)

Involucre sessile upon and continuous with the frond, obtusely conical or
pyriform, perforated at the apex, 1-fruited. Capsule globose, closely invested
by the calyptra. Spores round, muriculate. (Antheridia in folliculose bodies
on the surface of separate fronds. *Wilson.*) (Name composed of σφαῖρος, *a
sphere,* and καρπός, *fruit.*)

1. **S. Michélii,** Bellardi. Frond orbicular, 3″ – 6″ in diameter, lobed,
entirely concealed by the numerous aggregated inflated involucres, which are
about ¾″ long, and 4 – 5 times larger than the capsules. (S. terrestris *of authors.*)
— Cultivated fields, South Carolina, *Curtis, Ravenel.* (Tab. 20.) (Eu.)

Suborder II. ANTHOCEROTEÆ.

Terrestrial, frondose annuals, with the fruit protruded from the upper
surface of the frond. Perianth none. Capsule pod-like, mostly 1 – 2-
valved. Columella filiform. Elaters none or imperfect.

3. ANTHÓCEROS, Mich. Horned Liverwort. (Tab. 20.)

Involucre tubular. Calyptra conical, with a subsessile stigma. Capsule narrowly linear, siliquæform, 2-valved, exsertly pedicelled. Spores muriculate. Elaters flexuous, the spiral fibres imperfect or none. Inflorescence monœcious : antheridia dorsal, sessile in a cup-shaped involucre. — Frond orbicular-radiate, lacerate, with immersed gemmæ as in Notothylas. (Name formed of ἄνθος, a blossom, and κέρας, a horn ; from the shape of the involucre.)

1. **A. punctàtus,** L. Frond deep green, 5″-8″ in diameter, margins plicate, crenate, the surface papulose-reticulated ; involucre erect, cylindrical, with a scarious and obliquely truncate mouth. — Wet slopes, sides of ditches, &c. (Eu.)

2. **A. lævis,** L. Larger than the preceding species ; surface of frond smooth ; mouth of the involucre more broadly scarious. — In similar places. (Tab. VI.) (Eu.)

3. **A. laciniàtus,** Schwein. A still larger species ; the frond more laciniated, its surface smooth : distinguished from No. 1 and 2 mainly by the bilobed mouth of its involucre. — Wet gravelly places, Southern States : forming patches a foot or more in diameter.

4. NOTOTHÝLAS, Sulliv. (Tab. 20.)

Involucre a protrusion of a portion of the upper stratum of the frond, opening irregularly at the apex. Calyptra vanishing early. Capsule closely invested by the involucre, oblong-ellipsoidal, subcompressed or ovate-cylindrical, slightly pedicelled, either 2-valved from the apex half-way down, or rupturing irregularly. Columella linear. Elaters wanting. Spores roundish, smooth. Inflorescence monœcious : antheridia immersed in the frond. — Frond orbicular, laciniate, papulose-reticulated, undulate-crisped at the margin, and with dark green oval grains (gemmæ) scattered within its substance. (Mem. Amer. Acad. n. ser. 3, p. 64, t. 4. (Name formed of νῶτος, the back, and θυλάς, a purse or bag ; from the shape of the involucre and its position on the back of the frond.)

1. **N. valvàta,** Sulliv. Frond 3″-8″ wide ; involucre horizontal-elongated, tapering-deflexed ; capsule ovate-cylindrical, horizontal-incurved, 2-valved by a dark-colored suture ; spores light yellowish-brown. (Musc. Alleghan. No. 289.) — Moist ground, Central Ohio. (Tab. 20.)

2. **N. melanóspora,** Sulliv. Capsule often without any suture ; columella with short hooked appendages ; spores dark brown, larger than in the preceding, which in other respects it resembles. — Grows in similar localities. (Musc. Alleghan. No. 290.)

3. **N. orbiculàris,** Schwein., Sulliv. Involucre nearly erect ; capsule oblong-ellipsoidal, subcompressed, the suture evident or obscure : somewhat smaller than the others. — On the ground, North Carolina, Schweinitz : Pennsylvania, Lesquereux.

SUBORDER III. MARCHANTIÀCEÆ.

Frondose and terrestrial perennials, furnished beneath with imbricating colored scales, and numerous tubular radicels tuberculate within; receptacle raised on a peduncle springing from the apex of the frond (also from the back, in No. 12), capitate or radiate, bearing from the under side pendent calyptrate capsules which open variously, but are not regularly 4-valved : elaters with two spiral fibres.

5. MARCHÁNTIA, L. BROOK-LIVERWORT. (Tab. 20.)

Fertile receptacle radiated. Involucres alternate with the rays, 2-valved, lacerate; enclosing 3 – 6 one-fruited 4 – 5-cleft perianths. Calyptra opening at the apex, persistent. Capsule globular, pendulous, exsertly pedicelled, dehiscing at the apex by several revolute segments. Spores smooth. Elaters long, slender, and attenuated at each end. Inflorescence diœcious. Sterile receptacle peduncled, shield-like, lobed or rayed, papillose on the upper surface by the summits of the immersed antheridia. Lentil-shaped gemmæ in cup-like receptacles on the back of the frond. Frond expanded, forking, with a broad diffused midrib. (Named after *Nicholas Marchant*, a French botanist.)

1. **M. polymórpha,** L. Fertile receptacle deeply divided in a star-like manner; the rays 8 – 10, terete. — Shaded and moist places; very common. (Tab. 20.) (En.)

2. **M. disjúncta,** Sulliv. (Mem. Amer. Acad. l. c. p. 63, t. 3.) Fertile receptacle ¼-circular, radiately 7 – 9-lobed; the lobes cuneate, crenulate on the outer margin; sterile receptacle digitately lobed : about the size of No. 1. — Springy places, banks of the Alabama River, near Clairbourne : fruiting in May.

6. PREÍSSIA, Nees. (Tab. 20.)

Fertile receptacle hemispherical, 2 – 4-lobed, with as many rib-like rays alternating with and shorter than the lobes. Involucres attached to the under side of the lobes, 1 – 3-fruited, opening beneath by an irregular line. Perianth obconic-campanulate, angular, unequally 4 – 5-lobed. Calyptra persistent, opening obliquely. Capsule large, pedicelled, dehiscing by 4 – 5 revolute segments. Spores tuberculate. Elaters short. Inflorescence diœcious, rarely monœcious. Antheridia immersed in a peduncled peltate receptacle. Frond sparingly forked, increasing by joints from the apex. (Named for *L. Preiss*, a German botanist.)

1. **P. commutáta,** Nees. Fertile receptacle somewhat angled by the prominent keel-like rays; capsule conspicuous, dark purple. — Shaded, moist places, Niagara Falls (*Carey*), Lake Superior (*Loring*), &c. (Tab. 20.) (En.)

7. DUMORTIÈRA, Nees. HAIRY LIVERWORT. (Tab. 20.)

Fertile receptacle convex, 2 – 8-lobed. Involucre 1-fruited, opposite to and connate with the lower surface of the lobes, horizontal, oblong, opening by a vertical slit at the outer extremity. Perianth none. Calyptra obovate, rupturing at the apex, persistent. Capsule oblong-globose, dehiscing by 4-6 irregular valves; pedicel short. Spores muriculate. Elaters very long, attenuated at each end. Antheridia immersed in short-peduncled disk-like receptacles (Named for *B. C. Dumortier*, a Belgian botanist.)

1. **D. hirsùta,** Nees. Diœcious; frond 4'-6' long, 6''-10'' wide, forking, thin, deep green; fertile receptacle and involucres and margin of the male disk hairy; peduncles chaffy at the apex.—Faces of rocks, Southern States. The largest of our Marchantieæ: fruit rare. (Tab. 20.)

8. FEGATÉLLA, Raddi.   GREAT LIVERWORT. (Tab. 20.)

Fertile receptacle conical-mitriform, membranaceous. Involucres 5-8, tubular, 1-fruited, suspended from the apex of the peduncle, coherent with the interior surface of the receptacle, and with each other, opening at the lower end by a slit. Perianth none. Calyptra persistent, bell-shaped, 2-4 lobed at the apex. Capsule oblong-pyriform, dehiscing by 5-8 revolute segments, deciduous with its short pedicel. Spores muriculate. Elaters short and thick. Inflorescence dioecious. Antheridia immersed in sessile oval disks, near the apex of the frond. Frond forking, conspicuously reticulated, with a narrow distinct midrib. (A personal name.)

1. **F. cónica,** Corda. Fronds 3'-6' long, 5''-9'' wide.—Springy places. Among the largest of our Hepaticæ: seldom seen in fruit. (Tab. 20.) (Eu.)

9. REBOÙLIA, Raddi.   (Tab. 20.)

Fertile receptacle conic-hemispherical or flattened, 4-5-lobed. Involucres 4-5, 1-fruited, opposite to and coherent with the lobes on the under side, 2-valved. Perianth none. Calyptra minute, lacerate, persistent at the base of the capsule. Capsule globose nearly sessile, rupturing irregularly at the apex. Spores muricate. Elaters moderately long. Inflorescence monœcious. Antheridia immersed in sessile crescent-shaped disks. Frond rigid; the midrib broad, strong, and distinct. (Named for *E. Reboul*, an Italian botanist.)

1. **R. hemisphǽrica,** Raddi. Frond forking, and increasing by joints from the extremities, green above, purple beneath; the peduncle bearded at its base and apex; fertile receptacle papillose on the summit.—Hilly districts, in shady moist places. (Tab. 20.) (Eu.)

2. **R. microcéphala,** Taylor. Distinguished from the preceding (of which it may be a form) by the more delicate texture of the frond, and by the smaller size of all its parts, except the peduncle, which is very long (3'-4'), with broader paleæ at its base and apex.—Pennsylvania, *Lesquereux*.

10. GRIMÁLDIA, Raddi.   (Tab. 21.)

Fertile receptacle hemispherical or conoidal, 3-4-lobed. Involucres 3-4, each a distention of an entire lobe of the receptacle, and opening by a cleft below, 1-fruited. Perianth none. Capsule globose, filling the involucre, dehiscing by a circumcissile line near the middle. Calyptra persistent at the base of the capsule. Spores rugose, with a transparent border. Monœcious or dio-cious. Antheridia immersed in imbedded disks at the apex of the firm and rigid keeled frond. (Named for *D. Grimaldi*, an Italian botanist.)

1. **G. barbifrons,** Bischoff. Stems linear-wedge-shaped, 3″- 6″ long, subdichotomous, 2-lobed at the apex, channelled and pale green above, with whitish pores visible to the naked eye, purple beneath; peduncle profusely paleaceous at its base and apex; monœcious; staminate disks obcordate. — Iowa, *Dr. Hor.* (Tab. 21.)   (Eu.)

2. **G. séssilis,** n. sp. Agrees with the preceding, except that it is one third smaller; the pores of the frond not visible; the fertile receptacle (the capsule being fully mature) sessile, and entirely concealed by a dense mass of purplish paleæ; antheridia not seen. — Texas, *C. Wright.*

11. FIMBRIÀRIA, Nees.   SMALL LIVERWORT. (Tab. 20.)

Fertile receptacle hemispherical, concave beneath, expanded at the margin into 4 large and pendent bell-shaped 1-fruited involucres. Perianth oblong-oval, projecting half its length beyond the rim of the involucre; the projecting portion splitting lengthwise into 8 - 12 usually free, fringe-like segments. Calyptra with a long style, fugacious. Capsule sessile, globose, dehiscing by an irregular circumcissile line near the middle. Spores muricate. Elaters rather short. Inflorescence monœcious. Antheridia immersed in the substance of the frond, not collected into disks. Frond much thickened in the middle, with a keel-like midrib. (Name from *fimbria*, a fringe, alluding to the perianth.)

1. **F. tenélla,** Nees. Frond elongated-wedge-shaped, nearly simple, notched at the end (6″- 10″ long, 2″-4″ wide), green above, purple on the margins and underneath. (F. mollis, *Tayl.*) — Alleghany Mountains, in shady places. (Tab. 20.)

2. **F. élegans,** Spreng. Much smaller than No. 1: remarkable for the very prominent papillæ of the fertile receptacle; the lobes of the perianth cohering at the apex into a short tube. — Texas, *C. Wright.* (Eu.)

12. PLAGIOCHÁSMA, Lehm. & Lindenb.   (Tab. 20.)

Fertile receptacle arising from the back of the frond, deeply 2 - 4-lobed; lobes ascending. Involucres very large, subcompressed-ovoid, erect, 1-fruited, opposite to and concealing the minute lobes, 2-valved, dehiscing by a vertical slit. Perianth none. Calyptra fugacious. Capsule globose, subsessile, horizontal, rupturing at the apex by an irregular line. Spores enveloped in a transparent rugose membrane. Elaters of medium length. Antheridia immersed in sessile disks at the end or in the middle of the frond. Frond rigid, thick. (Name composed of πλάγιος, *placed sideways*, and χάσμα, *a chasm*, referring to the lateral dehiscence of the involucre.)

1. **P. Wrightii,** n. sp. Frond 5″-10″ long, 1½″-2″ broad, continuous at the apex, glaucous above, with dark purple scales beneath, the margins crenulate, ascending, convolute; involucres usually three; peduncle scarcely one line high, paleaceous at the apex and base. — Under overhanging rocks, along streams; Texas, *C. Wright.* (Tab. 20.)

SUBORDER IV. **JUNGERMANNIÀCEÆ.** SCALE-MOSSES.

Either frondose or foliaceous: leaves when distinct 2-ranked, and often with a third row of smaller ones (amphigastria) on the under side of the stem. Capsule on a cellular pedicel, dehiscent lengthwise into 4 valves.

    I. Vegetation frondose (stem and leaves confluent in a frond).

13. METZGÈRIA, Raddi. (Tab. 21.)

Fertile fructification arising from the lower surface of the midrib of the frond. Involucre 1-leaved, scale-like, at length ventricose and 2-lobed. Perianth none. Calyptra ascending, oblong-obovate, rather fleshy. Capsule ovate. Elaters with one spiral fibre, adherent to the tip of the valves. Inflorescence diœcious: antheridia 1 - 3, enclosed by a 1-leaved involucre on the under side of the midrib. Ovate gemmæ aggregated on the attenuated tips of the linear frond: midrib distinct. (Named for *J. Metzger*, a German botanist.)

    1. **M. furcàta,** Nees. Fronds linear, thin and membranaceous, forking or proliferous, with white pellucid hairs on the margins, and beneath on the midrib; calyptra hispid. — Hilly districts, on rocks and the bark of trees. (Tab. 21.) (Eu.)

    2. **M. pubéscens,** Raddi. Larger than the last, pubescent on both surfaces. — Mountainous localities. (Eu.)

14. ANEÙRA, Dumortier. (Tab. 21.)

Fructification arising from the under side near the margin of the frond. Involucre cup-shaped, very short and lacerate, or none. Perianth none. Calyptra ascending, nearly cylindrical, fleshy. Capsule oval or oblong. Elaters adherent to the apex of the valves, containing a single broad spiral fibre. Inflorescence diœcious. Antheridia immersed in the upper surface of receptacles proceeding from the margin of the frond; which is fleshy and destitute of a midrib (whence the name, from *a* privative, and *νεῦρον, a nerve*).

    1. **A. sÉssilis,** Sprengel? Fronds irregularly lobed (1' - 2' long, 3" - 5" wide); involucre none; calyptra papillose at the apex; pedicel 9" - 12" long, sometimes folded upon itself and remaining within the calyptra, thus making the capsule appear sessile; sterile receptacles elongated, and tapering deflexed processes. (Mem. Amer. Acad. n. ser. 3, p. 62, t. 5.) — Rotten logs, margins of swamps, Ohio; rare as high as lat. 40; very common in the Southern States. — This may not be Sprengel's plant, the leaves of which are described as having large oblong areolæ, and the calyptra as being smooth. (Tab. 21.)

    2. **A. pinguis,** Dumort. Much like the last; frond more linear and simple; involucre short and lacerate; sterile receptacles 2-lobed, lobes obtuse. — Among Sphagnum, in the Southern States (*Schweinitz*); and in Ohio. Fruit not seen. (Eu.)

    3. **A. palmàta,** Nees. Fronds usually crowded (2" - 3" high), ascending, palmately divided, the divisions linear and obtuse; sometimes prostrate and creeping extensively; calyptra tuberculate. — Rotten logs, &c.; common. (Eu.)

4. **A. multifida,** Dumort. Fronds prostrate, 2-pinnately divided; the divisions linear, narrow; whole plant brownish-green.—Alleghany Mountains, on moist, rocky banks. (Eu.)

15. STEÉTZIA, Lehm.   (Tab. 20.)

Involucre at first terminal, arising from the midrib of the frond, at length by the growth of the frond dorsal, cup-shaped, short, lacerate. Perianth elongated-tubular; the mouth denticulate. Calyptra equalling the perianth, irregularly torn at the apex. Capsule oval. Elaters filiform, free, with two fibres. Inflorescence diœcious. Antheridia dorsal on the midrib, covered by minute fimbriated perigonial leaves. Frond with a distinct midrib. (Named for *Dr. J. Steetz*, a German botanist.)

1. **S. Lyéllii,** Lehm. Frond simple or 2-cleft, delicate in texture, oblong-linear, the margin slightly waved, entire or obscurely serrate ($1'-4'$ long, $3''-5''$ wide).—On the ground, in wet or springy places. (Tab. 20.) (Eu.)

16. PÉLLIA, Raddi.   (Tab. 21.)

Fructification proceeding from the back of the frond near the apex. Involucre cup-shaped, short; the margin lacerate. Perianth none. Calyptra oval, membranaceous, longer or shorter than the involucre. Capsule globose. Elaters long, free, with two fibres. Inflorescence monœcious. Antheridia globose, immersed in the upper surface of the broad indeterminate midrib of the frond. (A personal name.)

1. **P. epiphylla,** Nees. Frond rather membranaceous, sparingly divided; its divisions oblong, somewhat wedge-shaped, repand-lobed; calyptra exserted.—Moist, shady places, on the ground, forming patches $2°-3°$ broad. (Tab. 21.) (Eu.)

17. BLÀSIA, Mich.   (Tab. 21.)

Fructification in an oval cavity in the midrib of the frond. Involucre none. Perianth a fusiform utricle, vanishing early. Calyptra obovate. Capsule oval-globose, bursting through the frond near its apex. Antheridia immersed in the frond and covered by dentate scales. Gemmæ globose, issuing by a slender ascending tube from their large flask-like receptacles, which are immersed in the frond.—(A personal name.)

1. **B. pusilla,** L. Frond $7''-12''$ long, $2''-3''$ wide, linear-obovate, simple or forked, or stellately expanded, the margins pinnatifidly sinuous.—On the ground, sides of ditches, &c., New York. (Tab. 21.) (Eu.)

II. Vegetation foliaceous (i. e. leaves and stem distinct).

● Leaves succubous; the apex of each leaf lying under the base of the next.

18. FOSSOMBRÒNIA, Raddi.   (Tab. 21.)

Perianth terminal, or by innovation dorsal on the main stem, subcampanulate; the mouth large, crenate-lobed. Involucral leaves 5–6, minute, subulate, coherent with the perianth. Calyptra pear-shaped, rupturing early. Capsule globose, irregularly 4-valved. Elaters short, containing two or three spiral fibres. Antheridia naked, borne on the back of the stem, which is prostrate, and either simple or forked, with somewhat quadrate 3 - 5-lobed undulate flaccid leaves. (A personal name.)

1. **F. pusilla,** Nees. Stem 6″ - 10″ long, thick; perianths conspicuous. — Moist places on the ground: mostly Southern. (Tab. 21.) (Eu.)

19. GEOCÀLYX, Nees. (Tab. 21.)

Perianth none. Involucre oblong, saccate, truncate, fleshy, attached by one side of its mouth to the stem, pendent. Calyptra membranaceous, partly connate with the involucre. Capsule oblong. Elaters with two spiral fibres. Antheridia on spike-like lateral branches, in the axils of small perigonial leaves. (Name formed of γέα, the earth, and κάλυξ, flower-cup; from the fructification becoming subterranean.)

1. **G. gravèolens,** Nees. Leaves ovate-quadrate, 2-toothed (light-green); amphigastria oval-lanceolate, 2-cleft to the middle; perianth subterranean. — On the ground, rotten logs, &c. (Tab. 21.) (Eu.)

20. CHILOSCÝPHUS, Corda. (Tab. 21.)

Fructification terminal upon a short lateral branch. Involucral leaves 2 - 6, different from and smaller than the stem-leaves. Perianth usually short, deeply 2 - 3-cleft. Calyptra globose, or somewhat club-shaped, slightly chartaceous, often longer than the perianth, rupturing irregularly at the apex. Capsule oval. Elaters with two spiral fibres. Perigonial leaves like the cauline, concealing antheridia in their saccate dorsal bases. Stem-leaves decurrent on the back of the stem; rootlets proceeding only from the base of the deeply 2-cleft amphigastria. (Name formed of χιλός, herbage, and σκύφος, cup; in allusion to the herbaceous calyptra.)

1. **C. polyánthos,** Corda. Stems procumbent; leaves ovate-quadrate; involucral leaves 2, slightly 2-toothed; perianth 3-lobed, the lobes short and nearly entire. — Rocks, &c. (Eu.)

2. **C. ascéndens,** Hook. & Wils. Stems prostrate; leaves ascending, roundish-oblong, slightly emarginate; involucral leaves 2, two-cleft; perianth 2 - 3-lobed; the lobes long and irregularly lacerate-toothed. (C. lubiatus, Taylor.) — On rotten logs, &c. — A large species, with pale-green foliage. (Tab. 21.)

3. **C. Drummóndii,** Tayl. (in Lond. Jour. Bot. 1846.) Densely cæspitose; stems branching, prostrate (the gemmiferous ones ascending, attenuated); leaves erect-patent, oblong, 2-cleft; amphigastria ovate, acute, connate with the adjacent pair of leaves; perianth oblong, inflated, bifid and subcompressed at the mouth, gibbous at the ventral base, terminal on short naked branches; involucral leaves 3 - 4, laciniate, scale-like: a small species. — "Bark of trees, North America, Drummond."

21. PLEURÁNTHE, Tayl.   (Tab. 21.).)

Fructification lateral. Involucral leaves 3, minute, scale-like, 2–3-cleft. Perianth elongated-fusiform, arising from the lower side of the stem, fleshy, solid and rooting at the base, membranaceous above; the mouth compressed or triquetrous, 2–3-cleft, lacerate. Calyptra concrete with the perianth, except at its apex. Capsule oval. Elaters with 2 spiral fibres. Antheridia unknown. Leaves 2-lobed or emarginate. Amphigastria lanceolate, entire. (Name from πλευρά, *the side*, and ἄνθός, *a flower;* the perianth being lateral.)

1. **P. oliváeea,** Tayl. Grows in close olive-green mats; stems creeping, 2″–3″ long, mostly simple, rooting profusely; leaves rotund-oblong, upwardly secund; pedicel 4″–5″ high: a small species, the perianth disproportionately large.— North America, *Drummond.* (Tab. 21.)

22. LOPHOCÓLEA, Nees.   (Tab. 21.)

Fructification terminal on the main stem or primary branches. Involucral leaves 2–4, large. Perianth tubular below, acutely 3-angular above, 3-lobed; the lobes tooth-crested. Calyptra short, membranaceous, circumcissile at the base, or rupturing irregularly at the apex. Capsule oblong. Elaters with two spiral fibres. Antheridia in the saccate bases of perigonial leaves. Stem-leaves decurrent on the dorsal side of the stem, flaccid, 2–several-cleft at the apex. Amphigastria 2–4-divided; the divisions more or less incised. (Name composed of λόφος, *a crest*, and κολεός, *a sheath;* from the crested calyptra.)

1. **L. bidentáta,** Nees. Stems (1′–2′ long) prostrate, sparsely branched; leaves pale green, ovate-triangular, spreading, 2-toothed at the apex; the teeth oblique, acute, with a crescent-like sinus; amphigastria minute, about 4-cleft, the segments entire. — Moist places, among Mosses. (Eu.)

2. **L. heterophýlla,** Nees. Stems much branched, ascending; leaves ovate, subquadrate, semi-vertical, entire, retuse, and bidentate on the same stem; amphigastria large, 2-cleft, the segments slightly dentate. — On decayed logs, and among Mosses. (Tab. 21.)   (Eu.)

23. SPHAGNŒCETIS, Nees. PEAT SCALE-MOSS. (Tab. 22.)

Fructification terminal, upon a short proper branch arising from the ventral side of the stem. Involucral leaves small, few, incised. Perianth ascending, terete, 3-angled at the apex; the mouth denticulate. Calyptra membranaceous. Capsule oblong. Elaters with two spiral fibres. Inflorescence monœcious: antheridia in the axil of the minute perigonial leaves of pendent proper branches. Stem leaves orbicular. Gemmæ collected in heads upon the attenuated tips of the branches. Amphigastria none, except upon the gemmiferous branches. Stems furnished with runner-like rootlets. (Name composed of Σφάγνος, *Peat-Moss,* and κοιτίς, *a little bed;* from its place of growth.)

1. **S. commúnis,** Nees. Stems creeping; leaves elliptical-orbicular entire, ascending. (Jungermannia Sphagni *of authors.*) — Upon moss and decayed wood. (Tab. 22.)   (Eu.)

24. JUNGERMÁNNIA, L. SCALE-MOSS. (Tab. 22.)

Fructification terminal on the main stem, or on a short branch. Involucral leaves free, like or unlike the stem-leaves. Perianth tubular, more or less angled; the mouth laciniate. Calyptra included, rarely projecting. Capsule globose or oval. Elaters with two spiral fibres. Antheridia in the base of inflated perigonial leaves. Stem-leaves entire, or 2 - many-lobed. (Dedicated to *Jungermann*, a German botanist of the 17th century.)

* *Leaves and amphigastria alike,* 2 - 4-*parted.*

1. **J. trichophÿlla,** L. Stems flaccid, branched; leaves and amphigastria 3 - 4-parted; the divisions straight, spreading, bristle-form, each composed of a single row of tubular cells; fruit-bearing branch lengthened; perianth nearly cylindrical, contracted and toothed at the mouth. — Decayed wood, &c. — A minute, pale-colored species. (Eu.)

2. **J. setàcea,** Weber. Leaves and amphigastria 2 - 3-cleft; the divisions incurved, each composed of two rows of cells; fruit-bearing branch short; mouth of perianth ciliate. — On the ground, &c. — Smaller than No. 1, brownish-colored. (Eu.)

* * *Leaves 2-cleft or (from No.* 7 - 11) 2 - 6-*cleft: amphigastria none, except in No.* 7 *and* 8.

3. **J. connìvens,** Dickson. Stems creeping, flexuous; leaves nearly orbicular, with a broad decurrent base, distant, a little wider than the stem, 2-cleft to ¼ or ⅓ of their length, the sinus obtuse; segments acute, connivent; areolation large; involucral leaves 3 - 5-cleft; perianth slender, the mouth lacerate-ciliate. — On rotten wood. (Tab. 21.) (Eu.)

4. **J. curvifòlia,** Dickson. Fruit-bearing branch short; stems creeping; leaves imbricated, ascending, nearly orbicular, inflated at the ventral base, lunately 2-cleft; the segments long-linear, inflexed; involucral leaves erect, 2 - 3-cleft, serrate; perianth narrow, plaited-triangular, the mouth denticulate. — Rotten logs, &c. (Eu.)

5. **J. bicuspidàta,** L. Fruit-bearing branch short; stems loose, procumbent; leaves distant or crowded, half vertical, ovate, a little wider than the stem, 2-cleft to the middle, the sinus obtuse; segments acute; involucral leaves spreading at the apex, 2 - 5-cleft, repand-serrulate; perianth elongated, the mouth denticulate. — A small and common species. (Eu.)

6. **J. divaricàta,** Engl. Bot. Fruit-bearing branch elongated; stems prostrate, rigid, thick; leaves distant, spreading, rather fleshy, equalling the stem in diameter, oblong, the sinus and segments acute; involucral leaves numerous, imbricated, 2 - 3-cleft, serrulate; perianth oval, plaited above; the mouth membranaceous, denticulate. (*J. byssacea of authors.*) — Among Mosses and on decayed woods. — A minute, dark green species. (Eu.)

7. **J. setifórmis,** Ehrhart. Stems erect or ascending, and, with the leaves, terete-sulcate; leaves toothed at the base, 3 - 4-cleft; the lobes channelled, ovate-oblong, acute; amphigastria ciliate-toothed at the base, deeply 2-cleft, with lanceolate segments; perianth oval, plaited. — Alpine regions of the White Mountains, *Oakes.* (Eu.)

8 **J. barbàta,** Schreber. Stems procumbent, sparingly branched; leaves roundish-quadrate, 3 – 5-lobed, the sinuses obtuse and undulate; lobes obtuse, acute, or mucronulate, variously directed; amphigastria (when present) broad, entire or 2-toothed; perianth angularly plaited to near the apex, the mouth denticulate. — Hilly districts, on the ground, rocks, &c.: variable. (Eu.)

9. **J. Michaûxii,** Weber. Stems ascending, flexuous by repeated innovations from below the summit; leaves crowded, erect-spreading, rather saccate at base and quadrate, 2-cleft, the sinus narrow; the lobes acute, incurved; exterior involucral leaves large, serrulate, the inner smaller; perianth oval, rather club-shaped, the obtuse apex plaited, the mouth fringed. — Alleghany Moun tains. (Eu.)

10. **J. incìsa,** Schrader. Stems prostrate, thick, rather flat, rooting copiously; leaves densely crowded, somewhat quadrate, waved, 2 – 6-cleft, the segments unequal; perianth oval or obovate, the mouth plaited, denticulate. — Damp, shaded places, on the ground. — A small, pale green species. (Eu.)

11. **J. intermèdia,** Lindenberg. Stems prostrate, almost simple; leaves roundish-quadrate, 2-cleft; the upper ones crowded into heads, and 3 – 4-cleft; involucral leaves 3 – 4-cleft, slightly serrate, connate at the base; perianth short, ovate-triangular, the mouth plaited, denticulate. — On the ground. — A small species. (Eu.)

     * * * *Leaves nearly orbicular, undivided; amphigastria different or obsolete.*

12. **J. scutàta,** Weber. Stems procumbent; leaves half vertical, emarginate-2-toothed; the teeth straight and acute; involucral leaves 2 – 3-toothed; amphigastria large, ovate-triangular, 1 – 2-toothed on the margin near the base; perianth obovate, the mouth plaited, denticulate. — Old logs, &c. — A minute species. (Eu.)

13. **J. Schradèri,** Martius. Stems creeping, flexuous; leaves elliptical-orbicular, ascending; outer involucral leaves large, elongated, entire or emarginate, spreading at the apex; the inner smaller, more or less laciniated; amphigastria obsolete; perianth oval-obovate; the mouth plaited-lobed, its lobes ciliate. (J. orbicularis, *Michx.?*) — Decayed logs, &c.; common. — Foliage often dark purple. (Eu.)

14. **J. Tàylori,** Hook. Stems erect, nearly simple; leaves orbicular, with large areolæ; amphigastria broadly subulate; perianth oval, compressed at the mouth, truncate and 2-lobed. — Bogs; mountains of New England. — A large species, with purple foliage. (Eu.)

15. **J. crenulàta,** Smith. Stems prostrate, branched; leaves orbicular, ascending, those towards the perianth larger and bordered by large marginal cells; perianth obovate, compressed-4-angled, the mouth much contracted, toothed. — Margins of ditches, Mobile, Alabama. (Eu.)

     * * * * *Leaves unequally complicate-2-lobed (i. e. folded together): the involucral ones 3 – 5-cleft: perianth oblong, obtuse, plaited.*

16. **J. exsécta,** Schmidel. Stems ascending; dorsal lobe of the leaves small, acute; ventral lobe concave, acute or 2-toothed. — Boggy places, decayed wood, &c. (Eu.)

17. **J. obtusifòlia,** Hook. Stems ascending, simple; lobes of the leaves oblong, obtuse or acute, minutely denticulate, the ventral scymitar-shaped; the dorsal smaller, oblique.— Dry, hilly situations, on the ground. (Eu.)

18. **J. álbicans,** L. Stems ascending: the dorsal lobe of the leaf ovate, the ventral larger, oblong-ovate, scymitar-shaped, both with a broad pellucid line in the middle; perianth obovate, cylindrical, the mouth plicate-dentate.— Moist banks, in hilly districts. (Eu.)

25. SCAPÀNIA, Lindenberg. (Tab. 22.)

Fructification terminal. Involucral leaves 2, larger than the cauline. Peri-antn compressed parallel to the plane of the stem, the mouth entire or ciliate-toothed. Calyptra membranaceous. Capsule oval. Elaters with 2 spiral fibres. Antheridia in the angles of small and saccate equally 2-lobed perigonial leaves. Stem-leaves complicate – 2-lobed; the dorsal lobe smaller. Amphigastria none. (Name probably from σκαπάνη, *a shovel;* from the shape of the lobes of the leaves.)

1. **S. nemoròsa,** Nees. Stems ascending, crowded; leaves ciliate-toothed, each lobe convex, obtuse; the ventral obovate, oblique, twice as large as the other.— Common on moist banks, &c.— A variable species, $\frac{1}{2}'$ to $3'$ long, pale yellow, green, or purple: texture of the leaf rather firm. (Eu.)

2. **S. undulàta,** Nees & Montagne. Leaves ciliate-denticulate or entire, loose, spreading; lobes rounded-trapezoidal, the upper half the size of the lower, except at the summit of the stem, where they are equal; of thin and flaccid tex-ture (green or purple.)— Mountainous districts. (Tab. 22.) (Eu.)

3. **S. breviflòra,** Tayl. (in Lond. Jour. Bot. 1846.) Stems ascending; leaves dentate, deeply 2-lobed, lobes rotund-triangular, the upper one much smaller, springing from the plane of the lower near its dorsal margin; perianth obconic, plicate, compressed, shortly 4-laciniate and dentate at its mouth, its narrow base surrounded by lanceolate, serrate scales; involucral leaves long as the perianth.— Near Philadelphia, *Dr. Watson.*

26. PLAGIOCHÌLA, Nees & Montagne. (Tab. 22.)

Fructification terminal or lateral. Involucral leaves 2, larger than the cauline. Perianth compressed at right angles to the plane of the stem; the mouth trun-cate, entire or ciliate-toothed. Calyptra membranaceous. Capsule oval. Ela-ters with two spiral fibres. Antheridia covered by small and ventricose-imbri-cated perigonial leaves. Stem-leaves with the dorsal margin decurrent and re-flexed, often turned to one side (whence the name, from πλάγιος, *sideways,* and χιλός, *herbage.*)

* *Amphigastria none: orifice of the perianth toothed-ciliate.*

1. **P. spinulòsa,** Nees & Montagne. Stems creeping, the branches as-cending; leaves remote, oblique, spreading, obovate-wedge-shaped; the dorsal margin entire, the ventral and the apex spinulose-toothed; perianth lateral.— Banks of rivulets, Alleghany Mountains. (Eu.)

2. **P. asplenioìdes,** Nees & Montagne. Leaves somewhat imbricated,

G. M.   7

oblique, spreading, rounded-obovate, entire or denticulate; perianth terminal.—Grows with No. 1. (Eu.)

* * *Amphigastria fugacious*, 2 - 3-*cleft*.

3. **P. porelloïdes,** Lindenberg. Stems divided; the branches ascending; leaves rather imbricated, convex-gibbous, rounded-obovate, those at and near the summit of the stem repand-denticulate, the others entire; perianth oblong, the mouth denticulate.—Among Mosses, at the base of trees in swamps.

4. **P. macróstoma,** Sulliv. Stems prostrate, rooting copiously, branched; branches not ascending; leaves nearly oval, horizontal, entire or slightly repand; perianth broadly obconic, the mouth compressed, margin repand; amphigastria lanceolate, 2-3-cleft.—Moist banks and decayed logs, Ohio. (Tab. 22.)

5. **P. Ludoviciàna,** Sulliv. Main branches ascending, flexuous, sparingly ramulose; leaves patent-divergent, semi-ovate, 2-3-dentate at the apex, their ventral margins decurrent and forming two parallel crest-like lines on the under side of the stem, the dorsal margins reflexed and entire, the ventral spinulose-dentate; amphigastria deeply 2-3-cleft, the segments ciliate-dentate.—Bark of trees, Louisiana.

6. **P. undàta,** Sulliv. Resembles the last; but is more rigid, with simple branches; leaves horizontal, triangular-ovate, obtuse, emarginate, or sparingly dentate at the apex, the dorsal margins reflexed and entire, the ventral repand-undulate and forming crest-like lines as in No. 4; amphigastria 2-cleft, the segments dentate.—Shaded rocky banks of the Savannah River, Georgia.

27. SARCOSCÝPHUS, Corda. (Tab. 21.)

Fructification terminal. Involucral leaves united nearly to the top into an oblong tube. Perianth 4-6-toothed, connate (except the teeth) with the interior surface of the involucral leaves. Calyptra membranaceous. Capsule globose. Elaters with two spiral fibres. Antheridia in the saccate base of perigonial leaves. Stems erect, producing from their base runner-like rootlets. Stem-leaves 2-lobed. Amphigastria none. (Name composed of σάρξ, *flesh*, and σκύφος, *a cup*; from the fleshy tubular involucre.)

1. **S. Ehrhárti,** Corda. Leaves erect-spreading, rather quadrate, embracing the stem by the broad base; lobes obtuse.—On mountains.—Plant of a firm texture, dark green or brownish-purple. (Tab. 21.)

28. GYMNOMÍTRIUM, Corda. (Tab. 21.)

Fructification terminal. Involucral leaves 2-4, convolute, emarginate. Perianth none. Calyptra short. Capsule globose. Elaters with two spiral fibres. Antheridia obovate, axillary. Stem-leaves 2-lobed. Amphigastria none. (Name from γυμνός, *naked*, and μίτριον, *a little cap*; the calyptra not covered by a perianth.)

1. **G. concinnàtum,** Corda. Stems erect, filiform, brittle, sparingly branched; branches thickened at the apex, obtuse; leaves densely imbricated, ovate, with a narrow membranaceous margin.—Alpine regions of the White

Mountains, New Hampshire, *Oakes.* — A small species, growing in compact masses, of a whitish or silvery hue. (Eu.)

* * Leaves incubous; the apex of each leaf lying on the base of the next.

29. FRULLÀNIA, Raddi. (Tab. 22.)

Fructification terminal on proper branches. Involucral leaves 2 or 4, two-lobed, not auriculate. Perianth oval or obovate, terete or 3–4-angled, mucronate at the apex by a tubular mouth. Pistillidia 2 or 4. Calyptra pear-shaped, persistent, rupturing below the apex. Capsule globular, 4-cleft half-way down. Elaters truncate at both ends, with one spiral fibre, adherent to the valves, erect. Spores large, irregular, minutely muricate. Inflorescence diœcious. Antheridia in the saccate base of closely imbricated 2-lobed perigonial leaves. Stem-leaves 2-lobed; the lower lobe usually an inflated helmet-shaped appendage (auricle). Amphigastria entire or 2-toothed, throwing out rootlets from their base. (A personal name.)

1. **F. Grayàna,** Montagne. Stems creeping, simply pinnate; leaves nearly orbicular, concave, decurved, marked in the middle by a necklace-form line; auricle oblong-club-shaped, emarginate at the lower end; involucral leaves unequally 2-cleft; the dorsal segment oblong, pointed, nearly entire, the ventral awl-shaped; amphigastria oblong, flat, 2-cleft, the sinus obtuse; perianth pear-shaped, 3-sided, obtusely keeled beneath. — On trees and rocks; frequent. — Foliage glossy, varying from deep purplish-brown to dark green. (Tab. 22.)

2. **F. Tamarísci,** Nees. Near No. 1; distinguished by its more rigid habit; bipinnate ramification; serrulate involucral leaves; and differently shaped amphigastria with revolute margins. — A variety only of this species is attributed to this country, with obtuse leaves, expanded auricles, and plane amphigastria. (*G. L. & N. Syn. Hepat.*) (Eu.)

3. **F. Drummóndii,** Tayl. Stems sparingly branched; leaves reddish, lax, patent, oblong, obtuse; auricles decurved; amphigastria minute, oblong, bifid; perianth ovate from a narrow base, retuse at the apex. — Bark of trees, Louisiana. — A small species.

4. **F. Caroliniàna,** Sulliv. Stem 6″–12″ long, rather wide, irregularly branched; leaves closely imbricating, oval-rotund; auricle small, elongated, distant from the stem, with a style interposed; amphigastria ovate-rotund, double the width of the stem, bifid, its segments repand: perianth pyriform, plane above, obtusely carinate beneath. — Trees, North Carolina, near the coast.

5. **F. Hutchinsiæ,** Nees. Stems (1′–2′ long, about 1″ broad) subpinnately branched; leaves dark olive-green verging on black, ovate, acute, dentate-serrate; amphigastria roundish, plane, bifid, subserrate, perianth oblong-obovate, plane above, keeled beneath. — On stones, in mountain rivulets of the Southern States. (Eu.)

6. **F. Virgínica,** Lehm. Stems creeping, vaguely branched; leaves nearly ovate, entire, concave, the auricle sometimes expanded into a lanceolate lamina; amphigastria round-ovate, double the width of the stem, 2-cleft; perianth pear-shaped, rather compressed, tuberculate, 4-keeled beneath, 2-4-keeled

on the back, the keels crested. (F. dilatata, *Musc. Alleghan. No.* 267, partly.) — Rocks and trees; common.

7. **F. Eboracénsis,** Lehm. Stems creeping, fasciculately branched; stem-leaves loosely disposed (the rameal imbricated), round-ovate; amphigastria ovate, a little wider than the stem; perianth smooth, pear-shaped, slightly compressed and repand, beneath obtusely keeled and gibbous near the apex. (F. microscypha, læviscypha, & nana, *Taylor.*) — Bark of trees; common.

8. **F. saxátilis,** Lindenberg. Near the last, but separated by its pinnately branched and more rigid stems, more crowded leaves, much larger amphigastria, and shorter perianth. — Trees, Massachusetts.

9. **F. plàna,** Sulliv. (in Mem. Amer. Acad. l. c.) Resembles No. 7, but is a somewhat larger species; the auricle very small, close to the stem, and covered by the plane rotund acutely bifid amphigastria, which are thrice the width of the stem; perianth oblong-oval, or nearly obovate, plane above, carinate beneath. — Rocks; East Tennessee.

10. **F. æolòtis,** Nees. Not unlike No. 8; leaves semi-vertical, subsquarrose, obliquely cordate, the auricle usually expanded into a lanceolate lamina; perianth unknown. — Grows in spongy masses on decayed logs, stumps, &c.; common.

30. LEJEÚNIA, Libert.   (Tab. 22.)

Fructification lateral or terminal, on proper branches. Involucral leaves 2, deeply 2-lobed. Perianth oval or obovate, terete or angular, winged or ciliate-crested on the angles, the mouth 3 – 4-lobed; pistillidium single. Calyptra obovate, persistent, rupturing below the apex. Capsule globose, membranaceous, pale, 4-cleft to the middle. Elaters persistent, adherent to the tips of the valves, erect, the upper end truncate-dilated, with a single spiral fibre. Spores large, irregular. Inflorescence diœcious. Antheridia on proper branches, lodged in the ventricose base of imbricated 2-lobed perigonial leaves. Amphigastria present. (Named for *Lejeune,* a French botanist.)

* *Amphigastria entire.*

1. **L. clypeàta,** Schweinitz. Stems (7″ – 10″ long) procumbent, somewhat pinnately branched; leaves (whitish-green, of a firm texture) with the upper lobe round-obovate and deflexed, the lower oblong, quadrate; amphigastria orbicular, approximate; perianth lateral, sessile, obovate, obtusely keeled on the back, 2-keeled beneath, the margin subcompressed. — Alleghany Mountains. (Tab. 22.)

2. **L. longiflòra,** Tayl.! Closely resembles the last species, but has leaves of a more membranaceous texture, and a 5-winged perianth. — On trees, Southern Ohio to Florida.

3. **L. calyculàta,** Tayl. Stems entangled, branched; leaves patent-recurved, oblong, obtuse, subdeflexed; the lower lobe involute, lanceolate; amphigastria rotund; perianth axillary, rather exserted, obcordate, 4-winged, the wings entire; involucral leaves narrow, acute. — On lichens; Alleghany Mountains.

4. **L. cyclostìpa,** Tayl. Stems (5″-7″ long) branched; leaves pale green, patent-recurved, oblong, obtuse; the lower lobe quadrate-ovate, involute, 1-toothed; amphigastria reniform-rotund; perianth terminal, obcordate, compressed, plane above, ventricose-4-winged beneath, the wings ciliate, the cilia dentate; involucral leaves nearly covering the perianth. — Bark of trees, near Cincinnati, Ohio.

5. **L. polyphýlla,** Tayl. Stems cæspitose (3″-4″ long); leaves olive-green, semi-cordate; lower lobe involute, lanceolate; amphigastria minute, reniform; perianth immersed, rotund-obovate, 5-6-angled near the apex, the angles dentate-crested. — Habitat same as the last. (We have not seen specimens of No. 3 and 5: the descriptions are from Lond. Jour. Bot., 1846.)

6. **L. auriculàta,** Hook. & Wils. Grows in dark green patches; stems 5″-8″ long; leaves closely imbricating, scymitar-shaped, complicate and somewhat 2-lobed at the base; amphigastria obovate-rotund, emarginate; perianth obovate-triangular. — Bark of trees, Louisiana.

7. **L. testudìnea,** Tayl. Stems 5″-7″ long; leaves whitish-green, very closely imbricating, patent-divergent, oblong, almost scymitar-shaped, obtuse, complicate-2-lobed at the base; the lobe small, lanceolate; amphigastria rotund, minute compared with the leaf. — Bark of trees, Southern Ohio.

* * *Amphigastria 2-cleft, or obsolete.*

8. **L. serpyllifòlia,** Libert. Stems vaguely branched; leaves with the upper lobe roundish-ovate, convex; the lower much smaller, obliquely ovate, involute; amphigastria rounded, 2-cleft, its segments obtuse; perianth obovate, acutely 5-angled. — On moist rocks and trees, Alleghany Mountains. — A small pale-green species, with transparent and loosely reticulated leaves. (Eu.)

9. **L. cucullàta,** Nees. Stems filiform, rather pinnately branched; leaves oblong-ovate, distant, the lower margin inflexed-hooded; amphigastria oval, 2-cleft; perianth obovate, rather compressed, obtusely keeled beneath, convex on the back and 2-keeled near the apex. (L. lucens, *Tayl.*) — Moist rocks, near the ground, Alleghany Mountains. — A minute, flaccid species, with light pea-green foliage.

10. **L. minutissima,** Dumort. Stem creeping, sparingly branched; leaves vertical, subrotund, imperfectly 2-lobed, the lower lobe an indistinct fold; amphigastria obsolete; perianth terminal, compressed, 5-angled; the mouth obtuse, papillose. — Roots of trees. — Small as No. 9. (Eu.)

11. **L. calcàrea,** Libert. Stems loosely and divaricately branched; leaves ovate, pointed, decurved, cellulose-echinate, inflexed at the base, saccate; amphigastria oblong, 2-cleft; perianth pear-shaped, with 5 crested wings. — On roots of trees, Ohio. — A very minute species, scarcely visible to the naked eye. (Eu.)

31. MADOTHÈCA, Dumortier. TREE SCALE-MOSS. (Tab. 22.)

Fructification lateral, nearly sessile. Involucral leaves 2 or 4, two-lobed. Perianth ovate, biconvex; the mouth 2-lipped, incised or entire. Calyptra globose, persistent, rupturing below the apex. Capsule globose. Elaters free, at tenuated at both ends, with two spiral fibres. Spores large, rather angular. Inflorescence diœcious. Antheridia in the saccate base of closely imbricated 2-lobed perigonial leaves. Stem-leaves deeply and unequally 2-lobed. Amphigastria large, decurrent. (Name formed of μαδός, *bald*, and θήκη, *capsule*; the elaters falling away from the valves.)

1. **M. platyphýlla,** Dumort. Stems irregularly 2-pinnate or nearly so; dorsal lobe of the leaf roundish-ovate, the basal margin more or less undulate; the ventral lobe smaller, oblique, heart-oval, margins reflexed; amphigastria round-obovate with reflexed margins; mouth of perianth nearly entire. — Trees and rocks, common; a large and variable species. (Tab. 22.)   (Eu.)

2. **M. porélla,** Nees. Stems 2-3-pinnate (2'-4' long), the forked branches divergent; leaves distantly placed; the dorsal lobe oblong-ovate, obtuse; the ventral much smaller, appressed to the stem, oblong, flat; amphigastria quadrate; mouth of the perianth crenulate. — Stones and roots of trees subject to inundation. (Eu.)

3. **M. Wataugénsis,** (n. sp.) Much like No. 2, but a smaller and more delicate species, with fascicles of rootlets springing from the base of the amphigastria, and the dorsal lobe of the leaf slightly repand-dentate; foliage light yellowish-brown : no fruit seen. — Closely adhering to decayed logs; banks of the Watauga River, North Carolina. (M. porella, var. ? *Musc. Alleghan. No.* 265.)

32. RÁDULA, Nees.   (Tab. 22.)

Fructification terminal on short branches, or in a fork. Involucral leaves 2, deeply 2-lobed. Perianth compressed or nearly terete; the mouth dilated. Calyptra pear-shaped, persistent, opening below the apex. Capsule oval. Elaters attenuated at both ends, with two spiral fibres. Spores large, globose. Inflorescence monœcious. Antheridia in the ventricose base of minute perigonial leaves. Stem-leaves 2-lobed, the small inflexed ventral lobe producing rootlets. Amphigastria none. (Name from ῥαδαλός, *pliant*, because these are mostly flaccid plants.)

1. **R. complanáta,** Dumortier. Stems flat, irregularly and somewhat pinnately branched, flaccid; leaves imbricated; dorsal lobe roundish; the ventral much smaller, triangular-ovate, appressed; perianth oblong, compressed, the mouth truncate and entire. — A large pale-green species; growing in orbicular patches on the bark of trees, &c. (Eu.)

2. **R. obcónica,** Sulliv. Stems indeterminately branched; leaves distantly placed; dorsal lobe obovate-roundish, convex; perianth clavate-obconic, the mouth obliquely truncate and entire. (R. complanata, var. ? *Musc. Alleghan. No.* 260.) — Trees, Cedar swamps, Ohio. — Much smaller than the last; well marked by the shape of its perianth. (Tab. 22.)

3. **R. pállens,** Nees. Stems rigid, divaricately fork-branched; leaves imbricated; dorsal lobe roundish, decurrent, the ventral lobe with an inflexed apex; perianth elongated funnel-form, the mouth entire. — Old logs, &c., Alleghany Mountains.

33. PTILÍDIUM, Nees. Fringed Scale-Moss. (Tab. 22.)

Fructification terminal on short branches. Involucral leaves 2 – 4, four-cleft. Perianth terete, obovate; the mouth connivent, plaited, denticulate. Calyptra pear-shaped, coriaceous. Capsule ovate. Elaters with two spiral fibres. Inflorescence diœcious. Antheridia covered by closely imbricated perigonial leaves. Stem-leaves complicate-2-lobed, each lobe divided. Amphigastria 4 – 5-lobed. (Name a diminutive of πτίλον, *a downy feather;* from the cut-fringed foliage.)

1. **P. ciliàre,** Nees. Stems crowded, somewhat pinnate; leaves (4-cleft) and amphigastria both lacerately ciliate, the fringe long and setaceous. — Rotten logs, in woods. (Tab. 22.) (Eu.)

34. SENDTNÈRA, Endl. (Tab. 22.)

Fructification terminal. Involucral leaves numerous, incised, free or connate at the base. Perianth tubular, deeply many-cleft. Calyptra chartaceous. Capsule globular. Elaters free, with two spiral fibres. Antheridia upon proper branches in the axils of ventricose perigonial leaves. Stem-leaves 2 – 5-cleft or entire. Amphigastria 2 – many-cleft. (Named for *O. Sendtner,* a German botanist.)

1. **S. junipérina,** Nees. Stems erect, nearly simple, slender, elongated; leaves and amphigastria almost alike, oblong, curved and one-sided, 2-cleft to the middle, the lobes lanceolate. — High mountains. — Plant rigid, reddish-brown. (Tab. 22.) (Eu.)

35. TRICHOCÒLEA, Nees. Downy Scale-Moss. (Tab. VIII.)

Fructification situated in a fork. Involucral leaves numerous, coalescent into an oblong and truncate coriaceous hairy tube, concrete with the calyptra. Perianth none. Capsule oblong. Elaters with two spiral fibres, free. Antheridia on the upper side of the stem in the axil of leaves. Leaves palmately divided; the divisions laciniate. Amphigastria present. (Name composed of θρίξ, *hair,* and κολεός, *a sheath;* from the hairy involucre.)

1. **T. Tomentélla,** Nees. Stems forked, 2 – 3-pinnately branched; divisions of the 4 – 5-divided leaves capillary-many-cleft; amphigastria setaceously many-cleft. — Moist places, in large patches. — Foliage pale green, soft-hairy. (Tab. 22.) (Eu.)

36. MASTIGÒBRYUM, Nees. Great Scale-Moss.
(Tab. 22.)

Fructification terminal, on short proper branches, arising from the axils of the amphigastria. Involucral leaves small, narrow, acutely incised at the apex. Perianth elongated, 3-angular, the mouth 3-toothed. Calyptra membranaceous. Capsule globose. Elaters with two spiral fibres. Antheridia on short branches from the axils of the amphigastria, two in the axil of each perigonial leaf. Stem-leaves usually 3-toothed at the apex. Stems flagelliferous (whence the name, from μάστιξ, *a whip or lash*, and βρύον, *Moss*).

1. **M. trilobàtum,** Nees. Leaves ovate, antrorsely gibbous at the dorsal base, broad and acutely 3-toothed at the apex; amphigastria 4 – 6-toothed, the teeth denticulate. — On the damp ground, Alleghany Mountains and northward. Stems 3' – 5' long; the foliage firm, varying from olive-green to brownish-yellow. (Tab. 22.)   (Eu.)

2. **M. tridenticulàtum,** Lindenb. Scarcely distinct from the pre ceding: described as having oblong, obtuse, shorter, less oblique, and less concave leaves, with minute and often obsolete teeth: its habitat (swamps of the Southern States) is different.

3. **M. deflèxum,** Nees. Leaves ovate or ovate-oblong, the dorsal margin arched, the narrow apex 2 – 3-toothed or entire; amphigastria 2-cleft, crenate or entire. — Rocky places. — Variable; much smaller than the last, fragile, of a dark brownish hue. — M. denudatum and M. ambiguum, *G. L. & N. Synop. Hepat.*, are probably forms of this species. (Eu.)

37. LEPIDÒZIA, Nees.   CREEPING SCALE-MOSS. (Tab. 22.)

Fructification terminal, on short proper branches arising from the under side of the stem. Involucral leaves numerous, small, broad, 2 – 4-toothed at the apex. Perianth elongated, obtusely 3-plaited, the mouth denticulate. Calyptra membranaceous. Capsule globose. Elaters with two spiral fibres. Antheridia on short spike-like branches, arising from the under side of the stem, singly lodged in the base of conduplicate 2 – 3-cleft perigonial leaves. Stem-leaves 4-toothed or 4-parted. Amphigastria present. (Name from λεπιδόω, *to cover with scales;* in allusion to the scale-like foliage.)

1. **L. réptans,** Nees. Stems creeping, pinnately compound or decompound; leaves decurved, quadrate, acutely 3 – 4-toothed; amphigastria 3 – 4 cleft. — Hilly districts, on the ground. (Tab. 22.)   (Eu.)

38. CALYPOGEÌA, Raddi.   (Tab. 22.)

Perianth none. Involucre oblong, saccate, truncate, fleshy, hairy, attached by one side of its mouth to the stem, pendent. Calyptra membranaceous, partly connate with the involucre. Capsule oblong, twisted; the valves narrow and contorted. Elaters with two spiral fibres. Antheridia on short lateral capitate branches, one in each of the scale-like perigonial leaves. Stem-leaves entire or 2-toothed. Amphigastria 2-cleft. (Name compounded of κάλυξ, *flower-cup,* ὑπά, *under,* and γαῖα, *the ground;* from the position of the fructification.)

1. **C. Trichómanis,** Corda. Leaves roundish-ovate, obtuse, spreading, imbricated; perianths imbedded in the soil. — Moist or springy places, on the ground. — Foliage delicate, pale glaucous-green. (Tab. 22.)   (Eu.)

ADDITIONS AND CORRECTIONS.

Page 12.

8. **Sphágnum sedoìdes,** Brid.—The form mentioned under this species has been found by Mr. James, in Ethan Pond, Willey Mountain, New Hampshire.

Page 19.

4. **Campýlopus víridis,** Sulliv. & Lesqx. (Musc. Bor.-Amer., No. 72.) Closely cæspitose; stems ascending, mostly simple; leaves erect-patent (when dry tortuous), lanceolate-subulate, very fragile.—In woods, on decayed logs, New England to Ohio.—A dark-green species, resembling Dicranum interruptum, remarkable for its fragile leaves, which are seldom found unbroken.

Page 24.

3. **Físsidens exíguus,** Sulliv.—Of this species, No. 39, Fissidens bryoides, and No. 40, Fissidens bryoides, var., of Drummond's 2d Coll. of American Mosses, are probably large forms. The bordering of its leaf is variable.

3b. **Físsidens synoícus** (n. sp.).—Hermaphrodite; stems simple, inclined, 3″-6″ long; leaves 12–14, oblong-lanceolate, oblique, shortly acuminate, bordered except at the denticulate apex, the blade shorter than the duplicature, the dorsal wing vanishing above the base; costa continuous; capsule terminal, oval-oblong, erect; operculum rather long-rostrate.—San Marcos, Texas, *Wright.*—A small species, distinct by its whitish-green leaves with a close areolation, regular erect capsule, and hermaphrodite inflorescence.

Page 31.

2. **Syrrhópodon Texànus** (n. sp.). Stems about 1′ high, simple; upper leaves pale green, serrated, ligulate, straight (tortuous when dry), spreading from a subciliate-dentate sheathing base, canaliculate, surrounded except near their point by a narrow pellucid border of linear cellules; areolation of

the sheathing portion composed of large oblong hyaline cellules, which elsewhere are very minute, subquadrate, opaque, and papillose; costa stout, terete,
percurrent, spinulose on its upper surface, often (the lamina being reduced or
nearly obsolete) bearing on its apex a dense roundish cluster of numerous
oval-oblong 6–7-articulated bodies. — San Marcos, Texas, *Wright.* — Sterile
plant only known: it may be a Calymperes.

Page 36.

3[b]. **Schistidium Agassizii,** Sulliv. & Lesqx. (Musc. Bor.-Amer.,
No. 137.) Near S confertum; but distinguished by its blackish, shining, denser
tufts; narrower, longer, and lingulate leaves, with an obtuse dentate apex;
and an elongated exserted perichæth.—Wet rocks, northern shore of Lake
Superior, *Agassiz.*

Page 54.

3[b]. **Fontinàlis Novæ-Angliæ** (n. sp.) Diœcious? stems 6′–10′ long,
divided from near the base into pinnately ramulose divisions; branchlets
numerous, equidistant, 1′–1½′ long, at right angles to the stem; leaves (the
cauline twice as large as the ramuline) erect-patent, rather distant or loosely
incumbent, evenly concave, ovate or elongated-ovate, acute or slightly obtuse,
serrated at the apex, auriculate and narrowly decurrent at the base, the areolæ
minute, linear (their length about seven times their width), acute at each end,
those near the summit much shorter and nearly rhombic, those of the auriculæ
large, oblong, pellucid, colored; perichætia on various parts of the plant;
perichætial leaves, capsule, peristome, and calyptra as in F. biformis, *Sulliv* —
In rivulets, Massachusetts, *Oakes, James:* Rhode Island, *Olney:* Connecticut,
D. C. Eaton. Stems reddish. Foliage clear shining green.

Our specimens are sterile, except those received from Mr. James since the
foregoing pages were printed. F. Novæ-Angliæ is a rather large species,
quite distinct from any before described, excepting F. biformis, the vernal state
of which it very closely resembles, and to which some sterile specimens collected near New Haven, Connecticut, by Mr. Eaton, were erroneously referred
on page 54. The two species differ from each other as follows: In numerous
specimens of F. Novæ-Angliæ (those from Mr. James collected in August),
there is no indication of a second growth of differently shaped leaves, such as
repeated observations during several years have shown to exist in F. biformis.
The first species has a pinnate, the second a fasciculate, ramification, with leaves
(in the vernal state) one half larger; their subflexuous areolæ have a length only
twice or thrice their width, and, being very obtuse at each end, are suggestive
of the name *sphagnifolium,* given to one of the forms of the species by Muller.
F. Novæ-Angliæ appears to be a more prolific species; some of the specimens
exhibiting fructification in all stages of growth, from the minute flower-buds,
cuspidate by the exserted styles of their two archegonia, and lodged in the axils
of nearly every leaf on the upper portion of the plant, to the mature capsules
of the present and the decayed ones of the preceding season. In the other
species the capsules are very rare, and found only near the base of the stem:
besides their opercula are longer. The peristome, usually supplying good dis

tinctive marks in this genus, is (as with F. antipyretica and F. squamosa) of no account in distinguishing the two species under notice.

In all the North American species of Fontinalis, and also in F. squamosa, L. (which has not yet been satisfactorily ascertained to be a native of this country), the leaves have auricles at their base, with an enlarged pellucid areolation. The sporules in all are of about the same diameter, namely $\frac{1}{555}$ of a line.

4. **F. dísticha,** Hook & Wils. Fine fruiting specimens collected by Mr. James in Saco River, Crawford Notch, of the White Mountains, New Hampshire, and sterile specimens found in Rhode Island by Mr. Olney, indicate for this species (heretofore deemed peculiarly southern) an unexpected northern range.

Page 59.

3ᵇ. **Léskea nervósa,** Myrin.—Sterile specimens collected on the White Mountains by the late Mr. Oakes, and at Trenton Falls, New York, by Mr. James, appear to belong to this species.

Page 64, under Pylaisæeæ.

Pterigynándrum filifórme, Hedw. — Diœcious; stems slender and with the fasciculate filiform branches arcuate-prostrate, villous, stoloniferous; leaves erect-patent, somewhat imbricated (appressed when dry), often subsecund, elliptical and obovate-spatulate, suddenly short-acuminate, concave, serrate above, papillose on the back, shortly bicostate, or unicostate half-way; areolation quadrate at the basal angles, rhombic at the apex, elsewhere linear-flexuous; capsule oblong, erect, long-pedicellate; operculum rostellate, with a conic base; annulus narrow, fragmentary; peristome small; teeth narrow-lanceolate, incurved, pale yellow, remotely 5–6-articulated, with alternate cilia short and fugacious; calyptra dimidiate, large, extending to the base of the capsule; perichætial leaves lanceolate, erect, sheathing, hyaline, ecostate.—On rocks and trunks of trees, White Mountains, New Hampshire, *James.*—A small cæspitose species, with thread-like branches, and greenish or yellowish lustreless foliage.

Page 69.

13ᵇ. **Hýpnum pilíferum,** Schreb. Diœcious; stems procumbent, extended, divided, subpinnately ramulose, the branchlets attenuated; leaves loosely imbricating, ovate-oblong, very concave, suddenly contracted into a long flexuous hair-point, serrulate above the slender costa, vanishing about half-way; capsule oblong, arcuate, annulate; operculum as long as the capsule; calyptra large; pedicels rough.—On the ground in dense woods, New England to Pennsylvania and Ohio.—A large species, with pale-green and shining leaves.

ERRATA.

Page 54, line 11 from bottom, and page 55, line 13, for "*D. E. Eaton*" read "*D. C. Eaton.*"

Page 56, line 12 from bottom, for "Dychelyma" read "Dichelyma."

INDEX.

EXPLANATION OF THE PLATES.

EXPLANATION OF THE PLATES.

N. B. — The figures of those genera of Mosses and Liverworts to which an asterisk (•) is prefixed, are from original drawings. The species selected for illustrating the genera are figured of the natural size: their details are more or less magnified. — The sign ♂ on the plates indicates the antheridia.

Genera of Musci.

TAB. I.

ANDRÆA. — Plant, capsule before dehiscence, the same after dehiscence, and calyptra of A. rupestris, *Turn.*: after Schimper.

• SPHAGNUM. — Plant, capsule with remains of the calyptra, the same cut lengthwise, and operculum of S. cymbifolium, *Dill.*

• ARCHIDIUM. — Plant, and a plant enlarged, capsule with base of the calyptra, and upper portion of the calyptra of A. Ohioense, *Schimper.*

PHASCUM. — Plant, the same enlarged, capsule, and calyptra of P. cuspidatum, *Schreb.* after Schimper.

• BRUCHIA. — Plant, and a plant enlarged, capsule, and calyptra of B. brevifolia, *Sulliv.*

GYMNOSTOMUM. — Plant, capsule, operculum, and calyptra of G. rupestre, *Schwægr.* after Schimper.

WEISIA. — Plant, capsule with operculum and calyptra, and five teeth of the peristome of W. viridula, *Brid.*: after Schimper.

RHABDOWEISIA. — Plant, capsule with operculum, capsule when dry, three teeth of the peristome, and calyptra of R. fugax, *Bryol. Europ.*: after Schimper.

DICRANODONTIUM. — Plant, capsule with the operculum, two 2-parted teeth of the peristome, and calyptra of D. longirostre, *Bryol. Europ.*: after Schimper.

ARCTOA. — Plant, capsule with operculum and calyptra, and two teeth of the peristome of A. fulvella: after Schimper.

SELIGERIA. — Plant, capsule with operculum and calyptra, and three teeth of the peristome of S. tristicha, *Bryol. Europ.*: after Schimper.

BARBULA. — Plant, capsule with operculum, the peristome, and calyptra of B. unguiculata, *Hedw.*: after Schimper.

CERATODON. — Plant, capsule with operculum, capsule when dry, two 2-cleft teeth of the peristome, and calyptra of C. purpureus, *Brid.*: after Schimper.

FISSIDENS. — Plant, capsule with operculum, two 2-cleft teeth of the peristome, and calyptra of F. taxifolius, *Hedw.* · after Schimper.

CAMPYLOPUS. — Plant, capsule with operculum and calyptra, two teeth of the peristome with a portion of the annulus, and calyptra of C. flexuosus: after Schimper.

TRICHOSTOMUM. — Plant, capsule with operculum, three teeth of the peristome, and calyptra of T. tortile, *Schrad.*: after Schimper.

CONOMITRIUM. — Plant, capsule with operculum pedicel and perichætial leaves, three teeth of the peristome, and calyptra of C. Julianum, *Mont.*: after Schimper.

● TREMATODON. — Plant, capsule with operculum and apophysis, two teeth of the peristome, and calyptra of T. longicollis, *Michx.*

TAB. II.

LEUCOBRYUM. — Plant, capsule with operculum, capsule dry, two 2-parted teeth of the peristome, and calyptra of L. vulgare, *Hampe: after Schimper.*

DICRANUM. — Plant, capsule and operculum, two 2-parted teeth of the peristome, and calyptra of D. scoparium, *Hedw. : after Schimper.*

● DESMATODON. — Plant, capsule, mouth of the same with peristome, two 2-parted teeth of the peristome with a portion of the annulus, operculum, and calyptra of D. plinthobius, *Sulliv. & Lesqx.*   .

DIDYMODON. — Plant, capsule, two teeth of the peristome with a portion of its annulus, operculum, and calyptra of D. rubellus, *Bryol. Europ.: after Schimper.*

● EUSTICHIUM. — Plants, one enlarged, male flower, an antheridium, fertile flower, and section of the leaf of E. Norvegicum, *Bryol. Europ.*

DISTICHIUM. — Plant, portion of stem and leaves enlarged, capsule with operculum, two teeth of the peristome with a portion of the annulus, and calyptra of D. capillaceum, *Bryol. Europ.: after Schimper.*

POTTIA. — Plants, capsule with operculum and calyptra, and capsule with operculum attached by the columella only, of P. truncata, *Bryol. Europ.: after Schimper.*

● SYRRHOPODON. — Plant, capsule with operculum and calyptra, three teeth of the peristome, and operculum of S. Floridanus, *Sulliv.*

● SCHLOTHEIMIA. — Plant, capsule with operculum, same covered by the calyptra, portion of the peristome (one tooth and two cilia), and the lower part of the calyptra of S. Sullivantii, *C. Mull.*

ENCALYPTA. — Plant, capsule with operculum, same covered by calyptra, capsule dry, and three teeth of the peristome with a portion of the annulus, of E. rhabdocarpa, *Schwagr.: after Schimper.*

TETRAPHIS — Plant, capsule with operculum and calyptra, the entire peristome, and operculum of T. pellucida, *Hedw.: after Schimper.*

● PTYCHOMITRIUM. — Plant, capsule with peristome and a portion of the annulus, two teeth of the peristome, operculum, and calyptra of P. incurvum, *Schwagr.*

● DRUMMONDIA. — Plant, capsule with operculum and calyptra, two teeth of the peristome, operculum, calyptra, and three spores of D. clavellata, *Hook.*

ZYGODON. — Plant, capsule with operculum, capsule without operculum and dry, and calyptra of Z. Lapponicus, *Bryol. Europ.: after Schimper.*

● MACROMITRIUM. — Plant, capsule, mouth of the same with the annular peristome, and calyptra of M. Dregei.

SCHISTIDIUM. — Plant, capsule with operculum and calyptra, two teeth of the peristome, operculum with columella, and calyptra of S. apocarpum, *Bryol. Europ.: after Schimper.*

RACOMITRIUM. — Plant, capsule with operculum and calyptra, one tooth of the peristome 2-parted to the base and with a portion of the annulus, and operculum of R. aciculare, *Brid.: after Schimper.*

HEDWIGIA. — Plant, capsule with operculum, same without operculum and dry, and calyptra of H. ciliata : after Schimper.

ORTHOTRICHUM. — Plant, capsule with operculum and calyptra, capsule dry, portion of the peristome (2 pairs of teeth and 8 cilia), operculum, and calyptra of O. Hutchinsiae, *Hook. & Tayl.: after Schimper.*

GRIMMIA. — Plant, capsule with operculum and calyptra, two teeth of the peristome with a portion of the annulus, of G. leucophaea, *Grev.: after Schimper.*

Tab. III.

BUXBAUMIA. — Plant, capsule with operculum, mouth of capsule with peristome, operculum with part of columella, and calyptra of B aphylla, *Haller : after* Schimper.

DIPHYSCIUM. — Plant, capsule, peristome, operculum with portion of the columella, and calyptra of D. foliosum, *Web. & Mohr. : after* Schimper.

ATRICHUM. — Plant, capsule with operculum, peristome, calyptra, and its point more magnified, of A angustatum, *Bryol. Europ :* after Schimper.

POGONATUM. — Plant, capsule and operculum, the same covered by the hairy calyptra, peristome, and four teeth of peristome, of P. urnigerum, *Brid.:* after Schimper.

POLYTRICHUM. — Plant, capsule with operculum, the same covered by the hairy calyptra, the same dry, and three teeth of the peristome, of P. commune, *L. :* after Schimper.

BARTRAMIA. — Plant, capsule with operculum and calyptra, capsule dry, portion of the peristome, and operculum of B. pomiformis, *Hedw. :* after Schimper.

MNIUM. — Plant, capsule with operculum, and portion of the peristome (two teeth, three perforated cilia, and five ciliolæ) of M. cuspidatum, *Hedw. :* after Schimper.

CONOSTOMUM. — Plant, capsule with operculum and calyptra, and peristome of C. boreale *Swartz :* after Schimper.

MEESIA. — Plant, capsule with operculum, same without operculum and dry, two teeth and two cilia of the peristome with part of the annulus, and a flower (of two antheridia, two archegonia, and four paraphyses) of M longiseta, *Hedw. :* after Schimper.

FUNARIA. — Plant, capsule with operculum and calyptra, the same with operculum only, one entire tooth of the peristome and two broken teeth opposite the two cilia, and the operculum, of F. hygrometrica, *Hedw. :* after Schimper.

AULACOMNION. — Plant, capsule and operculum, the same without operculum and dry, part of the peristome (two teeth, one cilium split along the middle, and two ciliolæ, with a portion of the annulus), and the calyptra of A heterostichum, *Bryol. Europ. ·* after Schimper.

TIMMIA. — Plant (calyptra attached to the pedicel), capsule with operculum, the same without operculum and dry, one tooth of the peristome and several appendiculate cilia united in pairs and a portion of the annulus, of T. megapolitana, *Hedw* after Schimper.

Tab. IV.

● **ENTOSTHODON.** — Plants, capsule with operculum, mouth of capsule with the entire peristome, three teeth of same with portion of the annulus, and the calyptra of E Drummondii, *Sulliv.*

● **PHYSCOMITRIUM.** — Plant, the same enlarged, capsule, operculum with columella, and calyptra of P immersum, *Sulliv.*

● **APHANORHEGMA.** — Plant, the same enlarged, capsule, operculum, and calyptra of A. serrata, *Sulliv.*

● **TETRAPLODON.** — Plant, capsule with its long apophysis, operculum with calyptra, four teeth of the peristome in pairs, and calyptra of T. australis, *Sulliv. & Lesqz.*

SPLACHNUM. — Plants, capsule with apophyses and operculum, mouth of the capsule with the reflexed teeth of the peristome and the exserted capitate columella, two teeth of the peristome, and operculum, of S ampullaceum, *L. :* after Schimper.

● **COSCINODON.** — Plant, the same enlarged, capsule with operculum, the same covered by the calyptra, two teeth of the peristome, with a portion of the annulus, and calyptra of C. Wrightii, *Sulliv.*

● **DICHELYMA** — Plant, capsule with operculum, perichætial leaves with the capsule laterally emergent, two teeth and two cilia (connected at the apex by cross-bars) of the peristome, and operculum, of D. capillaceum, *Bryol. Europ.*

FONTINALIS. — Plant, capsule with operculum, the same immersed in the perichætial leaves, peristome (the interior a tessellated cone), operculum, and calyptra of F. antipyretica, *L.*: after Schimper.

ANACAMPTODON. — Plant, capsule with operculum, dry capsule with peristome, two entire teeth with a portion of another reflexed and three cilia of the peristome, operculum, and calyptra of A. splachnoides, *Brid.*: after Schimper.

● FABRONIA. — Plant, capsule with operculum, two teeth of the peristome, operculum, and calyptra of F. Ravenelli, *Sulliv.*

ANTITRICHIA. — Plant, capsule with operculum, two teeth and three cilia of the peristome, operculum, and calyptra of A. curtipendula, *Brid.*: after Schimper.

● LEPTODON. — Plant, capsule with operculum pedicel and perichætial leaves, capsule with operculum and calyptra, and two teeth of the peristome of L. Ohioense, *Sulliv.*

● PYLAISÆA. — Plant, capsule with operculum, portion of the peristome, and calyptra of P. intricata, *Bryol. Europ.*

BRYUM. — Plant, capsule with operculum, portion of the peristome (one tooth, one perforated cilium, and three appendiculate ciliolæ), and a hermaphrodite flower (consisting of 2 antheridia, 2 archegonia, and 4 paraphyses), of B bimum, *Schreb.*: after Schimper.

● LEUCODON. — Plant, capsule with operculum pedicel and perichætial leaves, capsule with operculum and calyptra, three of the perforated teeth of the outer and the annular membrane of the inner peristome, and operculum, of L. julaceus, *Hedw.*

TAB. V.

● HOMALOTHECIUM. — Plant, capsule with operculum and calyptra, three teeth of the outer, with fragments of the membrane of the inner peristome and a portion of the annulus, and operculum, of H. subcapillatum, *Bryol. Europ.*

PLATYGYRIUM. — Plant, capsule with operculum and calyptra, four of the outer with as many cilia of the inner peristome and a quarter of the large annulus, and operculum, of P. repens, *Bryol. Europ.*: after Schimper.

● CYLINDROTHECIUM. — Plant, capsule with operculum and calyptra, two teeth of the outer and one cilium of the inner peristome, of C eladorrhizans, *Bryol. Europ.*

● MYURELLA — Plant, two capsules with opercula, two teeth of the outer with one cilium and three ciliolæ of the inner peristome, of M. Careyana, *Sulliv.*

● LESKEA — Plant, capsule with operculum and calyptra, five entire and three broken teeth of the exterior and three cilia of the interior peristome, operculum, a tooth and a cilium with a portion of its basilar membrane, and a part of the annulus, of L obscura.

● CLASMATODON. — Plant, capsule with operculum and calyptra, portion of the single peristome with part of the annulus, vertical section through the peristome, and two opercula of C. parvulus, *Hampe.*

● CRYPHÆA. — Plant, a perichæth enclosing the capsule with its operculum and calyptra, capsule with operculum partly removed, two teeth of the exterior and three cilia of the inner peristome with a portion of the annulus, two sporules, and calyptra, of C. glomerata, *W. P. Sch.*

HOOKERIA. — Plant, capsule and operculum, two teeth and two cilia of the peristome, and calyptra, of H. lucens, *Smith:* after Schimper.

● CLIMACIUM — Plant, capsule and operculum, two teeth and two cilia of the peristome, calyptra, and operculum, of C. Americanum, *Brid*

NECKERA. — Plant, portion of the stem with male flower and perichæth enclosing the capsule, two teeth of the exterior and three rudimentary cilia of the inner peristome, calyptra, operculum, capsule, pedicel, vaginula, paraphyses, and perichætial branch, all in connection, of N. pennata, *Hedw.*: after Schimper.

● ANOMODON. — Plant, capsule with operculum and calyptra, two teeth of the outer and the membranous rudiment of the inner peristome and a portion of the annulus, of A. obtusifolius, *Br. & Sch.*

* OMALIA. — Plant, capsule with operculum, part of the peristome (one tooth, two cilia, one ciliola, and a portion of the annulus), and calyptra, of O. Wrightii, *Sulliv.*

HYPNUM. — Plant, two capsules with opercula, part of the peristome (one tooth, one cilium, and two cilliolæ, with a portion of the annulus), and a calyptra, of H. salebrosum, *Hoffm.*: after Schimper.

Genera of Hepaticæ.

TAB. VI.

RICCIA. — Plant ; vertical section of the frond (showing two imbedded capsules and numerous large air-cavities) ; spores enclosed in a mother-cell ; three free spores ; and calyptra with its style, of R. natans, *L.*: after Bischoff.

* ANTHOCEROS. — Plant ; portion of the two valves of the capsule and the columella, together with spores and elaters ; two spores and two elaters, of A. lævis, *L.*

* NOTOTHYLAS. — Plants ; vertical section of the frond through the involucre, showing the capsule ; apex of the capsule protruding from the end of the involucre ; lower half of the capsule showing the columella ; upper half of capsule ; a gemma ; an antheridium ; twelve free spores and two clusters of spores (4 in each), of N. valvata, *Sulliv.*

REBOULIA. — Plant ; fertile receptacle viewed from above ; the same from below ; capsule dehiscing with remains of the calyptra at its base ; vertical section of the male disk, showing the imbedded antheridia ; an elater ; portion of the same ; and three spores, of R. hemisphærica, *Raddi*: after Bischoff.

SPHÆROCARPUS. — Plant ; a cluster of 5 involucres ; an involucre enclosing a capsule ; a capsule filled with spores ; and three spores, of S. Michelii, *Bellardi*: after Schweinitz.

* DUMORTIERA. — Plants (portions of), male and female ; fertile receptacle, showing three involucres, each with a capsule ; capsule partly covered by the calyptra ; vertical section of the male disk, showing the imbedded antheridia ; an elater, portion of the same ; and three spores, of D. hirsuta, *Nees.*

* PHAGIOCHASMA. — Plants ; triangular fertile receptacle with its three large involucres seen from above ; same viewed sideways ; involucre with one side cut away, showing the capsule and remains of the calyptra ; a capsule with remains of calyptra at its base before dehiscence ; same after dehiscence ; an elater ; a piece of same more magnified ; and two spores, of P. Wrightii, *Sulliv.*

FEGATELLA — Plants (portions of), male and female ; a vertical section of the fertile receptacle, showing two involucres, each with a capsule ; capsule with its calyptra ruptured at the apex ; vertical section of male disk showing the antheridia ; two elaters ; portion of an elater ; and two spores of F. conica, *Corda*: after Bischoff, partly.

PREISSIA. — Plants (portions of), male and female ; a vertical section of the fertile receptacle ; perianth, calyptra, and capsule ; two elaters ; portion of an elater ; two spores ; and vertical section of part of the male disk, showing the imbedded antheridia, of P. commutata, *Nees*: after Bischoff, partly.

MARCHANTIA — Plants (portions of), male and female ; vertical section of the fertile receptacle ; perianth, calyptra, and capsule ; an elater ; portion of the same ; five spores ; a vertical section of a part of the male disk, showing the imbedded antheridia, of M. polymorpha, *L.*: after Bischoff, partly.

FIMBRIARIA. — Plants ; a fertile receptacle ; vertical section of the same ; a capsule dehiscing ; two elaters ; and two spores, of F. tenella, *Nees.*

* STEETSIA — Plant ; portion of the frond, with involucre, perianth, and calyptra ; involucre and perianth cut away so as to show the young calyptra ; capsule before dehiscence ; the same after dehiscence ; antheridium with its perigonial leaf ; an elater and two sporules, of S. Lyellii, *Lehm.*

TAB. VII.

PELLIA — Plant; calyptra with lower part of the pedicel; capsule; an elater; portion of the same; two spores; and two antheridia, of P. epiphylla, *Nees:* after Hooker.

BLASIA. — Plants (fertile, male, and gemmiparous); end of a frond, showing the calyptra and capsule protruding from the apex of the midrib; male frond with two antheridia; a gemmiparous frond with two receptacles; a vertical section of one of the receptacles, showing the gemmæ enclosed, and the tube through which they issue; three gemmæ; four spores and three elaters; two spores, and portion of an elater; capsule dehiscing; vertical section of the cavity in the end of the midrib showing the perianth and the calyptra in a young state, of B. pusilla, *L :* after Hooker.

METZGERIA. — Plants (fertile, male, and gemmiparous); a fertile plant enlarged; the hispid calyx with the two-lobed involucral leaf and part of the pedicel; forked ends of the gemmiparous plant; a gemma; underside of a portion of the male plant, showing roundish perigonial leaves covering the antheridia; an antheridium; three spores and two elaters, of M. furcata, *Nees:* after Hooker.

* ANEURA. — Plant (portions of male and female); a vertical section of the fleshy calyptra, with the base of the pedicel; a portion of the frond, with two elongated deflexed male receptacles; one of these receptacles cut transversely, showing the imbedded antheridia; valves of the capsule bearded by tufts of elaters; three spores; one elater, and portion of the same, of Aneura sessilis, *Sprengel ?*

FOSSOMBRONIA. — Plant; and the same enlarged; capsule dehiscing, with pedicel, perianth, and involucral leaves; part of the stem, with two leaves and dorsal antheridia, an antheridium; two sporules; and two elaters, of F pusilla, *Nees:* after Hooker.

* GEOCALYX. — Plant; part of the stem, with the involucre, which is cut vertically, showing the calyptra and lower part of the pedicel; two pairs of leaves, with the amphigastria; portion of the stem, with one amphigastrium; four valves of the capsule; two elaters; and three spores, of G. graveolens, *Nees.*

GRIMALDIA. — Plants (portions of) male and female; end of a frond showing the palea and lower part of the peduncle; end of a frond with two male disks; one of the disks cut vertically, showing the imbedded antheridia; a fertile receptacle; a vertical section of the same; capsule dehiscing by a circumcissile line; two elaters, and two spores, of G. barbifrons, *Bisch :* after Bischoff.

* CHILOSCYPHUS. — Plant; portion of the stem, with involucral leaves, perianth and calyptra; a pair of leaves with antheridia in their dorsal bases; an antheridium; portion of the stem, with a leaf and an amphigastrium; capsule with its four valves; three spores and two elaters, of C. ascendens, *Hook. & Wils.*

* PLEURANTHE — Plant; the same enlarged; a portion of the stem, with a pair of leaves and an amphigastrium; perianth with involucral leaves and part of the pedicel; the same cut vertically, showing the calyptra; capsule with its four valves; five spores; three elaters, and part of an elater, of P. olivacea, *Tayl.*

* LOPHOCOLEA. — Plant; portion of the stem, with its leaves and the perianth; same, with one leaf having in its dorsal base an antheridium; the same with three pairs of leaves and three amphigastria; one amphigastrium; one antheridium; a cross-section near the mouth of the perianth; three spores and an elater, of L. heterophylla, *Nees.*

JUNGERMANNIA. — Plant; portion of the stem with two pairs of leaves; branch with involucral leaves and perianth; an involucral leaf; calyptra; capsule with valves closed; same with valves spreading; an elater and two sporules, of J. connivens, *Dicks :* after Hooker.

GYMNOMITRIUM. — Plants; portion of the stem with three pairs of leaves; the same with involucral leaves at the apex, pedicel, and capsule; calyptra with base of the pedicel, the involucral leaves being cut away; and two involucral leaves, of G. concinnatum. *Corda:* after Hooker.

SARCOSCYPHUS. — Plant; portion of the same with stem, involucral leaves, and base of the pedicel; involucral leaves and perianth opened so as to show the calyptra and lower part of pedicel; capsule with its 4 valves; an elater and two sporules, of S. Ehrharti, *Corda:* after Hooker.

TAB. VIII.

SCAPANIA. — Plant, perianth, enclosing the calyptra and part of the pedicel, furnished at the base with involucral leaves; part of the stem with three leaves; two antheridia; capsule open; an elater and two spores, of S. undulata, *N. & M.:* after Hooker.

• PLAGIOCHILA. — Plant; portion of the stem with five leaves; perianth, enclosing the calyptra and part of the pedicel; piece of stem with an amphigastrium and radicles; two antheridia; capsule; two spores and two elaters, of P. macrostoma, *Sulliv.*

SPHAGNŒCETIS. — Plant; portion of the stem with four or five pairs of leaves, and a short branch clothed with involucral leaves and bearing the perianth; an involucral leaf; the attenuated extremity of a branch, bearing gemmæ at the apex; four gemmæ; capsule; three spores and two elaters, of S. communis, *Nees:* after Hooker.

• LEJEUNIA. — Plant; perianth, with capsule and involucral leaves; portion of the pedicel; portion of stem with a pair of leaves, an amphigastrium and a male branch; an antheridium; a portion of the stem, with two pairs of leaves seen from above; the same with two amphigastria viewed from below; cross-section of the perianth; two elaters, and two spores, of L. clypeata, *Schweiniz.*

• FRULLANIA. — Plant; portion of the stem, with two pairs of leaves seen from above; the same, with the amphigastria and auriculæ, viewed from beneath; perianth and involucral leaves; cross-section of the perianth; an involucral leaf; capsule; two elaters and two spores, of F. Grayana, *Mont.*

• MADOTHECA. — Plant; portion of the stem, with a pair of leaves and an amphigastrium, seen from beneath; portion of the male plant, with four spikelets of perigonial leaves, containing antheridia; a 2-lobed perigonial leaf with its antheridium; an antheridium; perianth, with involucral leaves and capsule; an elater and two spores, of M. platyphylla, *Dumort.*

• RADULA. — Plant; a branch terminated by the perianth and capsule, with lateral male branchlets; a male branchlet; an antheridium; a perianth with two involucral leaves; portion of the stem with two pairs of leaves, seen from above; the same from below; a capsule; an elater and two spores, of R. obconica, *Sulliv.*

PTILIDIUM. — Plant; portion of the stem with a pair of leaves; same with an amphigastrium; perianth with its involucral leaves; a capsule; an elater and two spores, of P. ciliare, *Nees:* after Hooker.

MASTIGOBRYUM. — Plant; portion of the stem with two pairs of leaves, two amphigastria, and a male spikelet; portion of a spikelet with its perigonial leaf; an antheridium; capsule; four spores and two elaters, of M. trilobatum, *Nees:* after Hooker, partly.

TRICHOCOLEA. — Plant; leaf, amphigastrium, and piece of the stem; the fleshy involucre; a capsule; two spores and an elater, of T. Tomentella, *Nees:* after Hooker.

SENDTNERA. — Plant; portion of stem with leaves and amphigastria; tubular many-cleft perianth; capsules; an elater and three spores of S. juniperina, *Nees:* after Hooker.

LEPIDOZIA. — Plant; portion of stem with three leaves and two amphigastria; a perigonial leaf enclosing an antheridium; an antheridium free; perianth with involucral leaves; capsule; four spores and an elater, of L. reptans, *Nees:* after Hooker.

CALYPOGEIA. — Plants; portion of stem with three leaves and two rooting amphigastria; hairy involucre with the lower part of the pedicel; the same cut vertically, showing the calyptra; capsule with its spiral valves; an elater and two spores, of C. Trichomanis, *Corda:* after Hooker

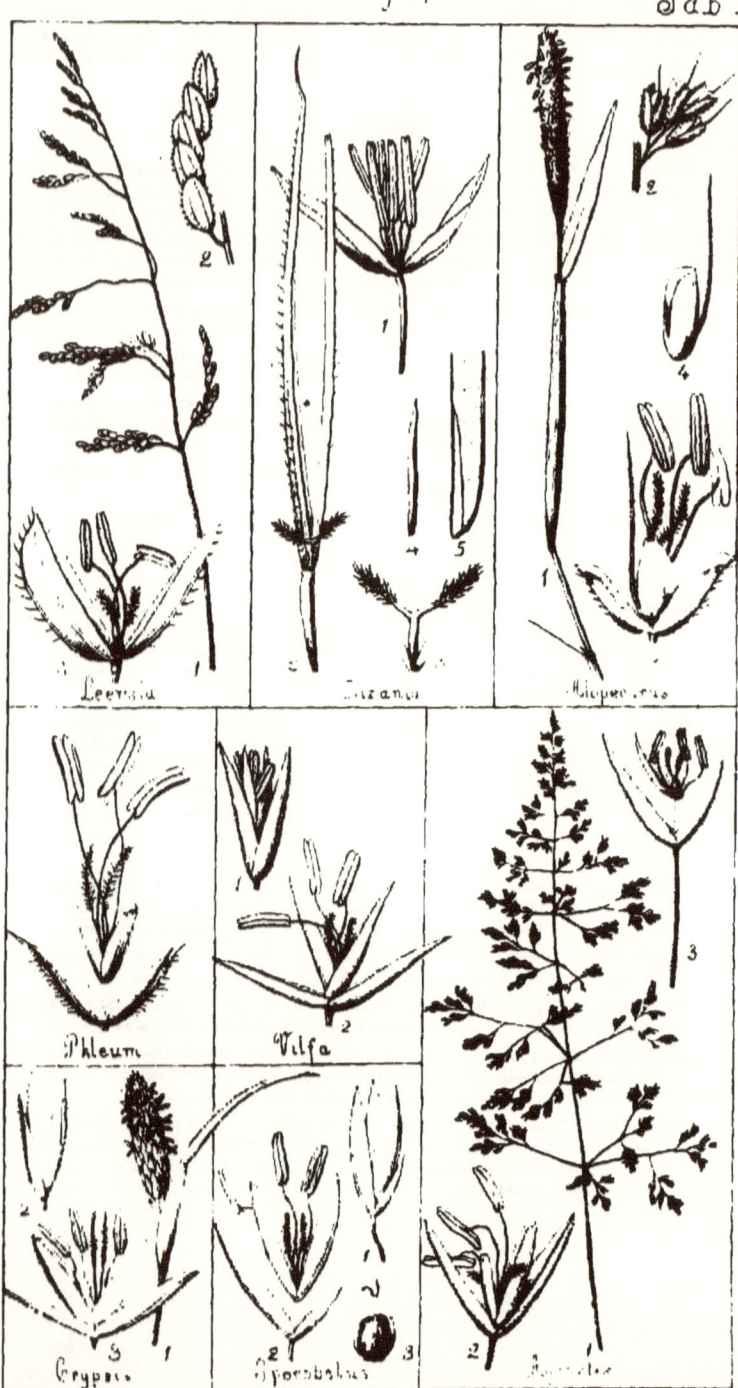

Leersia

Izania

Alopecurus

Phleum

Vilfa

Crypsis

Sporobolus

Agrostis

Sprague

Genero of Grasses

Tab. II.

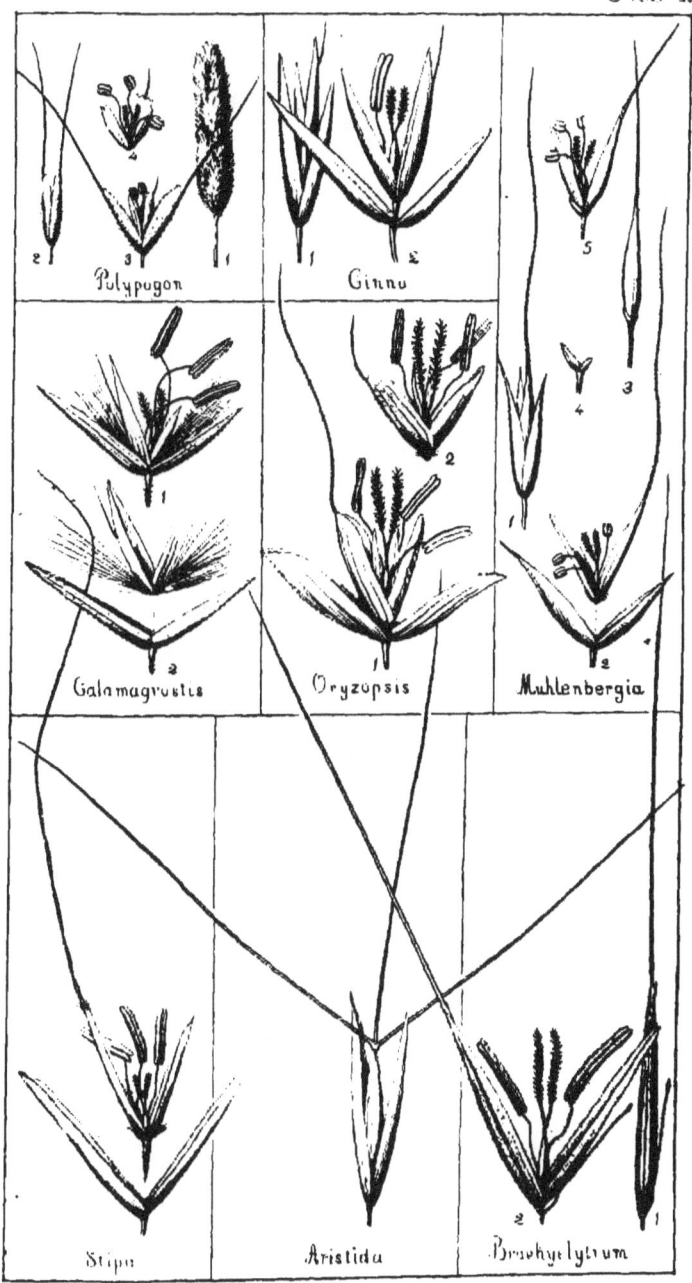

Polypogon

Cinnu

Galamagrostis

Oryzopsis

Muhlenbergia

Stipa

Aristida

Brachyelytrum

Sprague

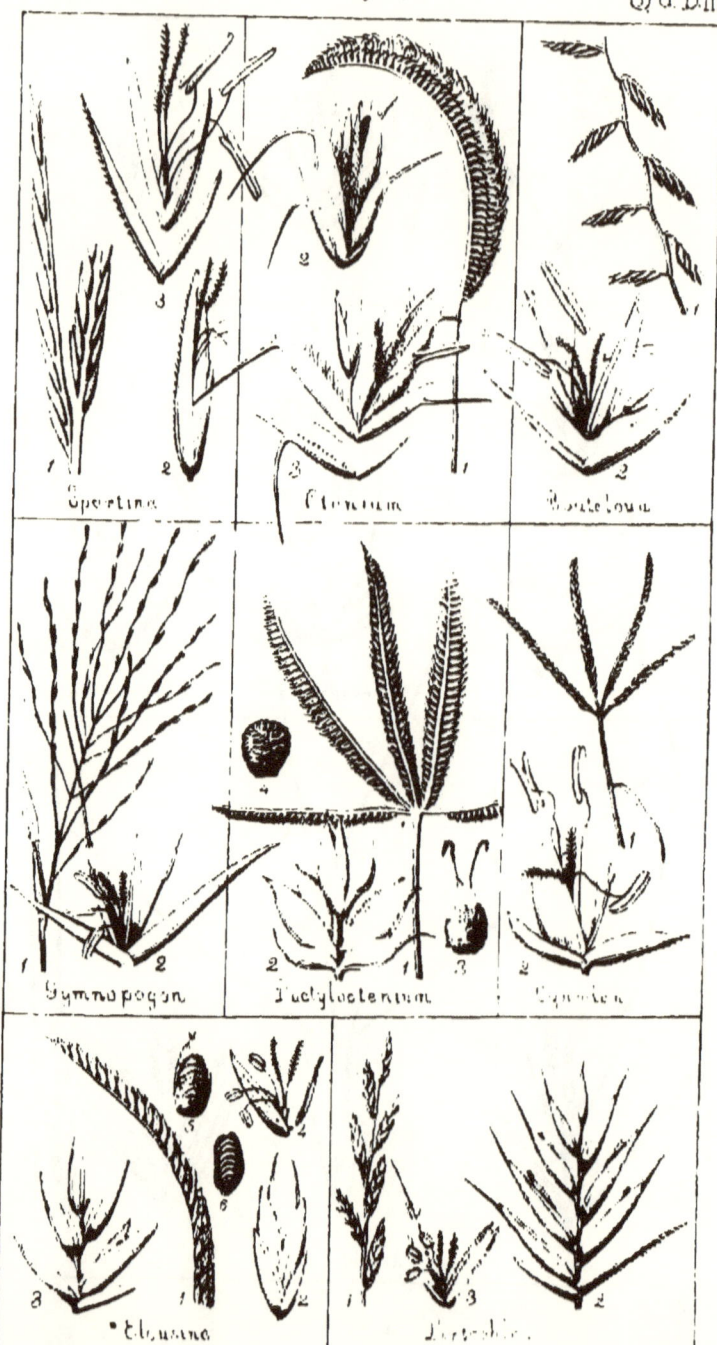

Spartina   Ctenium   Bouteloua

Gymnopogon   Dactyloctenium   Cynodon

Eleusine   Leptochloa

Genera of Grasses.

Tab. IV

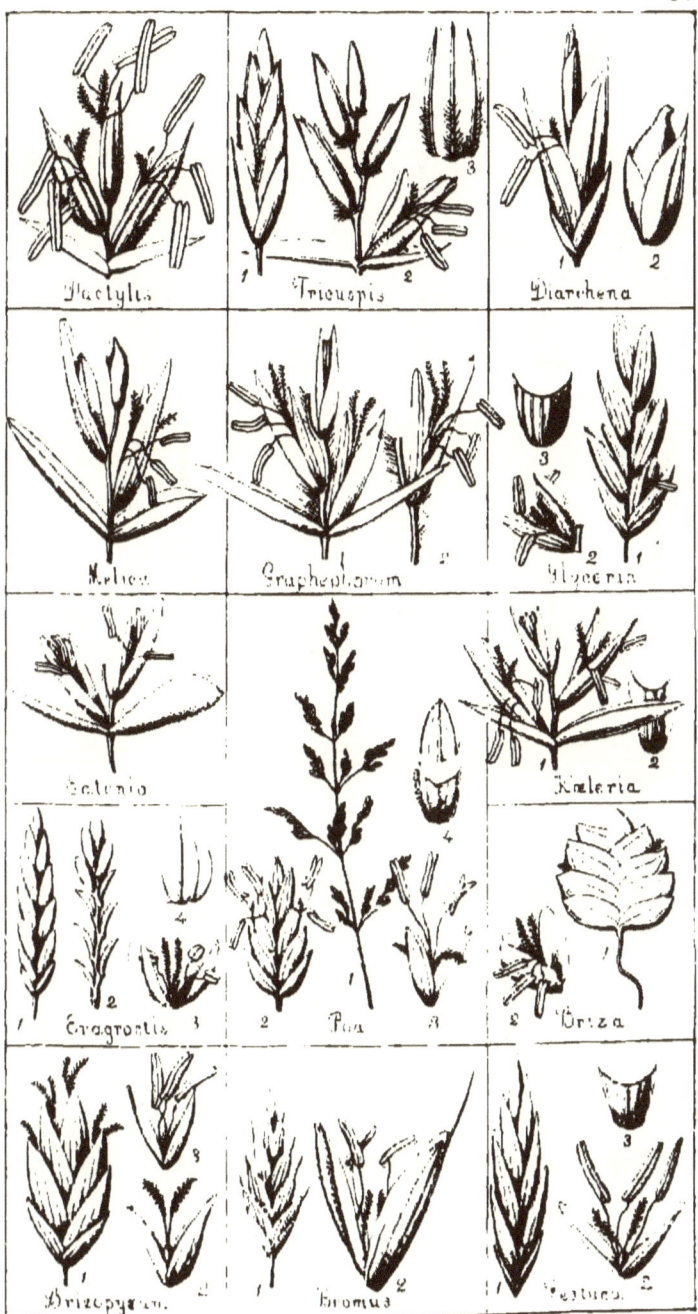

Dactylis   Tricuspis   Diarrhena

Melica   Graphephorum   Glyceria

Catenia   Koeleria

Eragrostis   Poa   Briza

Brizopyrum.   Bromus   Festuca

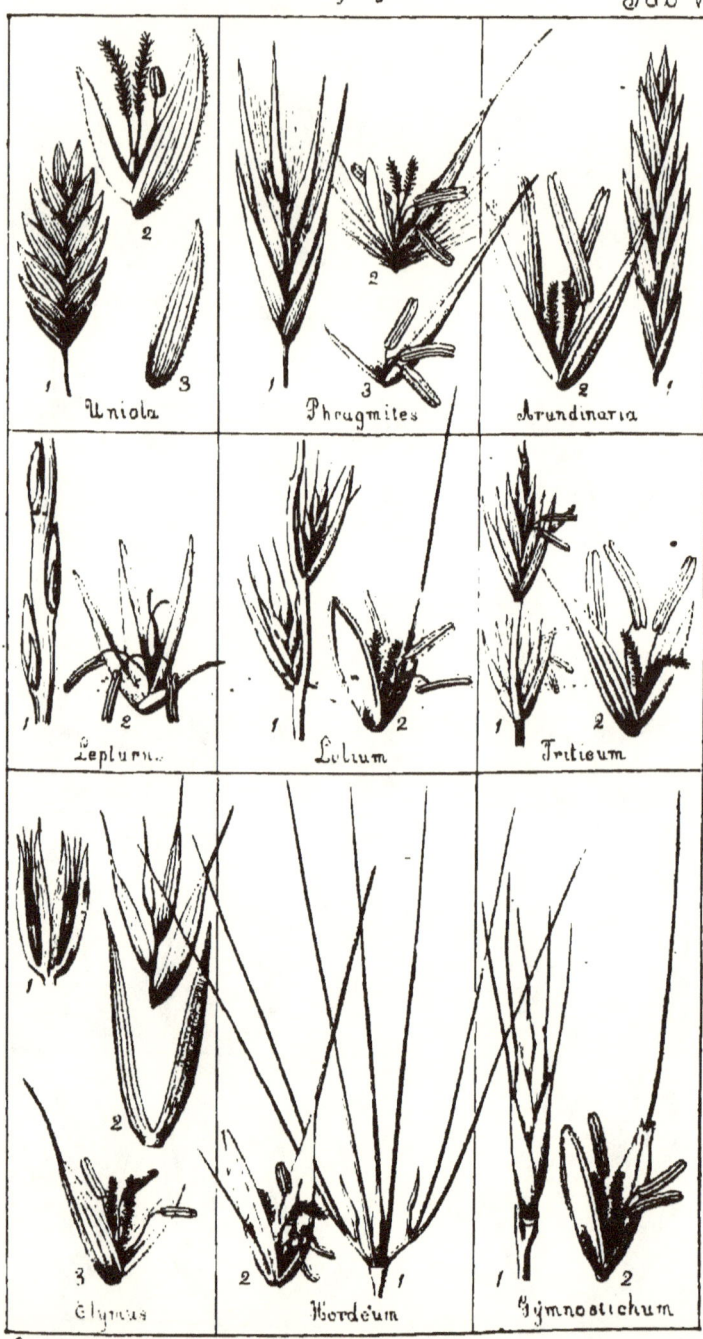

Uniola

Phragmites

Arundinaria

Lepturus

Lolium

Triticum

Elymus

Hordeum

Gymnostichum

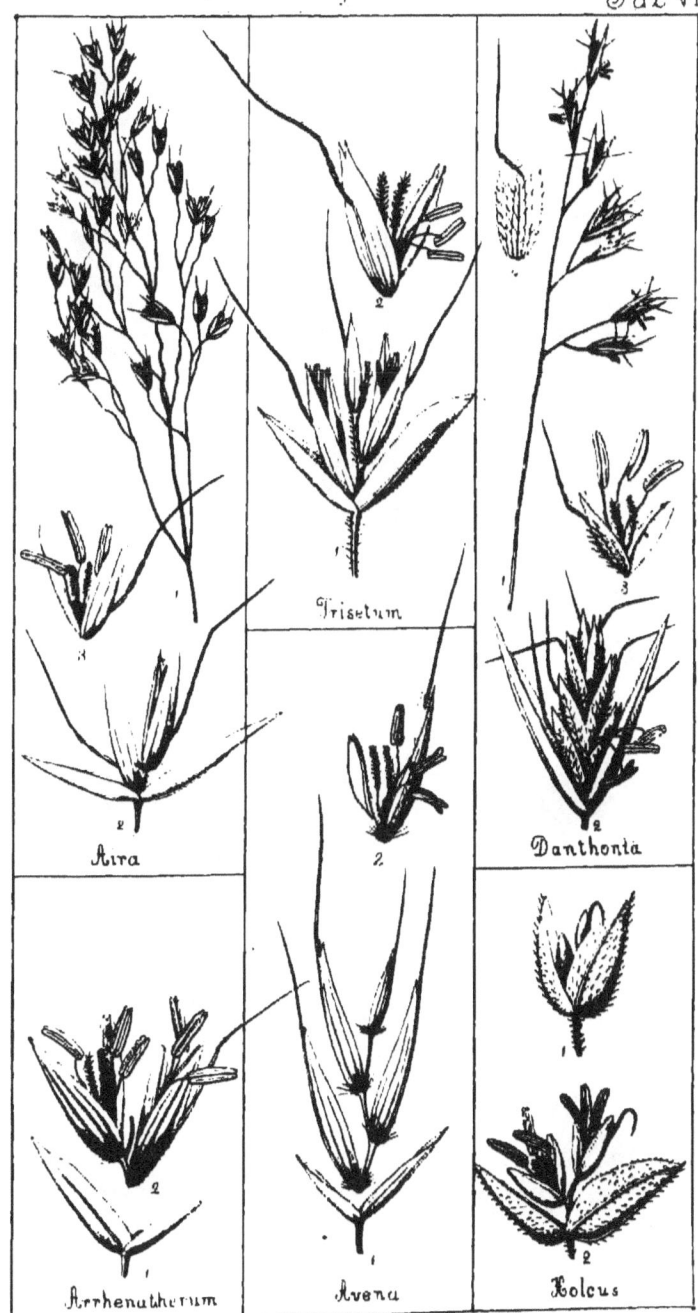

Trisetum

Aira

Danthonia

Arrhenutherum

Avena

Holcus

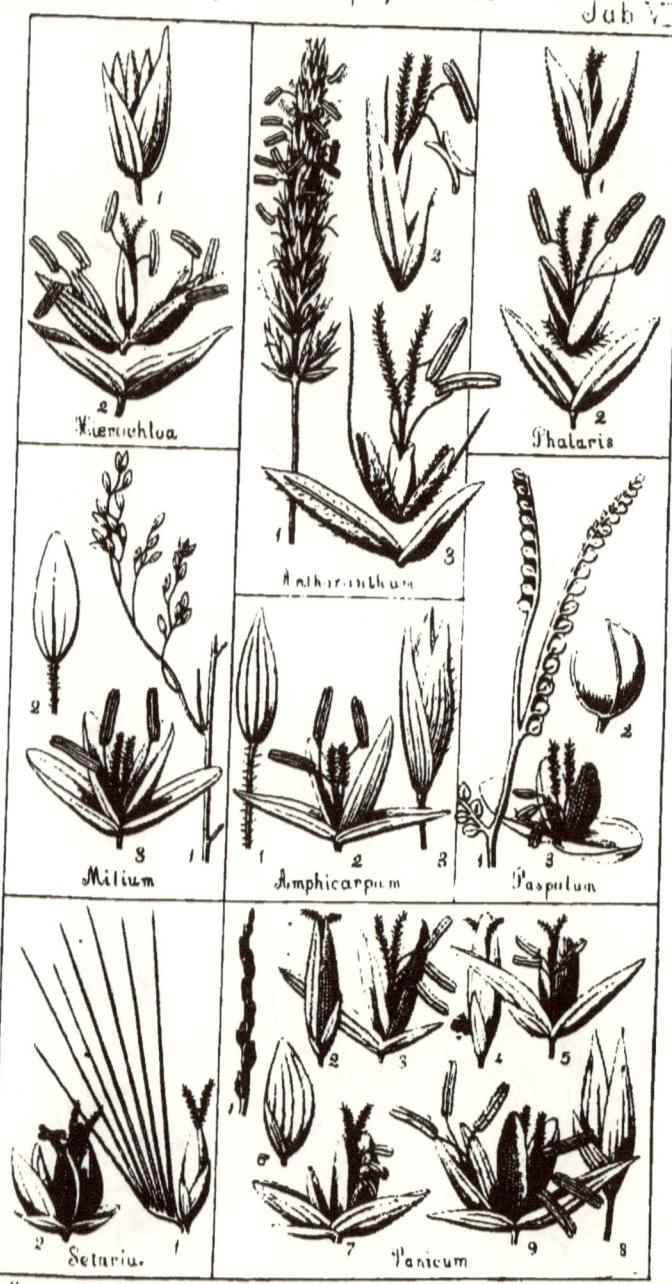

Sprague

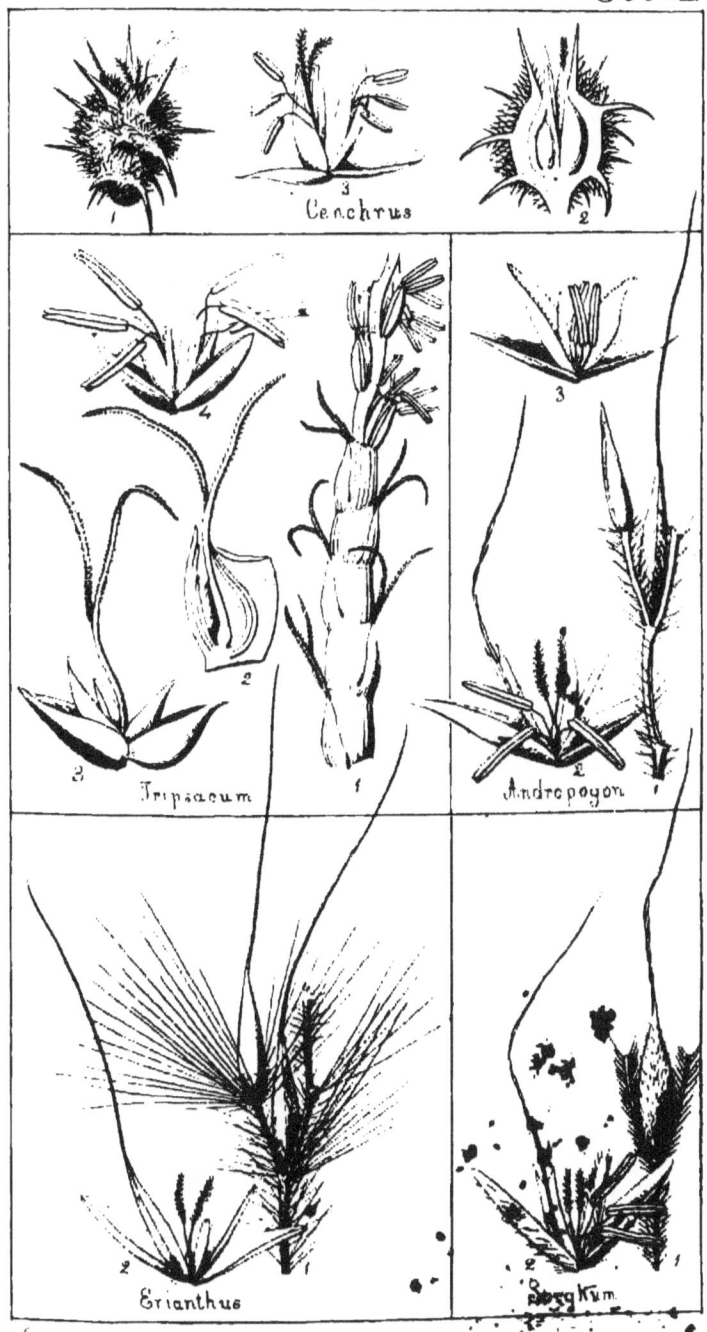

Cenchrus

Tripsacum

Andropogon

Erianthus

Sorghum

Sprague

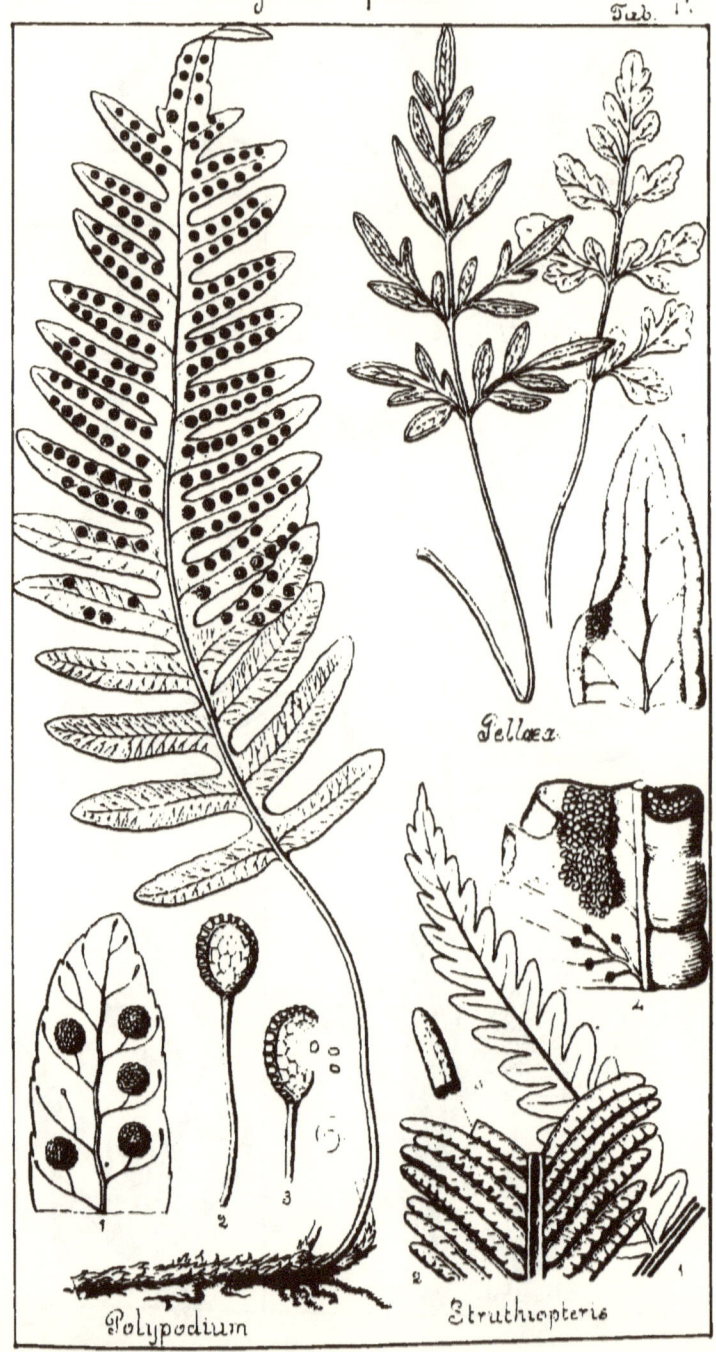

Polypodium

Pellæa

Struthiopteris

Sprague

Genera of Filices

Tab X

Pteris

Adiantum

Cheilanthes

Woodwardia

Sprague

Dicksonia.

Asplenium.

Camptosorus.

Scolopendrium.

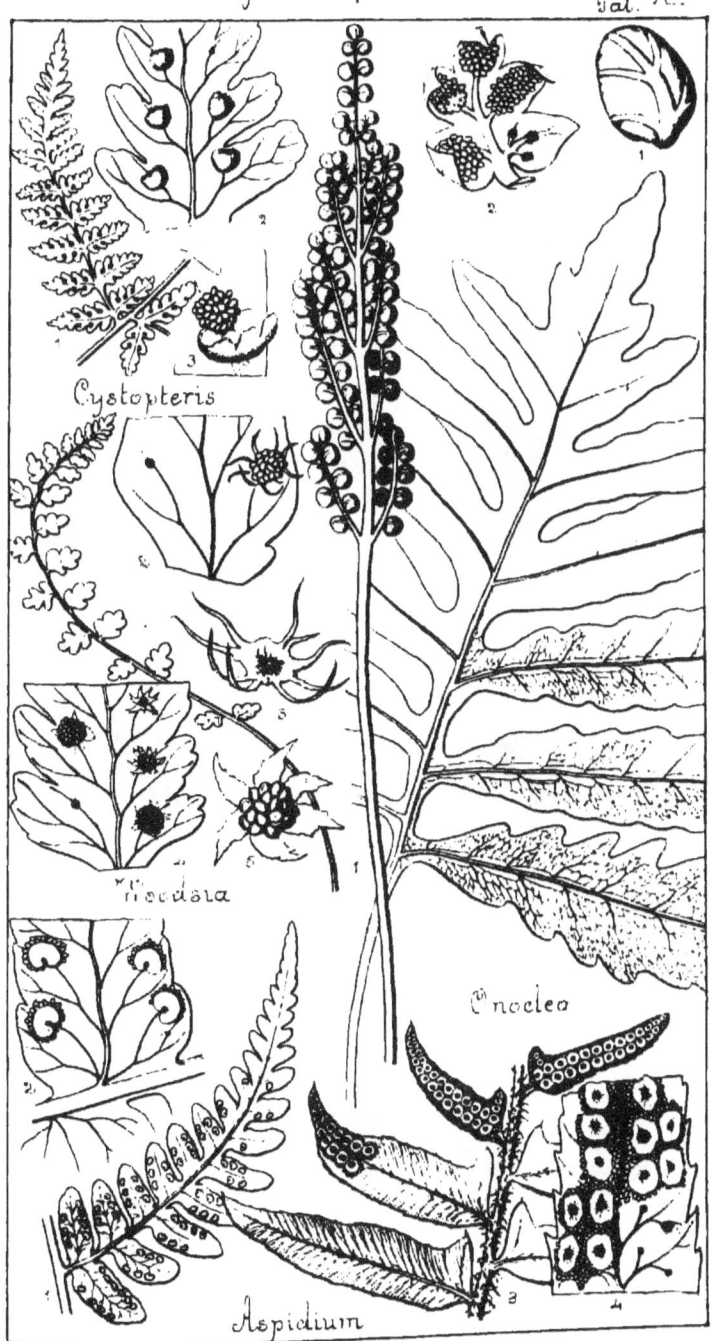

Cystopteris

Woodsia

Onoclea

Aspidium

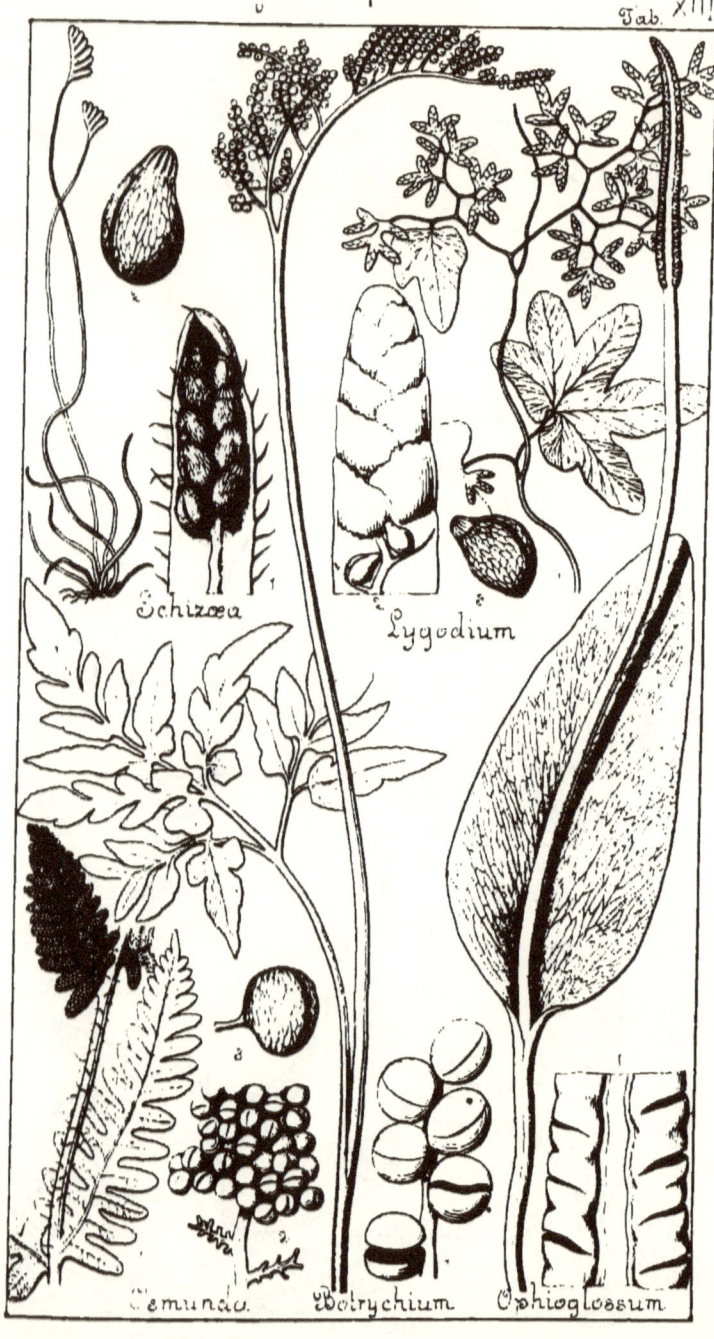

Schizœa

Lygodium

Osmunda.

Botrychium

Ophioglossum

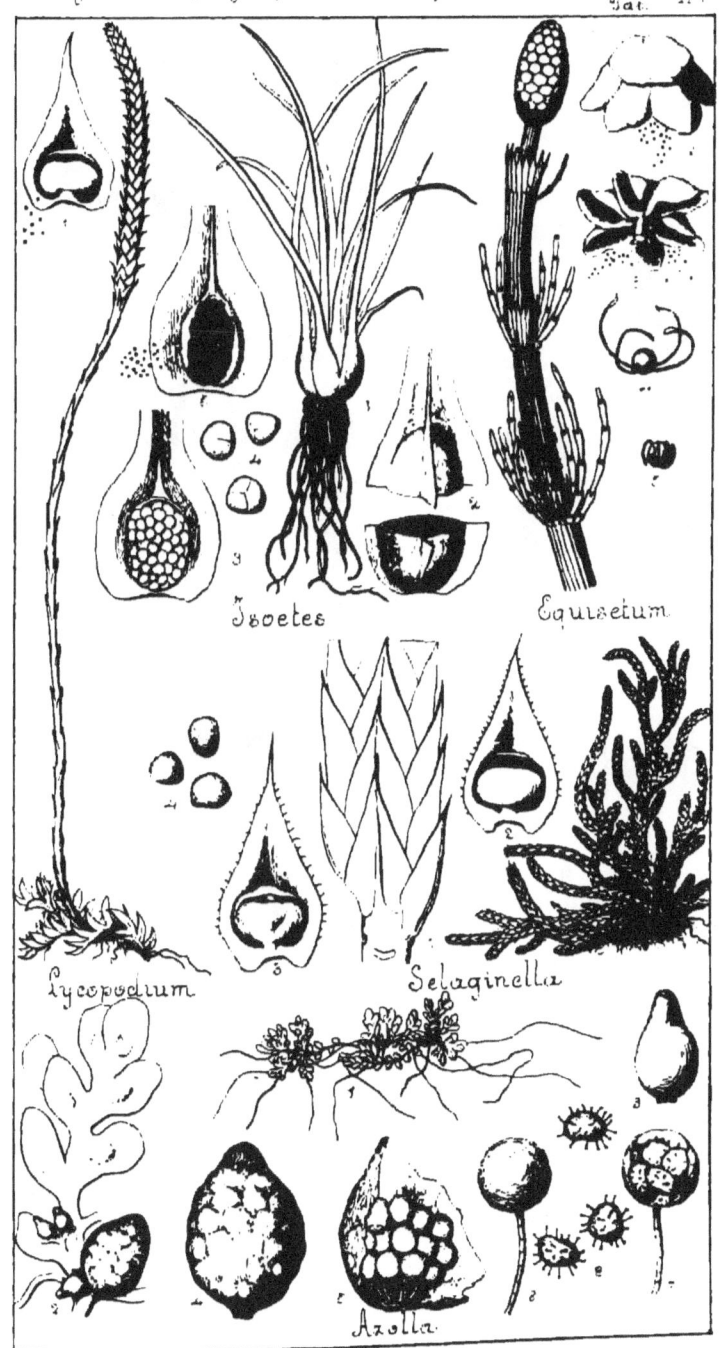

Isoetes

Equisetum

Lycopodium

Selaginella

Azolla

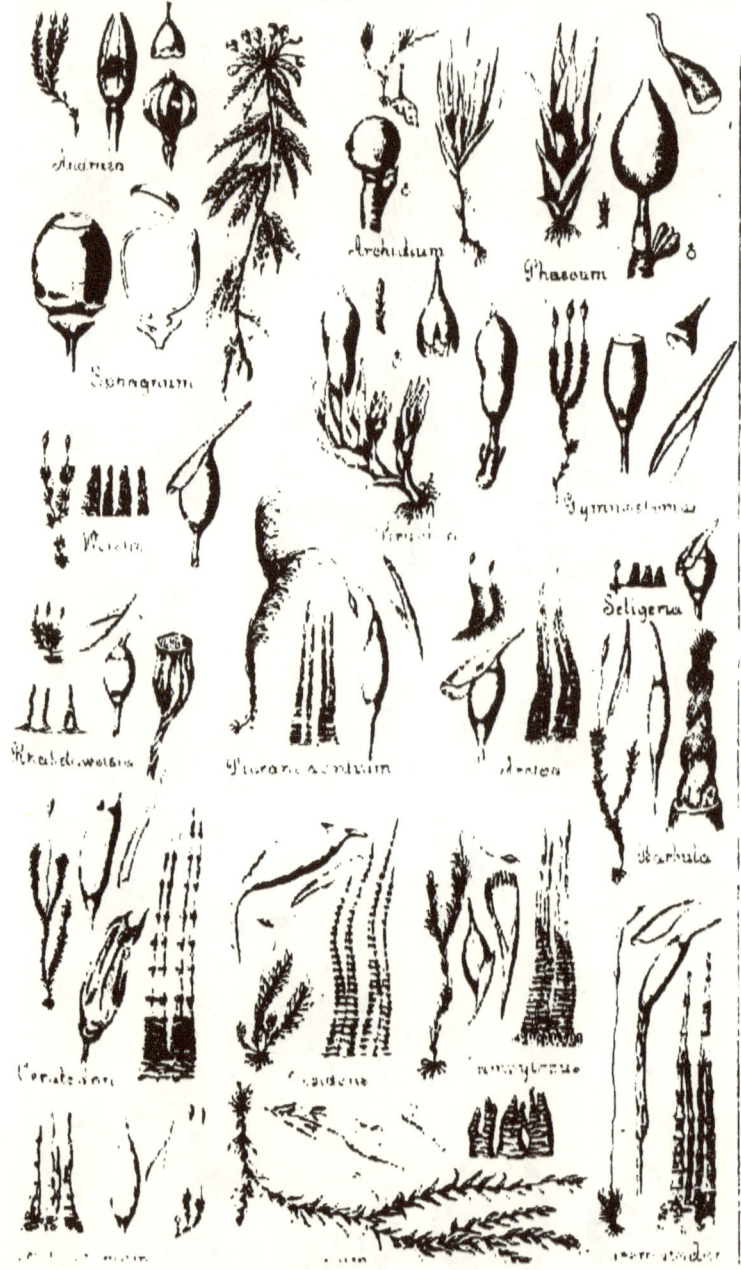

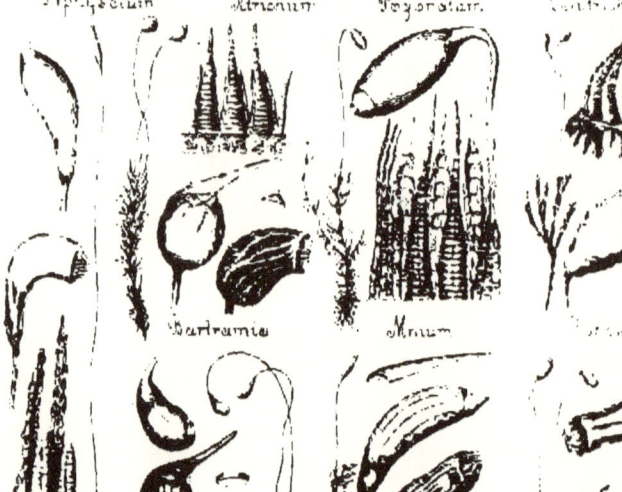

Buxbaumia

Diphyscium   Atrichum   Pogonatum   Catharinea

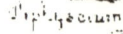

Bartramia   Mnium

Funaria   Aulacomnion   Tima

Tab. XVIII.

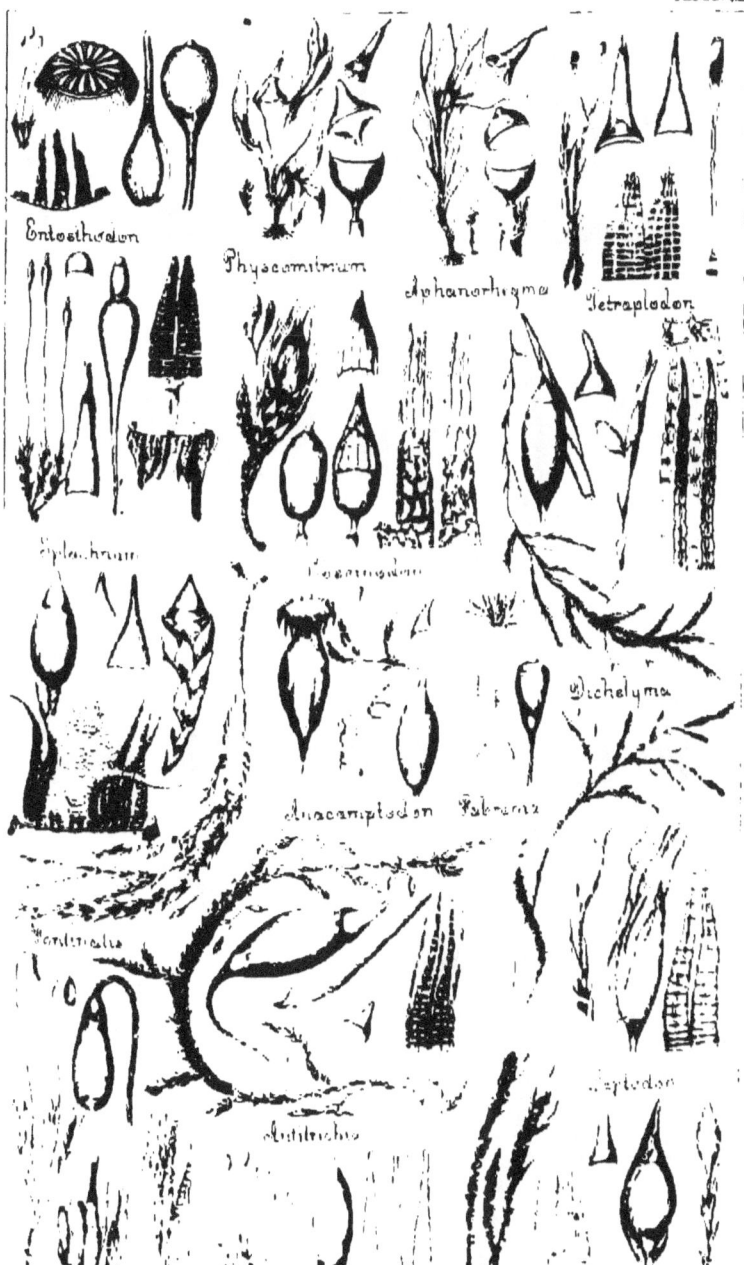

Entosthodon

Physcomitrium

Aphanorhegma

Tetraplodon

Splachnum

Dissodon

Dichelyma

Anacamptodon

Fabronia

Fontinalis

Antitrichia

Leptodon

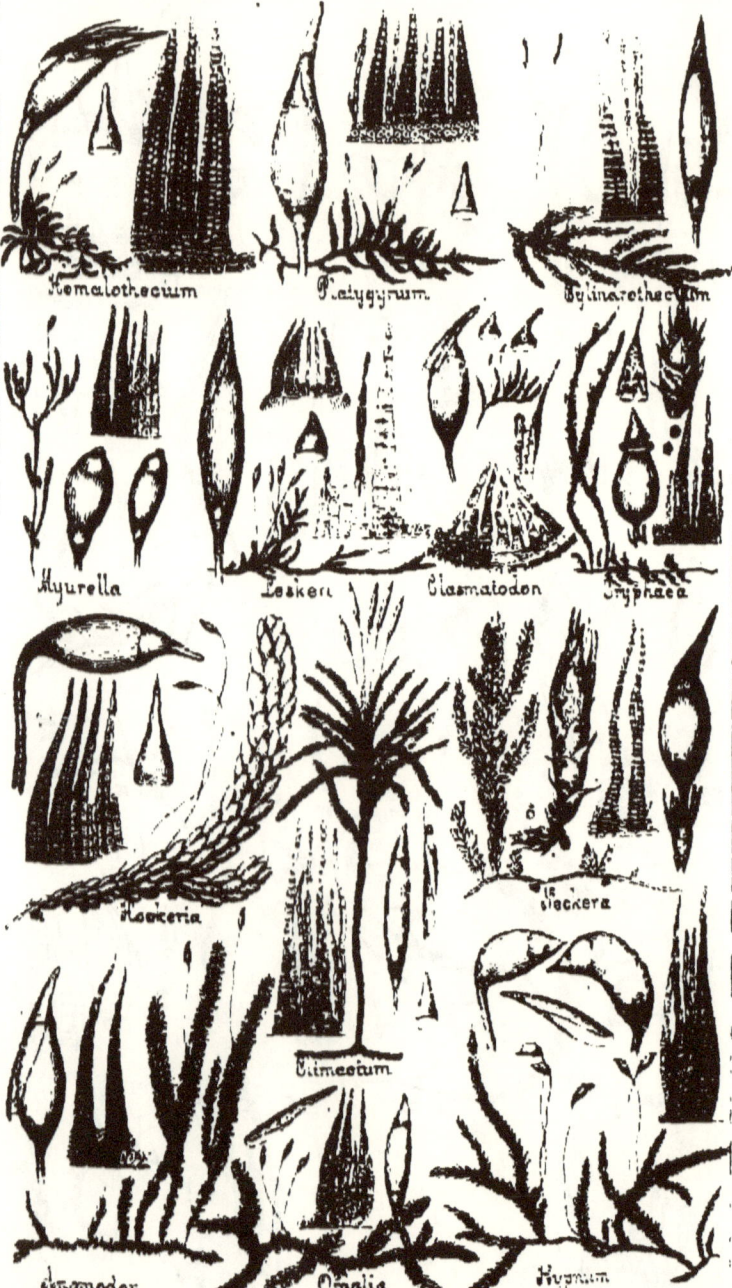

Hemalothecium   Platygyrum.   Pylinarothecium

Myurella   Leskea   Clasmatodon   Cryphaea

Hookeria   Climacium   Neckera

Anomodon   Omalia   Hypnum

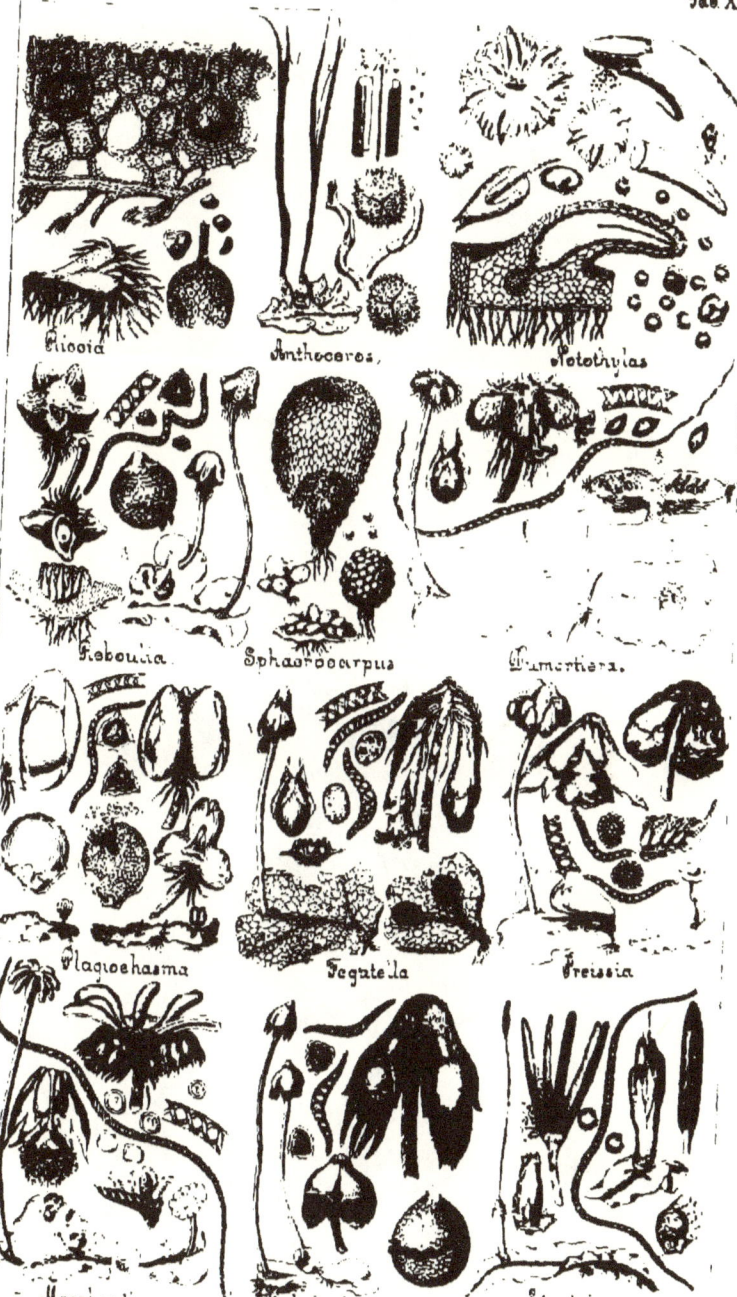

Riccia   Anthoceros,   Notothylas.

Reboulia   Sphaerocarpus   Dumortiera.

Plagiochasma   Tesatella   Preissia

Marchantia.   Fimbriaria   Steetzia.

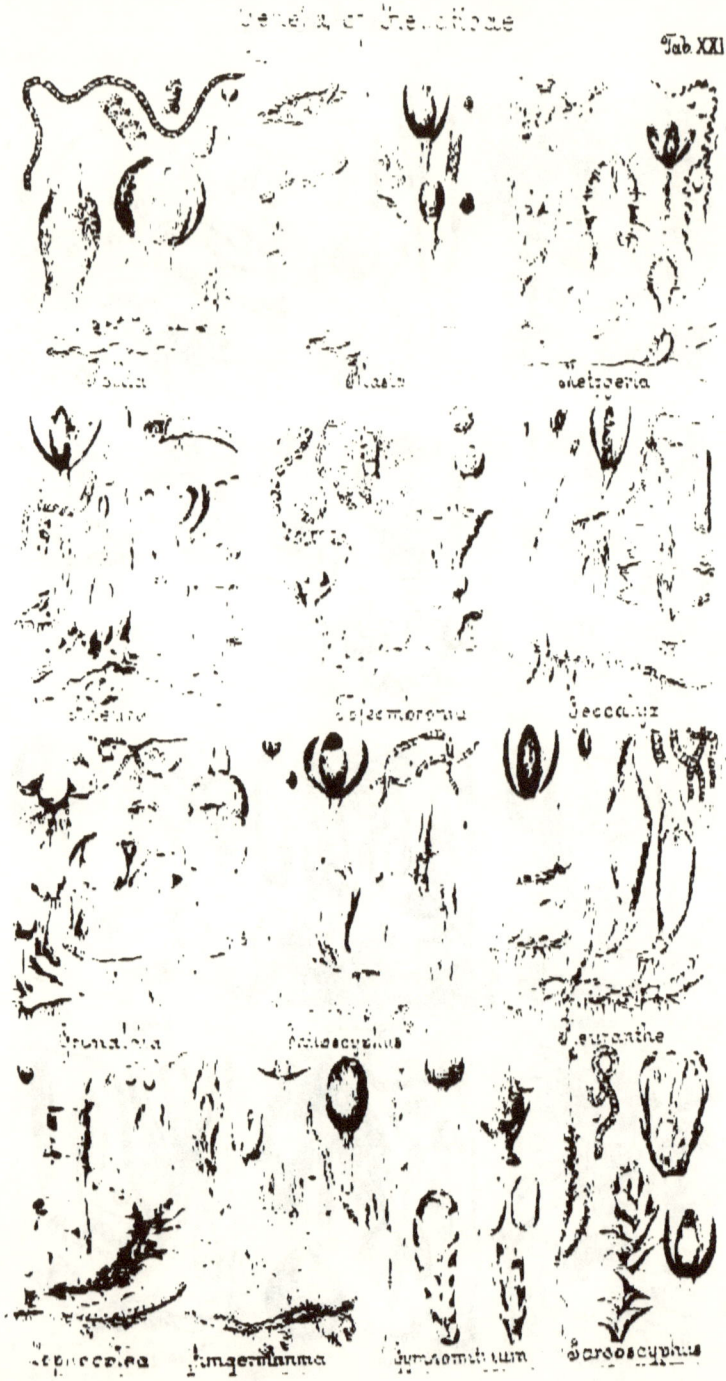

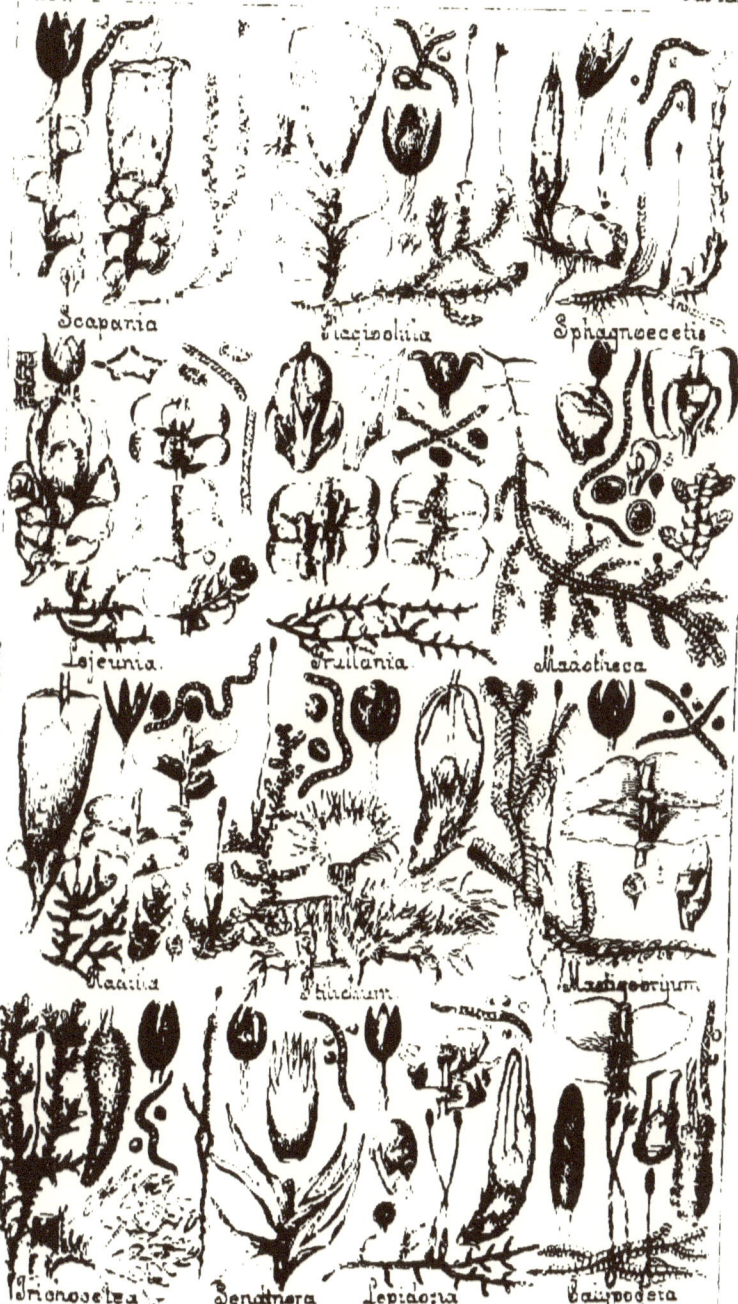

Scapania

Jacinolita

Sphagnoecetis

Lejeunia

Frullania

Maiotheca

Madiia

Thindium

Madigoorium

Trichosolea

Senathera

Lepidozia

Calypoosta